DECEPTION

Gordon Smart

Copyright © 2024 Gordon Smart

All rights reserved

The characters and events portrayed in this book are fictitious. Any similarity to real persons, living or dead, is coincidental and not intended by the author.

No part of this book may be reproduced, or stored in a retrieval system, or transmitted in any form or by any means, electronic, mechanical, photocopying, recording, or otherwise, without express written permission of the publisher.

ISBN-13: 9798324250263
ISBN-10: 1477123456

Cover design by: Art Painter
Library of Congress Control Number: 2018675309
Printed in the United States of America

For Maureen

PROLOGUE

Saturday 11th March

Brian opened the fridge door and took out a can of Heineken lager. He loved the satisfying *pssst* noise it made when he pulled on the ring-pull, the white foam bubbling out of the hole and over the surface of the can-lid. He scooped it up with his mouth then took a long swig. Ahh. There really was nothing to beat the taste of cold beer.

He'd been working all afternoon on the piece, sitting at the kitchen table. He thought it was coming together quite well, though he would have to wait until Monday to put the finishing touches to it. That was when he would have the meeting. He was a bit nervous about that, but he couldn't really finish what he was working on without it.

He'd stop soon and go and have a shower. It was Saturday after all. He was excited at the prospect of seeing Julie later. He'd even have a shave and put on his new shirt. She'd like that.

He was pretty keen on her, and she seemed to be serious about him too. He knew that she had been through some tough times, but he thought that he made her happy. Who knew, they might even have a future together. He hadn't had much luck with relationships previously.

He was about to go back to his laptop when he thought he saw a shape passing the window. The kitchen was at the back of the ground floor flat, located on an estate on the edge of Cambridge. A path led down the side of the building to the back garden, but it wasn't used much. Maybe it was a neighbour going to the bins that way. The only other person he could think of was Julie. He'd arranged to see her later, but they'd agreed to meet in the pub not for her to come here. She would go to the front door and buzz to be let in, though. Unless she wanted to surprise him by knocking on the kitchen window. He had a look out of the window but couldn't see anyone there.

He turned back towards the table where his laptop sat when suddenly there was an almighty bang, and he felt a massive force like a thunderbolt hit him in the back and throw him across the room headfirst. He collided with a set of kitchen cupboards and put his hands out to grasp the worktop as he felt his legs give way. Pain suddenly seemed to spread out from the middle of his back where he'd felt the blow; he collapsed to the floor on his knees, his head spinning wildly.

He tried to stand up, turned and looked towards the window. It had completely shattered, a gaping hole in its middle. A figure stood outside looking in, a balaclava covering his face, a pistol pointing straight at him. Another blast. This time at his chest. Then the room seemed to explode around him in flames, but he was unable to move. Darkness came rushing in like a swift tide swallowing up all his senses and sucking him deep below its waves.

MONDAY

ONE

A distinct sense of panic gripped Finn. The small plane juddered and battled with the wind to reach the clouds; the sight of the ground below quickly became smaller and smaller, intensifying his feeling of impending doom. Suddenly he felt sick. It was his second flight of the day, having already caught an early morning BA shuttle to Edinburgh and now the Loganair connection to Kirkwall. This was a big mistake, he thought. He should never have come. He closed his eyes, took some deep breaths and told himself to relax. It was only a spot of turbulence, after all. Don't panic. This flight must have happened hundreds of times without incident. OK, it was a bit breezy today but surely the pilot would have flown in much worse than this. It was just a normal day, not a storm. So, he tried to focus on something pleasant: walking along a beach came to mind. But that made him think of a holiday in Greece with Fiona. Fuck. That made things even worse. He didn't want to think about her.

He badly needed a drink. Time was, he

would have sneaked in a couple of pints of Peroni at the airport along with a fry-up, maybe even have had a few shots; but those days were gone. Instead, he had had a flat white and a panini and passed the time sipping from a bottle of mineral water.

He had a look at the news on his phone. The *Chronicle* website. The paper that he worked for, in fact. The lead story was on small boats overflowing with asylum seekers crossing the Channel. Sometimes they didn't make it. Only two days ago a boat had sunk with fifty souls on board. None of them had survived. It put his fears about the flight into perspective. It would be his first day back on the isles in fifteen years. What was it going to be like? he wondered. Being back there, after all this time. He'd resisted it until now. There had been the odd party and wedding he'd been invited to over the years but he'd always politely, or sometimes not so politely, declined. But this time he felt he had to return. His conscience left him no choice. But how would he really feel once he was there? The truth was that he was even more terrified of the memories it might bring back and what it would do to him than the fear he felt in his gut on this tiny plane. But one was imaginary at the moment; the other was very real. Too real. He suddenly had to grab the sick bag from the back of the seat and threw up the coffee and panini.

In the taxi from the airport into Kirkwall, as he saw all the old familiar landmarks - the standing stones, the coastline, the distinctive outline of St Magnus's cathedral - Finn's mind went back to his childhood and teenage years. He was surprised that the place looked mostly just as he remembered it. Nothing much seemed to have changed. That disconcerted him. It really felt like going back into the past. He had grown up on Mainland, the largest of the islands in the archipelago, which housed the towns of Kirkwall, where he had lived, and Stromness, as well as numerous villages. He didn't realise how much he had missed the landscape and stared out of the taxi window, feeling deeply moved at the sight of it.

There was a magical feel to the place, he had to admit. There really was nowhere else on earth like it. Partly it was to do with how ancient and unspoilt it was. Locations like Skara Brae were some of the oldest built places in Europe. For thousands of years the land had been inhabited here, long before even the likes of Stonehenge. Those ancient inhabitants developed skills and artwork that influenced communities across Europe. It was, at one time, the centre of civilization. Much later, the Vikings had come and left their mark with mystical-looking runes carved into stones. He was proud of all of that. In England, when anyone from abroad asked where he came from, he wouldn't hesitate to say Orkney, not Scotland. In fact, like Shetlanders, the people here, the Orcadians, didn't see themselves as Scottish. One local politician, the leader of Orkney council, wanted a referendum to decide whether Orkney should go back to belonging to Norway, as it had done hundreds of years ago when it was gifted to Scotland as part of a marriage dowry.

It was all so different from the hustle and bustle and the sheer human density of a big city like London, where the Tube in the summer was insufferably hot and crowded and the air stank of diesel and petrol, despite the mayor's attempts to improve things with the ULEZ. But, still, he was glad he had a return ticket in his pocket, booked onto flight back to London via Edinburgh, as he didn't intend to hang about after the funeral: a church service, followed by the burial in the churchyard's cemetery overlooking the sea. It wasn't so much that he preferred to live in London, than that he had personal issues with Orkney which overwhelmed him. Issues from his past. He almost hadn't come because of too many unsettling memories.

The taxi arrived at the church twenty

minutes before the service started. He couldn't have timed it better. It was a strange service. His gran belonged to the Free Presbyterian Church so there was no singing of hymns allowed, only Psalms and the minister telling the congregation all how they were all worthless sinners. In the church, there were a few faces he recognised and some he half-thought he knew. He was aware of the curious glances and knowing looks, saw folk whispering to one another and turning to discreetly cast their greedy eyes over him, sizing him up, judging him. He remembered how the life of the isles revolved around gossip and here he was at the centre of it. One or two came over to speak to him as he stood at the graveside and the wind blasted through the cemetery, but he couldn't remember many of their names, so completely had he blanked out that part of his past. One he did remember was a relative, Malcolm, a second cousin, the son of his mum's cousin Katy, who'd tracked him down and messaged him on social media to tell him about his gran's death; they exchanged a few polite words, but he didn't feel like talking much. They exchanged mobile numbers and said they'd keep in touch.

After the coffin had been lowered into the grave, everyone else left and he stood alone at the graveside for a few minutes with his thoughts. He remembered his gran as she had been when he was a child. She had been kind and loving to him. That was before they grew apart and fell out. He cursed the stupidity of his adolescent and teenage self for how he had behaved towards her and felt consumed by guilt. 'I'm sorry, gran,' he said.

The weather was deteriorating, and it was beginning to sleet. It didn't feel like spring, more like mid-winter with that icy blast coming from the north. He then joined the wake at a nearby hotel which was within walking distance. He answered the questions which were directed at him as curtly as possible without seeming rude, but he wasn't in the mood for any lengthy conversations.

'So, how does it feel being back, Finn?'

'What are you doing with yourself, Finn?'

'Where do you live these days. Finn?'

It was awful. All he wanted was to leave as quickly as he'd arrived. Everyone seemed to be downing pints and spirits. That also made him feel out of place, clutching an orange juice. He was tempted to have a pint. It would definitely take the edge off his anxiety at being here. But he managed to resist the impulse, knowing that there was no way he could stop at one. He reminded himself, as he often had to, how liberating sobriety was. How good it was to have a clear head and a clear conscience in the morning. How different that felt from the hangovers and the constant sense of self-disgust.

His mobile rang just as he was just about to get into a taxi to take him back to the airport. It was his editor, Iain Guthrie. 'It's come to my attention, Finn, that you've gone to Orkney,' he said. 'Are you still there?'

'Yes,' said Finn.

'I want you to stay on there for a bit. There's something you can look into while you're up there. The Jeremy Powell case. You'll have heard about it. His widow is kicking up shit about it on Twitter. Seems to think her husband was killed. Our proprietor has got wind of it and told me to get someone up there to speak to her. You're originally from that neck of the woods, I believe, so that might help. The local paper there, the *Orkney Times*, has all the background. Find out if there's anything in what she's banging on about.'

Fuck … He couldn't believe it. He was being told to remain on the isles. He felt like throwing up all over again. He was speechless.

Guthrie carried on. 'You're more experienced at this kind of thing than any of the local reporters. See what the story is. Even if she's bonkers, I'm sure you'll find an angle. Human interest stuff, that sort of thing. Probably nothing in it but maybe she's onto something. So go and meet the staff on the local paper this afternoon, they'll fill you in on what they know. I'll call the editor and tell them to expect you.'

'Listen, Iain, I don't think ...' Finn started to say.

'I'll ask admin to book you into a hotel room and have them text you the details,' Guthrie said, ignoring him. 'Look into the Powell case and see what you can come up with. I'll speak to the widow and ask her to meet with you. I'll let you know. Get taxis to get around but keep the receipts. Although from what I hear, the isles are so small maybe a bike would do! And keep any receipts for any other expenses as well- but don't go mad buying yourself an entire new designer outfit or anything. Not that they'll have many shops like that up there, I suppose. Anyway, good luck! Keep me posted.' With that, the call was ended.

It was the last thing he wanted. Being back on the isles for a day was bad enough. Plus, he felt exhausted. He'd hardly slept the night before. It wasn't just the neighbours upstairs, either, who insisted on enacting the Kama Sutra noisily every night: it was the noises in his head; it was the memories the place evoked. He had longed to get back on that awful plane and get the hell out of there, even though an empty flat awaited him at the other end.

TWO

The local paper, the Orkney Times, belonged to the same news organisation as the Chronicle. So, OK, he'd do as he was instructed: spend a few days looking into it, then get the fuck out as fast as he could. He also knew he wouldn't exactly receive a hero's welcome from the local reporters. Quite the opposite. They'd resent the fact that some supposedly hot-shot investigative journalist had been asked to take on one of their stories. Even if he did grow up locally. Well, fuck them, he didn't care about what they thought. They could think what they liked. He had a job to do.

Instead of making for the airport, he headed for the stores on Albert Street, such as they were. There wasn't exactly the kind of range you'd find in London, far from it, but there was some half-decent shops and, using his credit card, he managed to pick up some spare clothes, a backpack and a few essential toiletries like a toothbrush, toothpaste, disposable razors and shaving cream. He bought a pair of jeans, a woollen jumper, a couple of T-shirts, some underwear and socks. He was tempted to include a pair of shorts and trainers so he could go for a run in the mornings as he'd recently started doing that. Part of his new healthy-me kick, along with joining a gym. But he reckoned the eagle-eyed accountants back at the paper's finance department wouldn't stomach that, remembering Guthrie's words. Going running could wait until he got back home. Fortunately, he had worn a sturdy pair of Doc Marten shoes and he'd brought a good wind and water-proof North Face jacket as he knew what the weather could be like there regardless of the time of year, particularly standing by the graveside. He made sure he got the receipts to keep the bean counters at the paper happy. At least he had his notebook with him. He never travelled without it and a pen. You never knew when they'd be needed.

His mobile pinged, telling him that the paper had booked him into the Marine Hotel in Harbour Street. Fortunately, the hotel was close to the shops and the office of the *Orkney Times*. But then again, everywhere here was close; Kirkwall was no more than on overgrown village. He made his way to the hotel and checked in.

The hotel had three floors. It looked solid and respectable, built about a hundred years ago, thought Finn. He knew it only from having been in the public bar a few times to play darts when he was eighteen. He had a peek into the bar to see if it had changed. Instead of a dart board, there was now a large widescreen TV and a couple of elderly men propping up the bar.

The receptionist, a young friendly blonde woman with a Dublin accent, was expecting him and gave him his key card and told him about the times for breakfast. The room was on the top floor. He decided not to take the lift but made his way up the stairs with his bags of shopping.

In the hotel room, Finn had a quick shower and changed out of his funeral garb - suit, white shirt and black tie, which had made him feel as if he was in Reservoir Dogs - into his new casual gear. It was a relief to be wearing ordinary clothes again. He hadn't worn a tie in years. He'd almost forgotten how to tie one. No one did these days, not even in the office.

Then he used his phone and the hotel wi-fi to refresh his memory of the Powell case. A month earlier, in March, the body of Jeremy Powell had been found washed up on a beach about two miles from his home on the other side of Mainland. He had disappeared three days earlier. Powell was the forty-five-year-old author of a collection of highly successful thrillers, which had been made into a Netflix series. Literary critics weren't impressed by the quality of the plot or the prose. But that didn't stop Powell from achieving phenomenal sales, especially since the stories started to appear on TV.

The writer had seemingly fallen into the sea while walking his dog one day. Suicide was suggested. Even murder. The story had been all over the press, TV and internet at first, but had then quietly retreated into the background, occasionally appearing now and again as some new theory or speculation emerged. It was officially concluded that it was most likely an accident: that he'd stumbled on the coastal path or slipped on a rock and fallen from a cliff-top into the sea. The police weren't treating it as suspicious, it was reported. But was it simply an accident, some still wondered?

THREE

Finn walked from the hotel round to the offices of the Orkney Times in Burnmouth Road. A receptionist showed him through an open-plan area where two young women who barely looked out of their teens sat at desks staring at monitors and into a smaller room where two people, a young black woman and an older white man were seated in front of laptops, the man with a blank expression and folded arms. The woman smiled. Guthrie obviously must have forewarned them of his arrival, as he had said he would. As expected, he was about as welcome as a plate of sick. He wasn't even offered a cup of tea or a coffee. It was clearly straight down to business. He sat down and stared across the table.

The man, who looked to be in his sixties, said, 'So, you're Finn Morrison, then, are you?' He was wearing a checked shirt with a tie and a sleeveless pullover in a shade Finn could only describe as puke. Finn hadn't seen anyone wearing a tie in an office in a long time.

'Yes,' said Finn with an outstretched hand which was ignored.

'I'm the editor, Peter Nicolson. This is Grace Campbell.' Nicolson had a Shetland accent. And no trace of a smile. Unlike Grace, who gave him a warm grin. He grinned back and they at least managed to shake hands.

'Pleased to meet you,' said Finn.

'You found us alright then?'

'Yes. I'm staying in the Marine Hotel. It's quite handy.'

Then Nicolson slid a folder across the table. 'Here's the collection of cuttings. It's all in there,' he said. 'Save you the bother of looking them up online. You'll see we've covered this story extensively from day one. I don't think there's anything else you can add to what we've already done. You're wasting your time and ours, to be honest.'

'Would you care to give me a brief resumé?' Morrison asked.

'A resumé is it you want, eh?' said Nicolson, with a snarl. 'That'll be fucking right!' It was at that moment Finn decided the man was clearly an arsehole.

Grace Campbell also laughed. But it was a different kind of laugh. She was clearly laughing at Nicolson. And he didn't like it. Nicolson turned and stared at her, and her laugh suddenly ceased.

Nicolson stood up. Morrison actually thought for a moment that he was going to walk out of the room but instead he walked over to the window and stood staring out at the falling sleet. There was an uncomfortable silence in the room for what felt to him like minutes. Finn wondered if he should just pick up the folder and leave the room himself. He was just about to do that when Nicolson turned around and sighed. 'Jesus. We've worked bloody hard on this. What thanks do we get from our publisher? I'll tell you. None! Fuck all! Instead, we get the brilliant Finn Morrison helicoptered in from London to rescue us poor bloody local hacks, whom the proprietor in his wisdom obviously thinks are fucking useless.'

'Actually, I flew in on a fixed wing and...' Finn said.

'I don't give a flying fuck if you flew in on a fucking jetpack,' said Nicolson, his face turning a deep shade of purple and his eyeballs looking like they were about to pop. 'But, of course, you were once a local here too, weren't you?' said Nicolson. 'About five hundred fucking years ago. That'll come in really fucking useful. The London bosses probably think that's an advantage, eh?'

He had evidently looked into his

background. It wasn't easy to keep the past hidden in such a small place, of course, he realised. 'Look, Peter, I'm not any happier than you are that I am here. I didn't choose to take up this assignment. I'd sooner be back on a plane, believe me, but my editor has told me to do it and that's what I'll do. But I don't intend to hang about.'

Nicolson sighed. 'OK. Well, Grace has done the legwork on this story and knows most about it.' he said. 'Fill the esteemed visitor in, Grace. No doubt he'll have some brilliant insights that we haven't thought of.' He sat down, crossed his arms and stared at Finn with a face like thunder.

Grace nodded. 'Of course,' she said. She looked at Finn and smiled then looked down at her notebook and opened it. 'So, the police held a press conference after the body was discovered,' she said. Finn tried to place her accent. English. Northern. Possibly Lancashire? Could be Yorkshire? He had difficulty distinguishing one from the other. He did distinguish, however, that she had beautiful dark skin, black frizzy hair and dark brown eyes. She was the first black person he'd seen since arriving on the isles. Very different from London, he thought. That was the other thing about Orkney he remembered from the past. It had been a very white place to grow up. He'd got used to being around a diverse group of people and liked it. It was good to think that the place was changing.

Grace described what they had learned from the police investigation. 'Powell lived in the village of Yeswick, which is on the other side of Mainland, on the west coast, eighteen miles from Kirkwall. He disappeared on Monday 13th March. The author's widow said he'd taken their dog, a white labradoodle, out for a walk at about three o' clock. She assumed he had come back and gone straight to his office shed in the garden, to work. But, later, there was no sign of him. Or the dog. She tried ringing his mobile phone but got no answer. So, she went out to look for him but couldn't find him anywhere. His car was still parked outside the house and his wallet with all his credit and debit cards was still in the house along with his passport. That's when she contacted the emergency services.

'A team conducted a search along the route Powell was expected to have taken, a coastal path adjacent to a rocky shore, along the clifftops then down to a pebbly beach. An underwater search team was also brought in to search along the coast but there was no trace of a body. The dog, too, had disappeared.'

'Hmm,' said Finn. 'What was the weather like that day?'

'It was raining and there was a strong easterly wind all day and a high tide later that afternoon. Suicide was, of course, considered a possibility but there was no sign of a note or history of depression and his widow thought that it was very unlikely he'd taken his own life. The coastguard searched the coastal waters, but Powell and his dog had completely vanished. A check on the ferry passenger manifests and examination of the CCTV around the ports showed that he hadn't boarded any of the crossings to leave the isles.

'Three days later his body was found by some ramblers on the shore of a rocky cove two miles north of where he lived. The post-mortem revealed he suffered a subdural haemorrhage caused by blunt head trauma: head injuries consistent with hitting rocks on his way down. Then drowned. The assumption was that he had lost his footing, slipped and tumbled into the water and his body had been swept out to sea. Toxicology results confirmed he had no alcohol or drugs in his system. They never found the dog, either. The police reckon it must have tried to clamber down the cliff after him when he fell and been washed out to sea, probably to be consumed by sea creatures.'

'Did the police suspect any foul play? That's what his widow thinks, anyway, I believe?'

Grace said, 'There's a theory that it was a dognapping. Someone killed him to get the labradoodle. However, there was no sign of the dog afterwards, on the isles or that anyone remembered seeing on any of the ferries leaving for Scotland.'

'Hmm. OK. The dognapping angle is interesting. These dogs can fetch a lot of money and I suppose it wouldn't be difficult to smuggle a dog off the isles in a van without anyone seeing it.'

'I spoke to the pathologist. She said that the head injuries were consistent with the fall, hitting rocks on the way down. She did admit, though, that it was also possible that he could have been struck with a heavy object. So, she couldn't entirely rule out foul play. The fact that he had then been in salt water, though, for days meant that there wasn't any material for Forensics to pick up on. There was nothing on the footpath to indicate an assault, but there had been heavy rain and anything like blood traces there would likely be washed away anyway. A witness out walking her dog did report seeing a car travelling at speed out of the village later that afternoon. All she remembered was that it was a large dark car. Possibly an SUV. Unfortunately, she didn't get the make or any of the registration number. The police appealed for the owner to come forward, but no one did. It might have nothing to do with the case, of course.'

'I hate SUVs. Bloody planet-destroyers,' said Finn.

'Are you taking this seriously, Morrison?' said Nicolson, scowling at him.

'Yes, of course. What about his mobile phone?' asked Finn.

Grace said, 'It was never recovered. He may have had it in his hand when he fell, and it just got washed away. We don't know.'

Grace went on to detail the other actions that had been taken by the police including door-to-door enquiries around the area and an appeal for witnesses in the media.

'Any CCTV to go on?' Finn asked.

She shook her head. 'There's very little in the village itself. Nothing on the footpath.'

'Hmm. Did anyone else see him leave his house to go for a walk that day?'

'Not as far as we know. Just his widow. Though she says she saw someone else walking past just after her husband left the house. But the person was never identified. The route he usually took goes straight onto the coastal path.'

'Hmm, so there's only his widow's word that he went for that walk alone. And only her story about a stranger. What did the police make of that? I take it they treated her as a suspect and examined her house?'

'Yes. Forensics apparently checked every inch of their home and garden. And the coastal path. There was nothing to indicate anything suspicious had occurred there. You'll be aware of all the speculation online about her, no doubt. But the police seemed satisfied that she's entirely innocent. And she's the one who has been disputing that it's an accident.'

'Were they happily married?'

'Well, apparently so. There are no signs that they weren't, according to people who knew them. Certainly nothing to suggest otherwise. He had a few friends on the isles but mostly seemed to lead a fairly quiet life. I suppose being a writer, he would, wouldn't he?'

'I guess so. It's odd about the dog, though, isn't it? What could have happened to it?'

'No one knows. As I said, maybe it went in after its master and got washed out to sea.'

'Hmm. What about any debts? Drugs? Anything like that?'

Grace said, 'Not as far as we know. From what we can gather, he had plenty of money as you'd expect, a healthy bank balance and a portfolio of investments; a lavish house mortgage-free, only built in the last year, as you'll see if you go there. And there are no signs that he gambled away a fortune or misspent his savings on cryptocurrency or anything to cause him any financial problems. Quite the opposite, in fact. From what we've been able to find out about him, there's no evidence, either, for any involvement in drugs. No drugs showed up in the toxicology report or in a search of the house. He liked wine, had an extensive wine cellar in the house.'

'Maybe he was just very good at covering things up. Sometimes it just needs a fresh pair of eyes. That's why I'm here.'

Nicolson laughed and said, 'I don't really see the point of you being here, Morrison, to be honest. It's obviously just an accident. The man went for a walk on a wet and windy day, and he lost his footing, slipped and went over the edge. End of story. Either that or he topped himself. There's nothing more to it. I'm afraid you're wasting your time here. The widow is the anxious type. I think she's imagining there's more to this than there is.'

'Hmm. What about Powell's past?' Finn asked. 'Is there anything in his background that might provide a motive for an attack?'

Grace shook her head. 'Not as far as we

could find out. He was a reporter and a foreign correspondent in the Middle East for a while. But there's nothing that indicates he had been recruited as a spy or anything when he was at Cambridge University, though you never know, of course. But I doubt a Russian SVR team seriously wanted to bump him off. Anyway, isn't using Novichok on the door handles not more their style these days? And usually, it's one of their own ex-spies that they bump off. Not British citizens, unless it's by mistake.'

'Hmm. Probably. Maybe his next novel was going to portray Vladimir Putin as a really a nice guy. That would seriously piss off the Russians.'

Nicolson said, 'Look, I have no idea what your boss was thinking of when he told you to join us and I've unfortunately no choice but to grin and bear it. However, take this seriously and don't act the smart arse with me or you'll be sorry. You'll be on the first plane back to London and the bosses can like it or lump it. Understood?'

Finn nodded. 'OK. Message received and understood, Peter.'

He stood up. 'Right, I'll leave you to it. We've got other fish to fry. This isn't the only story we have on our books, you know. There's a desk you can have and a laptop for your use. If you want anything, I'll be next door in my office.' He left the room.

Grace stood up to go. 'Sorry about Peter. He doesn't take kindly to offers of assistance. He's used to doing things his way. He's been here a long time, over ten years in post and coming up for retirement soon. His bark is actually worse than his bite when you get to know him.'

'Not really sure I do want to get to know him,' Finn said. 'I'm allergic to bites by editors. They bring me out in a rash.'

She laughed. He liked her laugh. He noticed there was no ring on her finger. He stood up and stretched. 'Listen,' he said. 'I've had a long day. And I had an early start this morning. Before I head back to the hotel for the night, do you fancy a drink?'

'You've got a bit of a brass neck, haven't you?' she said.

He nodded. 'I'm renowned for it. Sorry, I don't mean to be so forward, it's just that you seem friendlier than Peter – although that's not saying much. But, if you'd rather not have that drink, that's OK. Sorry, I didn't mean to –'

'It's fine. I know somewhere we can go for a quiet chat.'

FOUR

He followed her out. They walked to a pub, the Bay Horse, on Bridge Street. It was an old establishment, traditional décor, with a long bar which stretched all the way from the front to the back. It was dimly lit so they took a seat near to the window where there was some light. There were a few other drinkers including a noisy group of laughing women at the far end of the pub, in an alcove. Finn remembered being in there when he was seventeen and getting served for the first time in a pub. That was when he'd first developed a taste for alcohol, something that became a habit, then an addiction. Now, he knew he couldn't risk touching a drop. He ordered an orange juice for himself and a gin and tonic for Grace.

'Do you not drink alcohol, then?' asked Grace.

'I *did*. I liked it too much, though' he said. 'Didn't know when to stop. But that's another story. In fact, I started my drinking in this very pub. We used to hang out here when I was still at school. Underage. But they weren't too bothered about checking ID then.'

'I see. Peter was right then; you are a local.'

'That's right. I was raised here. Not been back for a long while, though. From your accent, you're clearly not from these parts.'

She laughed. 'Yorkshire born and bred. Leeds.'

'So, what brings you up to this godforsaken part of the world?'

'Is that how you feel about it?'

'Not really. But I've got mixed emotions, some good memories, some not so good. So, why here?'

She shrugged. 'I just took a fancy to it. Saw a job and applied. I fancied something different. Liked the idea of Scotland. Maybe something to do with my surname. Campbell. Did you know lots of West Indians acquired Scottish surnames? Legacy of the British empire and slavery, of course. My grandad came over from Barbados as part of the Windrush generation. Had to fight the government to get accepted as a British citizen. Bastards! Anyway, I'd always worked in Yorkshire. I was sort of tired of it. Needed a change of scene. Didn't fancy London.'

I laughed. 'It's definitely a change of scene

here from Leeds. Isn't there anything you miss?'

'Not really. Though it's a bit weird being one of the few people of colour here. This place is so *white*! I go home every now and then to see Mum and Dad. But most of the people I grew up with all split to London or abroad anyway.'

'What about a boyfriend? A husband? Is there a mysterious Heathcliffe-type somewhere lurking on the moors back there?'

Now it was her time to laugh. Then she shook her head. 'Moors in Leeds? No. Well, not anymore. I was involved with someone but that's over. In the past. That was another reason to move here.'

He nodded. 'I get it. Fresh start and all that. And here? What about now? Is there someone here?'

She gave him a tap on the arm and smiled. 'You're getting rather too personal, now, Mr Morrison.'

'Sorry, I'm a bit of a nosey parker.'

'What about you? Are you married? Single? Divorced? Other?'

'I'm single. Like you I was in a relationship but that's finished.'

She took a drink from her glass and smiled. 'So, do you come back here much? It must have been a lovely place to grow up in, it's so beautiful.'

'Actually, I hated it, couldn't wait to get away. I wanted to get to a big city where you're anonymous, not like here where everyone knows your business.' He sipped his orange juice, wishing it had something else in it. Like vodka. 'In fact, this is my first visit back since I was eighteen. Fifteen years. I just came back for my gran's funeral today when I got the call from my editor.'

'Oh, I'm sorry, I didn't realise you were at a funeral. My condolences. Why have you never come back until now?'

'Good question. It's a long story. You don't want to hear about any of that, it would just depress you.'

'Try me.'

'My mum died when I was eleven.'

'Fuck, that's awful.'

'Yeah, it wasn't great, I suppose. Guess I've got used to it.'

'What happened?'

I shrugged. 'She was a single mum and junkie. She lived in Edinburgh, that's where I was born, but she brought me here when I was a baby and left me with my gran and grandpa to raise me. She went back to Edinburgh. I hardly ever saw her. She overdosed on heroin one night. I never knew who my dad was and maybe she didn't know either.'

'Oh my God! That's terrible.'

'Yeah, I know. She'd appear every now and again. Then she died. And Grandpa died too, when I was twelve. Then it was just me and my gran. When I was an older teenager, I went a bit wild. Lots of drink and drugs, you know the kind of thing. A party animal. I was probably a bit of a handful, no doubt about it. Rebellious. I think my gran was afraid I was going to turn out like my mum. We had a lot of arguments. So, finally, when I'd finished my exams, I left Orkney and never came back. I never saw my gran again. Now she's dead and it's too late for us to make up. I'm a bit sad about that.'

'That's tough. Sorry.'

'Yeah, like I said, I told you it would depress you. This place ... I don't know. It just has all those connections to a past that I'd rather forget.'

'Thanks for telling me, though. So, it must be hard being back here then, is it?'

'Kind of. I wasn't going to hang about for long, but my editor insisted I look into the Powell thing. Listen, I'm curious about this guy Powell. What do *you* think really happened? Accident or maybe something else? Suicide? Is there anything to lead you to think he could have been killed?'

'Not according to the police.'

'No mysterious Russian trawlers spotted that day, crewed by Moscow assassins ready to bump him off? So, there's nothing *fishy*?'

'Is that a joke?'

'Hah. Yeah, pretty poor, wasn't it? It was probably Peter's "fish to fry" remark that made me think of it. He's quite the raconteur, isn't he?'

'Listen, I don't mean to be rude, but Peter is right about one thing. We have looked at all the angles on this story.'

I nodded. 'I'm fully aware of that. Let's get one thing straight. I didn't choose this assignment. I'm not any happier than you about me being here.'

'Fair enough.' She knocked back her drink.

'Hey, you're a proper drinker! Want another one?'

'No thanks, I should be getting home.' She finished her drink, stood up and put on her coat.

'OK. I'm hoping to speak to his widow. And visit the area where he disappeared. My editor was going to contact her and let me know when I could speak to her. Hopefully tomorrow. I'll text you and you can come along too. Give me your number.'

'OK. I'd like to do that.' She told him her number and he put it into his phone.

'Listen, you don't need to rush off, do you? Maybe we could have dinner together? Talk some more about what other crime stories you've been covering here? There might be something that's useful.'

'Eh, I don't think so. I'll see you tomorrow, Finn. Thanks for the drink.'

FIVE

Grace headed for home and Finn walked the short distance to his hotel. In the hotel bar he ordered a mineral water and a chickpea and spinach curry. He sat at a corner table and had a look around the room as he waited for his meal to arrive. There was no one there he recognised. It was pretty quiet, just a few middle-aged guys propping up the bar and a handful of other folk dotted around the tables. On a wall, a large TV was showing a football match, but nobody appeared interested in it. It felt strange sitting in a bar, as it had done earlier with Grace, without some alcohol in his hand. For the past year he had been avoiding them as much as possible but occasionally, usually to do with work, he had had to venture into one. When he'd been at the bar waiting to order, he had glanced enviously at the barman pulling a pint of Guinness for a customer. It made his mouth salivate just thinking about how it would taste. That first pint of the day was always the best. Everything else was simply catch-up. That was the problem. He couldn't stop at one. Or two. Or three. Or four...

His curry arrived and he wolfed it down quickly while catching up with the news on his phone and then climbed the stairs to his room.

He got a text from his editor saying he'd spoken to Powell's widow, and he could visit her the next morning at 9.00 am. He texted Grace who replied that she would pick him up outside his hotel at 8.30. It would have been nice to have spent more time with her that evening, to have a bit of company. He didn't want to feel alone back here in this place where he had grown up, where there were ghosts that haunted him. She would have taken his mind off that. Maybe it could have led to more than that? he wondered.

That made him think of Fiona. The ghost from the more slightly more recent past. Memories of her still haunted him as well. He tried to think about where it all went wrong. His drinking obviously was a big cause. But it hadn't always been like that, he told himself. They had been happy once. For quite a while, in fact. After they got together, life seemed good. But then Finn started to hang out with workmates more. Drinking became more than just a few pints of the odd evening. It was every day after work, often at lunchtime too. Soon he reckoned it was easily over a hundred units a week, not that he was counting in those days.

The strange thing was that it didn't affect

his work. Not that he noticed anyway. He became what was known as a functioning alcoholic. Well, his working life functioned, if not his personal one. And there were so many other reporters who drank heavily that it was considered the norm to be a booze hound. It was embedded in the culture of the newspaper business and had been for decades, though things were changing now. He could see that in the younger generation, so many of them just had never been drinkers, weren't interested. What it did affect, though, was the rest of his life. That spiralled downhill.

Why? Why was he an addict? he asked himself now. He hadn't at the time. He didn't even consider himself to have a drinking problem. It was only after it had ruined his relationship, and his life was a mess and he decided to sober up for good that he could honestly reflect on it. Was it genetics? His mother had been an addict. Probably so had his biological father, he reckoned. He may have been another junkie, a heroin user in Edinburgh, most likely also dead, if that was the case. He'd probably never know for sure. He was fortunate he hadn't been born with HIV.

The good thing was that he had managed to stop drinking. Regular AA meetings helped to keep him on a sober path. It *was* an achievement. Not that he had any hopes that Fiona would take him back. She had since hitched up with another partner, he had learned from following her on Facebook. The surprising thing was that she hadn't blocked him. No, he had to move on with his life, not go backwards anyway. But what if... he asked himself. What if he had sobered up before their relationship hit the rocks. Maybe they would have been parents. Would he be able to handle that responsibility? He wasn't sure.

He decided to hit the sack. It had been a long day after all. He'd had to get up in the middle of the night to get to Heathrow. It was about midnight and was just brushing his teeth when there was a knock at the door. He had a mad idea that it was Grace wanting to make hot, passionate love to him after all.

But it wasn't her. Instead, he opened the door to find an attractive woman around his own age, clutching a bottle of white wine and two wine glasses. She was wearing high heels, a dark blue overcoat and a figure-hugging turquoise dress exposing plenty of cleavage. Someone he hadn't seen in about fifteen years but whom he recognised instantly: her hair was shorter but still a striking auburn colour, and those sparkling green eyes were a giveaway. How could he ever forget those?

SIX

'*Amy? What the fuck...*'

'Hello, Finn,' she slurred. 'I thought we could have a wee drinkie-winkie.' She waved the bottle and glasses and said, 'You're not very polite. The least you could do is invite me in.' She gave him a wide grin.

He opened the door wide, and she staggered in, bouncing off the sides of the doorway. It was clear she'd already had a skinful, he realised.

'You're the last person I expected to see,' he said. 'How did you know I was here?'

She put the bottle and glasses down on a table by the window, which had a couple of bottles of mineral water and two tumblers on a tray beside an empty ice bucket, took her coat off, threw it on the bed and collapsed on one of the two armchairs in the room. She unscrewed the wine bottle and poured the wine into one of the glasses she had brought. He stopped her before she filled a second glass

'Not drinking, Finn? I saw you in the Bay Horse with Grace Campbell earlier. Drinking orange juice. What's that all about?'

'I was an alcoholic, if you must know.'

'An alcoholic. Really? I would never have thought that you would end up like that. God, I'm sorry, Finn.'

'Anyway, how come you know Grace?'

'Come on, everyone knows who everyone else is here, have you forgotten?'

'Where were you in the pub? I didn't see you.'

'Hah, no. I was in a corner with a bunch of people at the other end of the bar. At first, I couldn't believe it was you, but I'd heard about your gran's funeral so realised that's why you were here. Sorry for your loss.' She hiccupped. 'I was confused how you knew Grace, so I googled you and found out you're also a journalist. On the *Chronicle, no less*. In London.' She raised the glass to her lips. 'You've done well with yourself, Finn. Congratulations.' She took a large slurp of the wine.

'Don't you think you've had enough, Amy?'

'Eh? No. Don't be a party pooper, Finn. Come on. Have a drink.' She waved the bottle invitingly.

'No. Didn't you hear me? I am an alcoholic. I go to AA meetings, for crying out loud. God, I can't believe I'm sitting here in a hotel room back in Kirkwall with you. You look plastered, incidentally. Do you normally get this drunk during the week? I should know all about it, I've been there, I know what it's like.'

'No. It was a special occasion. By the way, you won't get anywhere with Grace, if that's what you were after with that drink with her.'

He stared at her. 'What do you mean?'

'She's gay,' she said.

'Oh, really.' Finn felt stupid. Why had he assumed that she was heterosexual? And he'd asked her about boyfriends. Heathcliffe, for fuck's sake! 'How do you know?'

'Gossip. Yes, a lesbian. I can tell you didn't realise by the look of surprise on your face.'

'OK.' Finn shrugged. 'Not that it makes any difference to me. I only just met her. She's a colleague, that's all.'

She laughed. 'Hah! I can see you're disappointed. Hey, did you think that maybe I was her when I knocked on your door?' She smiled and took another drink, then topped up her glass.

'No, of course not.'

'You did, didn't you? You thought she was looking for a shag!'

'Fuck off, Amy!'

'Anyway, as a reporter I guess you're also hanging about with the likes of Grace for another reason. What is it? Why would a London-based journo be here? Hmm?' She put her finger to her chin and stroked it. 'I suppose you're interested in Jeremy Powell's death? The great mystery of the famous writer's death. Is that why you're staying on and haven't taken the first plane back? Trying to get an exclusive, maybe? The hot-shot reporter from London looking for a scoop?'

'Why would you think that?'

She laughed. 'Come on! This isn't London. We don't actually have that many famous writers who die in mysterious circumstances here. It doesn't take a genius to add two and two together. Thought you'd probably be staying here, or the Thistle and I'd find you in the bar downstairs, but I know Alan behind the bar, and he told me you were here, and you'd gone up to your room. Even told me which room it was. Think he's got a wee fancy for me.' She smiled and raised her glass. 'Here's to auld acquaintance!' She took another gulp of her wine. 'For auld lang syne!' She started to sing. 'Should auld acquaintance be forgot...'

Amy, be quiet, for God's sake. It's late. There's other guests next door probably trying to sleep.'

'Oh, Finn, you *are* a party pooper.'

'You're right about one thing, Amy. I have been asked to look into Powell's death. You always were quite sharp, I'll give you that. But you have a right cheek turning up like this. Last time I spoke to you, you told me you'd just got engaged. To my best friend. Great timing, especially as *we* were going out with each other at the time.'

Amy nodded. 'I know, I know. I'm sorry, Finn. I was a right bastard. Forgive me!'

'So, what happened between you and Alasdair then? I never spoke to him again.'

'Hah! That!' She laughed and took another gulp of wine. 'It was all a stupid mistake. The engagement that is. We broke up after six months. We both went off to Edinburgh University, Alasdair to do law and me English. But we quickly realised that being students engaged to each other was stupid. I wanted to have fun at university. I also realised how boring he could be!'

'So, what happened then?'

'Well, bit of a long story. After I graduated, I went off travelling with a girl friend from uni.

Somehow, I ended up in Perth, Australia, and got married to an Aussie bloke. A professional golfer, would you believe. That was another fucking mistake. Shit, my love life is a disaster. That lasted two years then I got divorced and came back here. Moved back in with mum and dad but then managed to get a job and a flat.'

'Any kids?'

'No. How about you?'

He shook his head. 'Currently unattached, as they say.'

'Fancy that, eh? We're like two peas in a pod. Zero luck on the romance stakes.'

'So, what were you doing earlier? The special occasion, in the pub.'

'It was a night out with folk from work, a leaving-do for someone I work with, and when it came to an end, I just had an idea to look you up.' She had finished her drink and started to pour another but knocked over the glass. Wine splashed across the table and onto the carpet. 'Oh, fuck!' she said. Finn grabbed a handful of tissues from a box on the dressing-table and mopped up the mess.

'Shit, sorry, sorry…,' Amy said.

'It's OK,' Finn said.

'Actually, I don't feel that well …,' she said.

She tried to stand up but staggered and then collapsed back in the chair. 'Fuck, I feel terrible.'

'Here, lie down,' he said, taking her arm and leading her over to the bed.

She threw herself down onto the duvet face down. He slid her high heels off. Soon, he could hear her snoring, so he pulled the duvet over her, found a blanket in the wardrobe, wrapped it around himself and settled down to try to sleep in the armchair.

SEVEN

Except he couldn't sleep. His mind went round and round, thinking of the past, remembering when he and Amy were an item. She had been his girlfriend since the start of Fifth Year at school, going out with each other for about eighteen months. She was the first girl he had sex with. They even had talked about a future together. But then she had dumped him. For his best friend at the time. He took it badly. Started drinking more and doing drugs. Mushrooms, cannabis, ecstasy.

At eighteen, after finishing his Sixth-Year exams, and after a final blazing row with his gran, he decided he'd had enough of Orkney and headed to the Scottish mainland. Though not that far. Aberdeen. He needed to get rid of the unhappy memories which the isles had meant for him. And it worked, mostly. He found a hotel job for the summer, which provided accommodation. Then he started university. That was where he met Linda. He remembered how excited he had been when she had agreed to go to a gig with him.

He had a spare ticket as his friend that he was going to go with had flu. So, he had asked her, and she had said yes. They were both on the same course and tutorial group but didn't really know each other that well. However, he knew that she liked the band, the Manic Street Preachers, as she had mentioned them once when they were part of a group of four having coffee together in the student refectory one day between lectures. The discussion was about which bands had decent politics. The Manics were an exception, one of the few, they agreed.

From then on, a romance took off. Nights in bed became days in bed. They made each other laugh and the sex was fantastic. They moved into a flat together for their final year. After university he got taken on as a trainee by the *Press and Journal* and Linda did teacher training at Northern College, aiming to become an English teacher.

Then he fell for someone else, Vicky, who was also a graduate trainee on the newspaper. One night when they both had had too much to drink, the inevitable happened and he went back to her place and didn't come home until the next morning. Linda asked him to move out immediately. He didn't blame her. He had been an idiot.

That was the end of that relationship. He

felt bad about it, the worst thing being that he and Vicky was just a meaningless physical relationship. Lots of great sex but they were just too different. It fizzled out after a couple of weeks. He really had nothing to be proud of as far as relationships went.

After that there was a series of one-night stands with colleagues and random women he met in bars and clubs. Life just seemed to be pretty unsatisfactory. He was bored with the job on the *P and J*; it was mainly court-reporting, which meant a lot of hanging around courtrooms and summarising proceedings. He wanted to get his teeth into investigations. So, he applied for a job on the *Chronicle* in London, as part of an investigations team. He didn't expect to get it but did and felt that his life was heading in a new direction. The job interested him, there were plenty of stories to draw him in, like investigating how organised crime syndicates in London were trafficking young women into Britain.

Fiona was a lawyer working with a unit that supported asylum seekers and victims of human trafficking. He interviewed her for a story he was working on and they got on well. He took the step of asking her out for a coffee and it developed from there. They moved in together, had great sex and went on some fabulous holidays. He was determined to make it work.

Except it didn't. He was constantly struggling with alcohol. From the moment he woke up until he passed out asleep, usually on the sofa. Their sex life declined. He took to spending far more time in the pub than at home. She finally gave him an ultimatum: her or the booze. Guess which he chose?

It was an illness, he had realised, after he lost Fiona. He had to sober up. So, he booked himself into a rehab clinic in the Cotswolds and blew his savings on getting sober. When he came out of there, he told himself he would stick to being sober. So far, he had. But it was never going to be easy. Each day felt like a fresh challenge.

And so now, here he was, back to where his relationships with women began, sharing a room with Amy, if not a bed. Something he'd dreamed about as a teenager. The first time they had made love, when they both lost their virginities, was in a bedroom at a party. At last, he wasn't a virgin. But it didn't last. She started going out with his best friend. He couldn't believe it.

After they'd broken up, each of his subsequent relationships didn't last, usually of his own making. He just couldn't commit. Then there was his love of alcohol, which didn't exactly help to sustain stable relationships. Maybe it was in his genes. Maybe it had something to do with a feeling of insecurity. He'd lost his mum. He'd lost this first girlfriend to his best pal. He couldn't afford to feel committed to anyone else in case they deserted him, abandoned him. The way Amy had. He hadn't been fair to the women he had gone out with. He let them down.

He felt guilty. Guilty for hurting those women he'd gone out with and disappointed; and guilt for never returning to Orkney to see his gran until it was too late. She'd lived to ninety-five years of age. He always remembered that she'd have a nightly dram she'd consumed all her life, and he liked to think that that explained her longevity, though as a former alcoholic he needed to be careful with such magical thinking. Why had he not come back to see her, even once? It was stupid. When he'd stayed with her, they'd got on fine until he was in his mid-teens. Then he would go out getting drunk, smoking weed and so and coming home late. Or not at all. There were rows. He felt she was too strict, but, looking back, she was probably only trying to protect him, look after him. In the end, he couldn't wait to get away, to sever the ties and the memories that the isles had for him. So, he'd jettisoned his past in an attempt to build a future.

At first, when he'd settled in Aberdeen, she had written letters, but he didn't reply. He'd consigned the early part of his life to history. He'd moved on, physically and metaphorically.

But last week he'd found out that his gran had passed away. He could have chosen to ignore the funeral but something inside him said he had to go back. Call it repentance, he thought. The dues he owed her. He'd expected to be there for a single day, but the isles seemed to have other plans for him, to involve him in a mystery; to surround him with the ghosts of his past.

TUESDAY

EIGHT

The next day, the weather had improved. There was no sign of the sleet from the day before and the sky was blue, though the wind was sharp and cold. Finn dressed in his suit. He thought he should look a bit smart to impress the widow. Grace picked him up as promised, just outside the hotel in a battered Renault Clio that looked like it had seen better days: there were several bumps and scrapes to the bodywork and one door was blue, the rest of the car red. He wasn't sure if it would make it the eighteen miles to Yeswick, never mind get back again.

She was waiting with a smile on her face. What was all that about? he wondered.

'Sleep well?' she said with a grin.

'I never sleep well away from home,' said Finn.

'Hmm.'

'What do you mean by that?'

'By what?'

'Hmm.'

'Nothing.'

'Come on, out with it?'

'I was just thinking about the woman you spent the night with last night!' She laughed.

'What? Jesus! How did you know about that?'

'I saw Amy leave your hotel this morning when I was waiting for you. She told me you'd be down in a minute. I wondered how she knew that.'

'It's not what you think. '

'Isn't it? What is it then?'

'Fuck's sake! This bloody place. There really are no secrets here, are there? Anyway, how do you know Amy Simpson?'

'She manages the bookshop in Albert Street. Everyone knows her. Those that read books, anyway. Which includes me. She also writes an occasional column for the paper. Descriptions of the natural world, you know, marine life, flowers and fauna on the islands. She's actually a pretty decent writer.'

'So, for your information, nothing happened. She's someone I knew back in the old days, from school. She was blind drunk last night and passed out on my bed. And before you ask, I slept in a chair! If you could call it sleeping.'

'Hah! If you say so. That must have been comfy!'

'Exactly. I needed three cups of strong coffee to get my head together.'

'Quite a welcome back to the isles, then, eh? Were you glad to see her?'

'I don't know. I guess so. Anyway, let's get back to why I'm here. Powell's widow, Laura. What's she like?'

'I don't really know her that well. Clearly, she's been through a terrible ordeal. Losing her husband suddenly. All of the attention from the media. Including us. And the police investigation. They treated her as a suspect to begin with which I'm sure unsettled her. That can't have been easy for her. Try to handle her with kid gloves, though. She's pretty fragile, I'm sure.'

'Of course. I'm well used to dealing with grieving spouses, as I'm sure you are too.'

Grace drove across Mainland for about half an hour until they reached Yeswick, and the Powell house. 'So, this is it, we're here,' she said.

Finn had visited the village once or twice before but it was a long time ago and the place had expanded with a lot of new houses, The Powell house was a spectacular place, built in a modernist style, a three-storey building clad in timber, the roof covered in solar panels, overlooking the ocean. However, to the front and both sides of the house, where you would expect a landscaped garden, was what resembled a building-site, with partially constructed walls and an incomplete patio with decking unfinished. There appeared to be no work going on at present as no workmen were about. A blue BMW sat on the driveway.

'Wow! Said Finn. 'Some place.'

'Yes, isn't it? I'd love to live here. I'd just sit and stare out of the window at that view all day long.'

Laura answered the door and showed them into a spacious, white-walled living room with floor-to-ceiling windows with a panoramic view out to sea. Finn and Grace sat down on one of the pair of matching cream leather sofas, Laura on the other. A large abstract oil painting hung on one wall. Another wall was shelved from floor to ceiling with an array of books and artefacts: oriental ceramics and delicate crystal vases. There was a hi-fi with a turntable and a pair of large floor speakers.

Laura was an attractive woman who, Finn

thought, looked in her thirties, a good ten years younger than her late husband had been. Her long dark hair was pulled back in a ponytail that made her look even younger. She was wearing a cream silk blouse and designer jeans. Her eyes had a slightly glazed look. It was only one month after all since she'd lost her husband and she still looked to be in a state of shock. There were bags under her eyes. She nervously fumbled with the wedding ring on her finger. She had made a cafetière of coffee which sat on a coffee table in front of them. Laura poured their drinks. She was wiping her eyes.

'Help yourself to milk and sugar,' she said.

'Are you OK? asked Grace.

Laura said, 'Sorry. It's just you both coming out here this morning has brought it all back. I thought I was over it. But it's a nightmare really. Jeremy and I had hoped to spend the rest of our lives together and were trying to have a baby. It hadn't worked, though, so we were talking about IVF treatment.' She looked like she was close to tears.

'I'm sorry for your loss,' Finn said. 'As I believe my editor has told you, I've been asked to speak to you. I understand that you'd like to know what happened to your husband. I have a few questions I'd like to ask.' He took out his notebook and pen and his iPhone. 'Is it OK if I record our discussion? I'll also need to make a few notes. I hope that's OK?'

Laura nodded. 'I know. He explained over the phone. I'm grateful to you for coming. Anything that can help get to the truth of what really happened.'

Finn had looked at Twitter that morning before leaving the hotel to find out what she had been posting. It was mainly her complaints about the police investigation and that she was sure it was not an accident. But she, inevitably, had received plenty of abuse from trolls. People dismissing her as deluded. As well as the usual misogynist hate speech. There were many who accused her of being behind the whole thing, saying she'd misled the police, that she was the one who had killed her husband, chasing after him and pushing him and the dog over the cliffs after a fight about alleged unfaithfulness or something else. They said she had a personality disorder. Was a psychopath. All sorts of things. He didn't know how she could cope with it.

'You think that someone may have killed him?' Finn asked.

'Yes. It's definitely possible.'

'I believe that the police investigation concluded that Jeremy's death was most likely accidental, but I'd like to know more about why you don't think so. Grace has already told me some things, but I'd like to hear it from you. But first, if you don't mind, I'd like to fill in a bit of background. First of all, I wondered why Jeremy chose to come and live here? I understand he was born in London, and lived mostly in big cities until he moved here. It's quite a change, when you're used to the big city. Any idea why he wanted to live somewhere so remote?'

She had picked up her cup and sipped the coffee while he had been talking. He was struck by her eyes. They were bright blue and fixed on him as he spoke. Then she answered, 'It was because it helped his writing. Fewer distractions. The peace and quiet. Having moved here myself from London, I appreciate that. It's so beautiful. Calm.'

Finn nodded. He felt acutely aware of the difference between London and Orkney himself and could understand the attraction, even if he wasn't sure he would ever want to move back there himself. 'Did he miss anything? There's so much to do in London. I live there myself but am originally from up here. It's quite a change. What about the social side of things? Didn't he miss his friends?'

She shook her head and smiled. 'No, not at all. Jeremy was actually really quite an introvert. Naturally, he had a few people he was close to back in London. He kept in touch with them, of course, but he was really a very solitary person. He liked his own company more than hanging out at parties. This place suited him.'

'Can you tell me much about Jeremy's past before he became a full-time writer? He was a journalist to begin with, wasn't he?'

'I can't tell you much. I didn't know him then, of course and he didn't talk about it, apart from saying he had always wanted to be a writer; he'd dabbled part-time and so on, but he just made the decision to take a gamble on it and wrote his first book in nine months. It paid off though, didn't it? As you can see by this place.' She waved her hand.

Finn looked around and nodded. It certainly was an impressive place. 'It's a beautiful place you have here.'

'Thanks. When we got married and moved up here, we lived first of all in a cottage facing the harbour. It was lovely but small. We were lucky to be able to purchase some land here from a local farmer. He wanted to get rid of a field and we bought it up. We have a friend in London who is an architect and he designed it. Then we hired a local builder to build it. That's when the problems started.'

'Problems? I see there's still work going on

beside the house. What's that all about?'

She ran her hands through her hair. 'That? Fuck, you don't want to know about that. It's a long story.'

'I'd like to hear it. But first, tell me how you got to know Jeremy.'

'It was when his agent sent the manuscript of his debut novel to the publisher where I worked as an editor. I still do that, though freelance now for different publishers. It's easy to do it remotely anywhere and I work from home here now but in those days pre-pandemic everyone worked in offices, didn't they? So, Jeremy came to our London office for a meeting with us and we struck it off together immediately. His first book was an instant bestseller as have been all the rest in the series; I like to think that my editing was a factor! Anyway, we had a few meetings and he asked me out on a date and that was it. We quickly fell in love.' She started to cry and wiped the tears from her eyes with a tissue.

'So, let's talk about what happened the day he disappeared. How did he seem?'

'He did seem to be preoccupied by something. He wouldn't talk about it, though. I asked him several times what it was, but he just said it was nothing. I'm sure that there was something bothering him, though. I told the police this.' She sighed and picked up her cup and took a sip of coffee.

'But you don't know what it was that was bothering him?'

'No.'

'What time did Jeremy leave the house that day?'

'It was just after three.'

'Tell me, did he always take the dog for a walk in the afternoon about that time?'

'About then. I usually walked the dog early in the morning and Jeremy in the afternoon. He liked doing it, said it helped him to gather his thoughts for his writing. He liked to work in the mornings, but he said that ideas came to him as he walked the dog. Then he'd go to his desk and do a several more hours' work before supper. Sometimes he would even work again for a few hours in the evening. If he had a lot of ideas in his head, he said he just wanted to get on with writing. He'd occasionally do the odd all-nighter when he'd sleep in his office shed. There's a sofa bed there. I like to put my light out early so he often wouldn't want to disturb me if he was going to work late. Anyway, that day I was working in my office upstairs in the attic and just assumed he'd come back and gone into his office with the dog to work until suppertime but when I went downstairs, he and Charlie were nowhere to be seen.'

'Charlie?'

'Our labradoodle.'

'So, you don't believe that it was an accident. What do you think happened that day?'

'I don't know. It just seems so odd. He walked that path every day. How could he just fall into the sea? But even if he had, how do you explain Charlie's disappearance?'

Finn nodded. 'There was speculation that the motive could have been to steal the dog. What do you think about that?'

She nodded. 'The police thought it was a possibility. I don't know. Would someone really kill someone for a dog? But I suppose it's possible.'

'You think someone killed Jeremy?'

'Yes. I do. I'm sure of it. He was always very careful on that footpath. How could he fall into the sea and Charlie just disappear? It doesn't make sense.'

'Why would someone want to harm him?'

'I have no idea.'

'Is there anyone who bore a grudge against him or that he fell out with?'

She nodded. 'Yes. David Laing.'

'Who's that?'

Grace said, 'He's a builder and property developer. Owns one of the main building companies on Orkney.'

'Why did they fall out?' asked Finn.

Laura said, 'Laing's company built our house. It went well at first but then there were all sorts of squabbles over money. He was supposed to add a conservatory to the side of the house and do the landscaping and patio, but Laing said he wanted more money. He claimed the cost of materials had gone up. But Jeremy said they had an agreement from the start and wouldn't give him it. As a result, Laing stopped the work.'

'How much more money did the builder want?' asked Finn.

'Twenty thousand We could have afforded it, but it was the principle. Jeremy felt he was trying to rip us off.'

'Did things ever get heated between them?'

'There was a bit of shouting one day, then Laing just stormed off and took his workmen with him. Jeremy phoned him but he wouldn't discuss it. No other builder on the isles would take on the job to complete it. They're all afraid of Laing.'

'Did you tell the police about this?'

'Yes. Of course.'

'Grace told me that you said you saw someone else pass by your house that day after Jeremy went out. Is that right?'

'Yes. It was just after Jeremy left the house with Charlie. I happened to glance out of the window and saw someone walking past the house in the same direction that Jeremy would have gone, along the coastal path.'

'What was this person like?'

'Definitely a man. He was wearing a black denim jacket and jeans. And a dark baseball cap.'

'And no one has any idea who this person was?'

'No. The police appealed for witnesses and issued my description, but no one came forward who knew anything. I found that very strange.'

'I see. So, you think maybe this person had something to do with what happened to Jeremy?'

'I don't know, but it's suspicious, isn't it? Why would no one come forward who was on the path around that time?'

'Maybe they're worried they'd be implicated in something that had nothing to do with them?'

She nodded. 'I suppose that's a possibility,

but I still find it strange.'

'Could it have been Laing?'

'I couldn't be sure. But it might have been. The police told me they had ruled him out. I don't know why.'

'What is he like?'

Grace said, 'He's a tough cookie. Got a bit of a reputation.'

'A reputation?' said Finn. 'For violence?'

'He's just a bully,' said Laura. 'A bully. That sums him up. If he doesn't get what he wants he throws his toys out of the pram.'

'Hmm. What about other theories? Has suicide definitely been ruled out in your mind? Did Jeremy have any history of substance abuse or mental illness?'

'No. He liked a drink. We both did. But he didn't take drugs and he wasn't drunk that day. And there was nothing to make me think he was going to take his own life.'

'Sometimes it's hard to tell if someone is suicidal.'

'I know, but I still can't believe that. I'm sure Jeremy wouldn't have killed himself.'

'You said he walked the dog every afternoon. So, if someone wanted to attack him on his own, they might know when and where to find him?'

'I suppose so.'

'Did he always take the same route?'

'Yes. Along the coastal path.'

'Do you know what he was working on?'

'I don't know. He didn't like to talk about what he was working on until he had finished it, then he'd show it to me. But he was probably basing it on a real event. He often did that, you know. People have these strange ideas that writers come up with entirely original ideas all the time, out of their own heads. That's not true. They're magpies, scavenging the media for stories. Jeremy would spend more time researching than writing, actually. He carried his notebook everywhere with him so he could jot down any ideas that came into his head. He even kept it next to the bed.' She laughed. 'Many is the time he'd woken me in the middle of the night putting a light on to write something down in that bloody notebook. When he'd finally got enough material, it wouldn't actually take him long to write the book.'

'Had he done anything different recently before his death?'

'The only thing was his trip to England just

before his death. He went down to give a talk at his old Cambridge college then spent a few days in London. He came home on the Sunday, the day before he disappeared.'

'Do you know how that went? The trip to England.'

'OK, I think. He gave a talk at the college about his latest book and there was a Q and A session afterwards. He seemed happy with it all when he came back.'

'What did he do when he was in London?'

'He said he caught up with a friend and saw his parents.'

'OK, that's useful to know. Could we see his office shed now before we go?'

'Yes. It's an outhouse in the garden. I'll show you where it is.'

'You don't have any CCTV around the place, do you?'

'No. I wish we had. We were pretty lax about security. It seemed such a safe place to live. Until now.'

'Did anyone else in Orkney know Jeremy that well? Did he have any close friends here whom he might have talked to?'

'You could speak to Callum Maclean. He

was probably his closest friend here. He's a poet. Jeremy used to go and visit him from time to time. He lives in Stromness. I have his address somewhere.' She got up and rummaged in a drawer and found an address book. 'Here we are,' she said. She jotted down the details on a post-it note and passed it to him. 'I've given you his phone number. It's a landline. He doesn't have a mobile.'

'Thanks, that's very helpful.'

'If you go to see him, take a bottle with you. Callum likes a drink. Malt whisky is his tipple. It might help.'

'Thanks, I'll bear that in mind. One last question. I'm sure you've been asked this before but maybe you've had more time to think about it. Can you think of anyone else apart from Laing who might want to harm your husband?'

She sighed and shook her head. 'No. I have absolutely no idea. Jeremy wasn't an angel. He could be difficult at times, got frustrated when things didn't work out, but I don't think he could ever have annoyed anyone so much that they wanted to kill him. The whole thing is preposterous. He was a writer, for God's sake. He spent most of his life holed up in a room on his own staring at a laptop. Who would want to kill him? But I'm convinced someone did.'

NINE

They left the house and Laura showed them to the office shed in the back garden. Like the rest of the garden, it hadn't been landscaped. There was just a path from the house across the rough ground beside a partially built wall. She left them there and returned to the house. It was actually quite a bit more than a shed: a designer-built timber construction with sliding glass doors and oak flooring. The writer's desk and chair were positioned facing the window: on the desk sat a printer and an Anglepoise lamp.

The place looked very cosy. There were even electric panel heaters. Quite a comfortable place to work, or even spend the night. As Laura had said, there was a sofa which presumably could be pulled out into a bed. On one wall, there was a large cupboard which contained some bedding, a bottle of malt whisky, tumblers, and a stack of blank printing paper. A tall bookcase held a large collection of books: dictionary, a thesaurus and an assortment of fiction – much of it crime and thrillers. There were books by Ian Rankin, John Le Carré, Peter May, Mick Herron and others of the crime and thriller genre. Also, of course, copies of all of his own titles, both in hardback and paperback. A few framed photos of Orkney were hung on the walls but apart from that it was a purely functional space.

They called in to see Laura again. Finn said, 'Thanks, Laura. It's been very useful talking to you. I'll keep in touch with you and let you know if I find out anything interesting. Here's my card. Call me if you think of anything else.' He handed her his business card and they left.

They walked along the coastal path in the direction the writer had gone on that fateful day. The path ran north from the house and meandered up and down sometimes close to the sea and even along the beach in places. They came to the highest spot where the path ran along the cliff tops. It was about a mile from his house, maybe a little more. Finn could see how the investigators might have thought he'd stumbled and fallen about there, especially on a wet and windy day. hitting his head off rocks as he went down and disappearing beneath the waves. It was slippery and once or twice he nearly lost his footing and Grace put out a hand and grabbed him. He wasn't used to this, though once, when he'd lived on the isles, he had been. Out of practice. Nowadays he rarely ventured to the countryside.

Finn felt unsafe. He had never liked heights. He always had a fear that some invisible force was going to suck him over the edge to fall to his death. The cliffs tumbled for hundreds of metres down to the sea below. There wasn't much to see. Just lots of rocky shore, pebbles and sea. Seagulls screeched. The noise was deafening, with the wind and the waves crashing on the rocks below. Finn tried to imagine what it would have been like that day that Powell took a tumble into the sea below. Powell might not have easily heard anyone creeping up behind him until they were standing close enough to hit him over the head with a rock or a hammer. Especially if he had been wearing headphones or earbuds, listening to music or a podcast on his phone, or on a call. It wouldn't take much to then push him over the edge.

'So, perhaps somebody did follow him up here,' Finn said. 'Just as Laura says. But who? Maybe he upset someone. Or he had a fling with someone else's wife and the husband found out? Or it really was all just to get hold of the dog. It could have been smuggled off the isles easily, I'm sure, in the boot of a car or in a van.'

'Hmm. I suppose so. Do you really think someone could have murdered him? I'm not sure.

She's sure someone did, but there's really no proof. I do think she might be imagining it. She strikes me as a bit paranoid.'

'I don't know. What about this guy, Laing, the builder? Any juicy stories about him?'

'The rumour is he has the police in his pocket. There are tales of brown envelopes being passed to councillors to get him planning permission for his housing developments.'

'Have you run any stories about him?'

She shook her head. 'No. It's impossible to substantiate any of the stories. Plus, he's a golfing buddy of Peter's.'

'Oh, right, I get it! Fucking hell. This place.'

'Don't tell me that doesn't happen in London? It does in Leeds. All the time. Councillors on the make.'

'True.'

They walked back to the car.

After that, Grace drove while he stared out at the landscape. You were never far from water, that was the thing that he remembered about here the most. They passed the odd standing stone. He'd forgotten how soothing the gentle hills and views of the sea were. In the distance a flock of birds were flying across the sky. His mind drifted back to when he was a teenager riding a moped along this road, his girlfriend on the pillion seat. A sense of freedom.

Further on, they passed near the Ring of Brodgar, a ring of standing stones, where as a child and a teenager, he'd often stood in the middle of that stone circle, closing his eyes and trying to think himself into the minds of the people from thousands of years ago who'd built this ancient place of worship. He'd cycled there often when he was troubled, and it eased whatever pain he was feeling inside; it was a magical place. Somehow it connected him mysteriously to the rest of the universe. At the age of seventeen, he'd once smoked a joint here with friends, the vast expanse of the Milky Way over their heads making him feel like a tiny speck in a huge universe spinning around him.

It was as if Grace could read his thoughts. 'Remembering the past? she asked, catching him staring out of the passenger window.

He nodded. 'There's a lot of memories. Some good, some bad. I didn't realise how much coming back here would bring them back.'

'So, will you be seeing her again?'

'Who? Laura?'

'No! Amy!'

'It's not like that. As I told you, she was

drunk. We're just old friends. There's nothing between us.'

'You sound bitter.'

'I'm not.'

'I don't believe you.'

'Think what you like.'

'But there once was?'

'What?'

'There once was something between you?'

'Well, yes. When we were young. Ancient history.'

'Do you want to talk about it?'

'No.'

'OK.'

After that there was an awkward silence for the rest of the journey. When they got back to Kirkwall, Grace parked the car and they walked to a shop in Albert Street to pick up sandwiches for lunch which they took quickly back to the office as the rain came on.

In the afternoon, he researched Powell a bit more and found out that he came from a very privileged background. His parents were wealthy, father a stockbroker, mother a journalist. He had a sister, who had emigrated to Canada who was married with two sons. He attended Cheltenham College, a top public school Then he went to Cambridge University. Took a degree in French and Arabic. After he graduated, he did a journalism course at City University, London and then worked on a local paper in Brighton before becoming a foreign correspondent, working for Associated Press before he decided to become a full-time writer.

At three o' clock, he left the office, walked to the nearest supermarket and bought a bottle of Highland Park, keeping the receipt for expenses. Though, how he'd manage to explain that it wasn't for personal consumption, he didn't know! Then he picked up a taxi from the rank to take him to Stromness.

TEN

Later that afternoon, Grace saw a post on social media that looked interesting. The post said there had been a break-in at a house in Kirkwall; a man had sustained an injury and there was also something about a missing dog. That intrigued her, thinking of what had happened at Yeswick. When she phoned the police, the media spokesperson wouldn't give her any more details other than the name and address of the owners. She decided to follow it up, so put on her coat and headed out.

The address was on the other side of the town in a newly built estate of three, four and five-bedroomed houses on a site which had previously been a fish processing factory. There were maybe ten or twelve houses in total. Grace was aware that it was one of David Laing's developments. Of course, it had to be! The builder was everywhere on the isles these days.

She hadn't actually visited the place before

but quickly found number six Marine View. She supposed you could just about see the sea from some of the attics, but it certainly wasn't visible from the ground. A nice bit of estate agent disinformation, she thought, to entice buyers. And it had worked. The houses had been snapped up even before they were built, buyers buying them off-plan, she had heard.

She rang the doorbell and waited. It was possible that the Lockharts wouldn't want anything to do with her and tell her to go away. She was well used to that kind of reception when doorstepping victims of crime. On the other hand, maybe they would see her interest and the resulting publicity as helpful in drawing attention to what had happened and finding the perpetrator.

A man in his sixties with a bandaged head answered the door. He was wearing a checked shirt, a thick grey cardigan and baggy black corduroy trousers. He had a white beard, equally white hair to match and large round spectacles, through which he peered at her with curiosity. A Santa lookalike, thought Grace.

'Mr Lockhart?' she said.

'Yes? What do you want?' he said, in an English accent. It sounded like a Yorkshire one, Grace thought, though not Leeds. Sheffield, possibly.

Grace put on her best smile and said, 'Hi. My name is Grace Campbell. I work for the *Orkney Times*. I've heard you had a break-in. I'm sorry to hear that. I wondered if I could have a word?'

Maybe it was her smile. Maybe it was her politeness. Maybe it was her Yorkshire accent. Whatever it was, Mr Lockhart nodded and said, 'OK. Come in.'

He led her through to the kitchen diner where a woman about the same age as him was standing at the sink wearing rubber gloves and washing dishes.

'June, this is someone from the local paper,' said Mr Lockhart. 'She wants to talk to us about the break-in.'

'Hello,' said June, removing her gloves and shaking Grace's hand.

'This is my wife, June,' said Mr Lockhart. 'I'm Bill.'

'Pleased to meet you. Would you like a cup of tea?' said June.

'Oh, I'm gasping for one, thanks,' said Grace.

'You don't sound like you're from round here. Is that a Leeds accent?' said June.

'Yes. Where are you from?'

'Rotherham,' said June, as she filled the kettle. 'Have a seat. Would you like a biscuit?'

'No thanks. Tea's fine,' said Grace. 'How long have you lived here?'

Joan said, 'Just over a year. We were both teachers. Bill was a secondary maths teacher; I was a primary depute head. We turned sixty and decided to retire and take our lump sums and pensions and do something different. Our two grown-up children are married and live in the south of England, and we rarely see them anyway. So, we sold our place in Rotherham and moved up here last year. Best thing we've ever done.'

'Until now,' said Bill.

'Until now, yes,' said June.

'Can you tell me what happened?' asked Grace.

'Well,' said Bill. 'Last night, June went to bed about ten. I stayed up watching TV until about midnight then let the dog out into the garden for a pee before I went to bed.'

'What kind of dog do you have?' said Grace.'

'An English springer spaniel. Henry,' said June.

'Yes,' said Bill. 'Henry sleeps in here. That's his bed over there.' He pointed to an empty dog basket covered with a red tartan rug in the corner of the room. 'I left Henry in here and went upstairs to bed. As I said, that was just after twelve. Next thing I hear is the dog barking.'

June touched Bill on the arm gently. 'You didn't hear him, dear,' interrupted June, looking at Bill. 'You were fast asleep.' She turned back to face Grace. 'And his hearing's not as good as mine. He doesn't wear his hearing aid at night. I heard Henry and woke you up. It was ten past three. I looked at the time on my phone.'

Bill nodded. 'Yes, that's right. Anyway, then I heard him too then. And it sounded like someone was walking around in the kitchen. I got out of bed and went downstairs. I grabbed a golf club from the cupboard in the hall. A three iron. Nice and heavy. I opened the kitchen door and saw someone wearing a balaclava. With a baseball bat. And there was another person there, also with a balaclava on. He had Henry in his arms. I say he. I'm pretty sure they were both men but I can't be certain.'

'What did you do?' said Grace.

'I said, "Get out of my house," and brandished the club at him but the one with the bat, he swung it at me and hit me. Next thing I know I'm coming to, lying flat out on the floor here with a sore head and June standing over me.'

June said, 'I heard a commotion and came down, but the intruders had gone. Bill was just coming round. Well, obviously I phoned the emergency services right away. They were very quick, I must say, both the police and the ambulance. The paramedics were lovely. The ambulance took Bill to hospital and the police wanted to talk to me. I hadn't seen the men so I couldn't tell them much. They must have had a car outside. They'd disappeared by the time I came downstairs. I looked out into the street, but they were gone. But it was obvious how they got in. The lock on the French doors had been forced open.' She pointed at the glass doors which led out to a decked area of the garden. 'Fortunately, I got a locksmith out who could repair it.'

'Are you alright?' said Grace to Bill.

'I've got concussion, the hospital said. But fortunately, that's all. The bastard could have killed me. I'm lucky he didn't fracture my skull.'

June said, 'They did all sorts of tests, even gave him an X-ray. I was really worried until the hospital said he could come home.' She turned to face Bill. 'You should be resting, you know. I don't know if answering all these questions is good for you.'

Bill said, 'I'm fine. There's no brain damage. I've just finished the crossword today in record time.' He grinned.

'Did either of them say anything?' asked Grace.

'No. Not a word.'

'And your dog is missing, is that right?'

'Yes,' said June. 'Nothing else. They took Henry. That's terrible, isn't it? Why would anyone do such a thing?'

ELEVEN

Callum Maclean lived in a cottage on the outskirts of Stromness. Finn had phoned him earlier to ask if he could visit and get his address, so he wasn't unexpected. When he answered the door, Finn thought Maclean looked to be in his seventies, his grey hair tied back in a ponytail and a pair of wire-framed reading spectacles perched on the end of his nose. His face lit up when presented with the bottle. He was holding a ginger cat in his arms when he came to the door but immediately put it down and took the bottle.

'Thanks,' he said with a grin. 'I didn't realise it was my birthday! I take it you're the newspaperman? Well, whoever you are, with a bottle in your hand, you're very welcome.'

'Yes. I'm Finn Morrison. As I explained on the phone, Jeremy Powell's widow suggested I had a word with you. I'm helping her find out what happened to Jeremy. I understand you were a friend of his.'

'Finn Morrison? You wouldn't originally be from these parts, would you?'

'Yes. A good while ago now.'

'Come on in, son.'

Maclean led the way through to a living room, each wall packed with books. Books overflowed every surface. Maclean even had to clear some off the sofa to let his guest sit down while he took the armchair. He took off his reading glasses and put them into a case. He said, 'I knew your mum, Anne, you know. A tragedy. So many people lost to the drugs. That must have been terrible for you at the time, son.'

'I was very young. I don't really remember her very well.'

'Your mother had a lovely singing voice when she was a teenager. I was involved with the folk club here then and she was a great singer. I played a bit of fiddle. I remember her singing at some Hogmanay parties. Aye, I remember listening to her at many a session and ceilidh. Such a waste. Aye, that was a terrible thing happened, son. They drugs are a menace, so they are. But you've grown up well and that would make her proud.'

'Thanks. Can you tell me a bit about Jeremy? I believe that the two of you were quite close,' Finn said, as Maclean opened the bottle and poured himself a generous two fingers of the amber liquid. Finn had explained to him he was a teetotaller.

'Poor old Jeremy. A great guy,' said Maclean. 'We had some good times together. He loved to come out fishing with me. Bloody awful thing that happened to him.' He took a sip of the ten-year-old malt. 'Good stuff this. You're sure you don't want a wee nip?'

Finn shook his head. 'How did you get to know him?'

'I run the local writer's workshop. We meet one a week in the library here. I asked Jeremy if he would come and give a talk to the group about his writing. He did and it was really inspiring. He was very generous with his time, and we all went to the pub afterwards. We hit it off and became friends. I once wrote a novel myself, you know, oh, over forty years ago now. Very autobiographical. About growing up here. It was a bit experimental. No punctuation! The London Review of Books described it as "Joycean". It never sold more than a few hundred copies. Nothing like Jeremy's books. But at least my poetry has been better received. Jeremy said he liked my poems, though maybe he was just being kind, I don't know.'

'How often did you see each other?'

'About once a month. We'd have a wee drink, play chess and chew the fat.'

Finn said, 'His widow thinks someone might have harmed him. What do you think?'

Callum rubbed his beard and shook his head. 'I know she does. Poor lassie. She must miss him very much. We all do but to lose a partner suddenly just like that...Well, I don't know why anyone would want to harm Jeremy. He was a gentle soul, despite all that violence in his books. He just had a very good imagination.'

'I know you say you had no idea who might want to harm him but, I wondered, did he ever tell you anything that might give a clue about any worries he had or anything from his past that troubled him? Anything at all?'

'Not much but he opened up sometimes. After a few drams, you know. Told me he couldn't be accused of just making stuff up in his books. I don't know much about what he did, but he was angry whenever a reviewer said his plots were too far-fetched and unrealistic. "What the fuck to they know about it?" he'd say.'

'When did you last see him?'

'Oh, it would be about two weeks before he died.'

'How was he then? Did he seem concerned

about anything? Worried?'

'I don't think so. No.'

'Did he ever talk about anyone he'd fallen out with?'

'Oh, aye, that man Laing!'

'David Laing, the builder?'

'Aye, that's him, the toerag! Jeremy thought he was ripping him off. I wouldn't put it past the guy. He's a right chancer! I've had my own run-ins with that bastard.'

'Yes, Laura told me about Laing. Was there anything else that disturbed him? Did he ever talk about anything else that bothered him?'

'Oh, aye, there was one thing. Must be the taste of this whisky that's making me recall it. One night we sat up into the wee hours, drinking and blethering, right here, round this fire. Just like you and I are doing now. Having a few drams. He would order a taxi to bring him over here and another to take him back again, so he didn't need to worry about getting stopped and breathalysed. That never used to happen here in the old days. Didn't trust himself driving after having a few. Though that never stopped me. God, the only thing you're likely to hit is a bloody sheep. Or something isn't it?' Callum picked up the bottle and poured himself another generous two fingers' worth, took a sip then placed the glass back on the table and leaned back in his chair and sighed. He closed his eyes. Finn wondered if the old man was going to fall asleep.

'Anyway, you were saying something about Jeremy telling you something.'

Callum opened his eyes and stared at Finn for a moment as if he hadn't ever seen him before. He frowned then seemed to suddenly remember who he was with and smiled. 'Sorry, did ye say something, son?'

'You said Jeremy mentioned something else that troubled him.'

'Oh, aye, aye, that's right. A woman. He once mentioned a woman he was very fond of who died. It was a long time ago but he never got over it, he said.'

'Did he tell you what happened to her?'

'Not really. He said it was while he was in Beirut. He said he was working there as a journalist. That's before he became a fiction writer, you know.'

'Do you know what happened? How did she die?'

Callum took another swig of whisky. 'Ah, that's good stuff. Ah, how did she die, eh? I'm not sure. I don't really know, but if you read his first novel, *The Beirut Affair*, I wouldn't be surprised if he used some of what happened in there. I think that experience, in fact, is what gave him the idea to start writing thrillers. There's a young woman in it who dies. I tried to ask him once if that's based on real life but he didn't seem to want to talk any more about it. I could tell, though, that the subject really upset him. He said he'd never forget her.'

'You don't remember if he said her name?'

Callum shook his head. 'No, son. Sorry.'

They chatted some more but Callum appeared to becoming less talkative. 'Thanks for your time, Callum,' said Finn. 'If you think of anything else, give me a call, OK? Here's my card.' He handed him a business card. 'My mobile number is on it.'

'Callum laughed. 'Oh, aye, a mobile. Everyone's got one of them these days, right enough.' He laughed. 'Except me. And that internet thingy! Never saw the point of that either. Ye cannae beat a good book, that's what I say.'

Finn said his goodbyes and left.

TWELVE

Finn took another taxi back to Kirkwall. He had to admit it was beautiful here, he thought, gazing toward the sea. Fresh air. The sounds of nature: seagulls, the waves. A flock of geese made their way across the sky above, honking. What was there not to like? So unlike the noise and fumes of London, all the traffic and noise there. Could he live here again? he wondered. No. He couldn't imagine it. Surely, he'd be bored out of his mind. And there were so many bad memories.

On his way back to the hotel, he wandered into Amy's bookshop in Albert Street just as it was about to close and picked up a copy of *The Beirut Affair*.

He asked the assistant if Amy was in. 'No, she's gone home early. She wasn't feeling well', she said. 'Maybe she's coming down with a virus. I hope it's not Covid.'

Finn had to smile as he picked up the book and made his way out the door, thinking to himself: 'I know what it is and it's called a stinking hangover!'

Then he started thinking about Powell, moving here to write his books. When he got back to his hotel room, he took out the book he'd picked up in the bookshop, lay back on the bed and started to read:

Chapter One

James Frost stepped off the plane in Beirut with feelings of both excitement and anxiety. He was twenty-seven years old, with a degree in French and Arabic from Cambridge University and local newspaper experience behind him. He was excited at the prospect of his new post as a Middle East correspondent but also anxious. What if he wasn't good enough? He'd always suffered from imposter syndrome. Maybe this would be where he'd be found out. He tried to dismiss these negative thoughts, though, as he waited for his luggage at the carousel in the hot, stuffy airport building.

Reporting was what he liked best and there was plenty going on here to interest him. The political situation was a powder keg with rival groups vying for control and the area was a hub of international tension, with various states trying to exert their influence: the Iranians, the Syrians, the Americans and other western powers, like the French and the British. Then there were the Palestinians. It was impossible to ignore the plight of the refugees from Palestine who, since 1948 had formed a diaspora around the region. Lebanon's neighbour, Israel, was regarded with hostility and there was the ever-present fear of war. All this was going through James's head in the taxi from the airport taking him through the congested streets of the city towards the apartment he had rented, when he heard a huge explosion coming from a few blocks further ahead and saw smoke rising above the buildings. The driver didn't seem to take much notice.

'What was that?' James asked him in Arabic.

'Probably a car bomb,' the driver replied nonchalantly with a shrug and executed a rapid U-turn. 'We can go a different way.'

He was immediately struck by the parallels with Jeremy Powell's own career. Powell, too, had taken up the job of Associated Press's Beirut correspondent at the same age after working on a local newspaper.

Later that evening, Finn got a call from his cousin Malcolm who had told him about his gran's death. Malcolm said that they were looking for a home for Maggie's dog, Kiki, a cockapoo. The dog was being looked after temporarily following the old woman's death and Malcolm couldn't take her as he had cats. No one else seemed able to take her and he asked him if he was interested in having a dog.

He was about to refuse. A dog would be an encumbrance in his life, a complication which he could do without, surely. But then again, maybe the companionship of a dog would be good for him. Yes, it would mean all sorts of hassle and having to look for dog-sitters, dog-walkers and so on but surely most of the time he could manage to look after her. It would also be a link to his gran. So, for sentimental reasons he didn't want to rule it out.

'I don't know. Can I think about it, Malcolm?' Finn said.

'Of course. Think about it.' said Malcolm. 'She's being looked after by Hamish Anderson who runs a kennel. I'll text you his address. It's a farm on the north side of town. But that's only a temporary arrangement. If you don't take her, I'll have to phone the refuge and see if they can take her'

'OK. I'll sleep on it and phone you tomorrow. OK?'

'Brilliant!' Malcolm said.

They chatted for a bit about how he was and how it felt being back after such a long time.

'Maybe we can have a pint some time before you go?' asked Malcolm. Finn didn't mention that he didn't drink. But they could meet for a coffee, surely.

'Aye, good idea. I'll give you a ring.'

Slowly, it felt like the isles were reeling him back in. But he wasn't sure if he wanted to be reeled in or not.

WEDNESDAY

THIRTEEN

*T*he next morning, Finn got another phone call. This time on the hotel's room phone just before he was about to go down to breakfast. It was someone he definitely didn't expect to hear from.

'Hi, Finn. It's Alasdair.'

'Alasdair?'

'Alasdair Semple.'

Finn wasn't sure what to say. Alasdair had once been his closest friend. Until he had stolen his girlfriend from him.

'Oh, hello, Alasdair.'

'I heard you were back on Orkney, Finn. For your gran's funeral, of course. I'm sorry for your loss.'

'Thanks, Alasdair. Good of you to call.'

'No problem. But that's not the only reason I called. I believe you're staying on here a bit longer, is that right?'

News travelled fast on the isles. If this was purely a social call, he wasn't interested. He was happy to meet Malcolm for a coffee but hanging out with Alasdair was definitely not on the agenda. At the time, when he'd stolen Amy from him, he would gladly have pushed Alasdair off the cliffs at Yeswick. Time had mellowed his feelings and he knew that it wasn't just Alasdair who was to blame. Amy had a responsibility too. It was all a long time ago but that didn't mean he was ready to become best buddies with Alasdair again.

'That's right. I'm actually kind of busy. What was it you wanted?' He knew his response was rude but he didn't really care.

'Oh, OK. Well, Finn, what it's about is this. I was your late gran's solicitor and I'm handling her will. I do need to speak to you about it. There's something that concerns you in it.'

Finn was stunned. He hadn't expected Maggie to have left him anything after the breach between them. 'Her will? Really? That comes as something of a surprise. Can you tell me what it is?'

'I'd rather we discussed this face to face. Can you come to see me? My office is in Victoria Street. Number twelve. When would you be able to come? I realise you're busy but what about later today? I'm free this afternoon at four o' clock.'

He thought about what he wanted to do today. 'Alright. I could manage four o' clock.'

'Yes, that's perfect. I'll see you then.'

Alasdair Semple. Another ghost from the past. First Amy, now Alasdair. They were definitely coming back to haunt him.

After breakfast, Finn made his way round to the newspaper office. Grace immediately cornered him.

'How did you get on with Callum Maclean yesterday?' she asked.

'OK. He didn't really tell me anything that useful, though. He'd heard that Laing upset Jeremy. He also told me that there was something from the past that Jeremy couldn't get over. The death of a woman in Beirut. I'm reading his first book which is set there to see if there's anything in it that might help. But otherwise, I don't feel like I'm making much progress. How about you? You look like you've got something to tell me?'

Grace nodded. 'I do. After you left the office, I read a post on a neighbourhood social media site. So, I went off to investigate and it's rather interesting. It might have something to do with the Powell story.'

'OK. Let's have a coffee and you can tell me more.'

There was a kettle in the kitchen corner of the office. Grace made the coffee and they sat down at her desk.

'Well,' said Grace, 'it was about a break-in at a house on the Marine View housing estate. The house belongs to a retired English couple, June and Bill Lockhart. Anyway, Bill disturbed the burglars but got a smack on the head from a baseball bat in the process from one of the intruders. He was knocked out and had concussion but seems to be alright now. He said there were two of them, though he didn't see their faces as they were both wearing balaclavas.'

'OK, so that's bad for him but where's the Powell connection?'

Grace smiled. 'They only stole one thing. Guess what?'

'Did they have a dog?'

'Correct! They made off with their spaniel. What do you think about that?'

'Hmm. So, sounds like there is a gang of dognappers operating here after all. '

'Yes. So, then I came back to the office and looked up the archives. There was one other incident two months ago, in Stromness. A poodle disappeared. Apparently, the owners had left it on its own in the garden for a bit and had gone into the house but when they came back out it was gone. They thought at the time that it must have escaped. It's never been seen since.'

'So, if it's the same guys going round places stealing dogs, that makes one a month, if we include Powell's dog.'

'That's right.'

'What are the police saying?'

'I rang them. They aren't sure the cases are connected. Of course, they regard what happened to Powell as an accident. But they're not ruling out that it could be the same thieves that stole the poodle as the spaniel in Marine View. I filed the story and it's online. Here, you can see for yourself.' She brought up the page on her laptop to show him.

POLICE HUNT DOG THIEVES

By Grace Campbell

Police are searching for a pair of dognappers after the theft of a spaniel in the middle of the night in Kirkwall which left an elderly man with a serious head injury. There is speculation that the thieves may have carried out a spate of such thefts in Orkney recently, including the disappearance of a poodle in

Stromness two months ago.

The couple, Bill Lockhart, 61, and his wife Joan Lockhart, both 61, of Marine View, Kirkwall, were disturbed by two burglars just after 3 a.m. on Tuesday 18 April. Bill was assaulted by one of the men wielding a baseball bat and sustained concussion.

The thieves, who wore balaclavas, made off with the couple's treasured springer spaniel, Henry. Police are appealing for any information leading to the arrest of the suspects and the safe return of the Lockharts' dog.

Meanwhile, the Lockharts are heartbroken over the loss of their beloved pet. 'They took Henry. Why would anyone do such a thing?' said a tearful Joan.

'A baseball bat, eh? Hmm. Could someone have come up behind Jeremy and whacked him over the head with a baseball bat? Maybe. Then made off with his dog?'

'Yes. Perhaps they just meant to stun him but he stumbled and fell off the cliff. Or, he put up a fight and they pushed him over.'

Finn said, 'Well, it's a possibility, I suppose. Let me know if there are any other developments. In the meantime, I'm going to look into Jeremy Powell's past and see what I can dig up.'

At lunchtime he was coming down the stairs on his way out to fetch a sandwich when he ran into Amy entering the building.

'Finn. I wanted to come and see you to apologise. I am so sorry about the other night,' she said. 'I had a wee bit too much to drink and was stupid. '

'That's OK. If it makes you feel any better, I've done much more stupid things when I was drunk. Which used to be quite often.'

'Oh Finn, you are so nice. Listen, can we go for a walk. Maybe grab some lunch? I'd like to talk to you.'

They left the building and walked towards the harbour.

Finn said, 'You didn't tell me that you were a bookseller. And a columnist!'

'God, Finn, I can't remember what I told you that night. I was blootered! But I've never been called a columnist before! That sounds a bit grand.'

'I've been reading some of your pieces in the archive. They're very good.'

'Thanks.'

'You should consider a career in journalism. Or some other form of writing. I like your style.'

'Hah. You are still a flatterer, Finn. Some things never change!'

'I'm serious. Anyway, tell me how you got into bookselling.'

'It was when I got back here from Oz. I thought, what the hell am I going to do? There was an advert for a sales assistant. I applied. Then a few years later the manager left and I took over. That's all there is to it.'

'Do you enjoy it?'

'Yes. I love books. Always have. And I love being surrounded by them though I don't like all the boring admin, but I guess every job has its down side. It also pays the bills and the rent on my wee flat. Saves me from living with Mum and Dad! They were driving me mental!'

It suddenly just felt like old times, when they were going out with each other, as if the intervening fifteen years hadn't happened. They turned into Laing Street and found a café. Finn ordered a panini and a flat white, Amy a bowl of soup and a latte.

'I wanted to talk to you about the Powell case,' she said. 'There's something I wanted to tell you, so that's why I came to see you.'

'OK. Go on then.' Finn stuffed a mouthful of panini into his mouth and chewed.

Amy said, 'At the start of the year, when Powell's last book was about to be published, his publisher was keen on as much publicity as possible. So, we were to have a book launch in the shop. Wine and nibbles, a talk from the author, a reading of an extract, a Q and A session, that sort of thing, you know. I went to talk about the arrangements with him.'

'OK. So, what happened?'

She paused and thought about this for a moment. 'I went to his house. His suggestion. His wife wasn't in, I'm not sure where she was, out somewhere. At a yoga class, I think. Anyway, in the course of the meeting he brought coffee over to the sofa and sat down beside me and put his hand on my thigh.'

'Really?'

'Yes.'

'What did you do?'

'I lifted his hand and asked him what the hell he thought he was doing? He immediately became apologetic.'

'Did you do anything about it, report it?'

'No. I thought about it but then I thought, there were no witnesses. It would just be he said she said, that sort of thing. It wasn't worth all the hassle. But I told myself that I'd never be alone with a client like that again. Anyway, that's what I wanted to share with you. Maybe the fact he was a lecher might have something to do with what happened to him. His widow thinks he didn't die in an accident, doesn't she? I was thinking, maybe he was having an affair and there was a jealous husband?'

'Wouldn't you know? You're the gossip queen after all, from what I remember.'

'Ha, ha. But that's not all. When I was there, just after that happened, someone came to the door and Powell went to answer it. I looked out of the window. It was the woman who lived next door. Maria. She's Spanish. I don't know what she wanted as I couldn't hear what they were talking about but when Powell came back in, he looked a bit embarrassed. Flustered, as if I'd caught him doing something he shouldn't have.'

'So?'

'Well, she's young and attractive with long dark hair and a great figure. Really stunning. Her husband's a company director of a pharmaceutical firm. Works from home but has to travel so he's away a lot.'

'So, you're thinking that they were having an affair and the husband found out and bumped Powell off?'

Amy raised her eyebrows. 'What do you

think?'

'Hmm. It's a possibility. I'll speak to Laura about it. You'd think the cops would have looked into that.'

Amy said, 'OK. Anyway, now we've got that out of the way, what do you say to dinner at my place tonight? Part of my apology. I'd like to make up for my bad behaviour.'

Finn nodded. 'OK. That would be nice.'

'Any allergies? You're not veggie, are you?'

'No, you're alright, thanks. Though I have been trying to be a bit healthier, eat less red meat.'

'Great. See you later. Give me your mobile number and I'll text you my address.'

Finn told her his number.

'Seven o' clock. OK?'

'It's a date. Oh, before you go, guess who phoned me this morning?'

Amy shook her head. 'No idea.'

'Alasdair.'

'Alasdair? You're joking.'

'No. He was my gran's solicitor, apparently. He says there's something in her will which concerns me. I'm meeting him this afternoon.'

'I'm sorry, Finn.'

'What about?'

'You know what! Alasdair! Me and Alasdair.'

'It's water under the bridge, Amy. We were young. These things happen.'

'Oh, Finn, you're a darling.' She looked at her watch. 'Oh, shit, look at the time. I've got to get back to the bookshop. See you later.'

She stood up and leaned over the table to peck him on the cheek then she was gone.

Finn watched her as she left. He felt surprised and confused by how much he was still attracted to her.

FOURTEEN

Finn arrived at Semple's office at four, as agreed. It was up a flight of stairs above a gift shop in the High Street. There was a small reception room with two chairs and a desk at which a receptionist was typing on a computer. She was a young dark-haired woman in her mid-twenties. When he told her who he was, she said 'Mr Semple is expecting you. But he's on the phone just now. Please take a seat. He shouldn't be long.'

She asked if he would like tea, coffee or water but he declined the offer. He suddenly felt annoyed. It was typical of Alasdair to make him wait on him, he thought. Then he reminded himself that what had passed between them was fifteen years ago, water under the bridge and all that, as he had said to Amy. However, there was still a part of him that wanted to take a slug at him for cheating on his girlfriend. He had been his best friend up until then. They'd shared everything, made plans together for their futures and so on. They had the same taste in music, read the same books, did the same drugs, drank together, partied together. He had felt so badly let down by him, when Amy had broken the news about the two of them, that he hadn't spoken to him again. Until today. Now here he was sitting outside his office.

At that moment, Alasdair opened the door of his office.

'So sorry to keep you waiting, Finn. Come on in.'

He looked different. Not only because of what he was wearing. Gone was the denim jacket and jeans, replaced with a smart pinstripe suit, shirt and tie. In contrast with Finn's casual attire of jeans, T-shirt and jumper. The years hadn't been kind to him, Finn was glad to see. His hair was receding. His long curly locks were long gone. He'd also put on weight. Once, he'd been a good-looking young man, a star striker in the school football team and an athletics champion on Orkney. A few inches taller than Finn. But he'd let himself go. He had a noticeable paunch, a beer gut, his waistline now making the buttons on his shirt look as if they were about to pop at any minute. He also had a ruddy complexion which looked like he enjoyed the drink a bit too much. Finn knew the look.

It was all a bit awkward. The past hung

between them like an invisible curtain. They shook hands and sat down on opposite sides of a large desk. The room felt stuffy and warm. The central heating must have been on full blast. On the wall behind the desk was a framed certificate. Finn couldn't make it out but presumed it was certifying Alasdair's legal qualification. The other walls had several paintings and the window had a view of the car park opposite.

Alasdair said, 'Would you like a tea or a coffee? I can ask Jessica to make us some.'

'No thanks. You wanted to tell me about my gran's will?' Finn said. He knew he was being abrupt but wasn't in the mood to hear his pleasantries. He felt as if the last fifteen years hadn't existed. He wanted this to be over and done with.

'Eh...oh yes, that's right. Better get down to business. Let's see.' He picked up a folder from his desk, opened it and flicked through some papers.'

'Here it is, yes, well. It's very simple. Your gran has left you the entirety of her estate.'

'What? You can't be serious!' said Finn.

'I am. Her house in Skene Close, and her savings, though in terms of savings, there isn't a fortune. But the house is worth quite a bit, I would say, on the open market.'

Finn rubbed his hands over his head. 'I can't believe this.'

'Absolutely. It's all yours. Her home. The estate. There's not much in the way of savings, though, as I said. Most of that went on employing carers for the past few years. She wanted to stay in her own home rather than move to a nursing home, but there's the house. Obviously, it will take time to go through, but I can guarantee it's all yours. I can even hand you the keys now if you like, so you can have a look at the property. You can even move in there, if you like. It might be more comfortable than the hotel. You can decide.'

'I didn't expect any of this.'

'Really? Oh, and she also left this for you.' He handed Finn an envelope with his name written on it in an unsteady hand. Written in her handwriting. Inside was a short note, the writing also looked unsteady but careful.

Dear Finn

I'm sorry that we fell out all those years ago. You were always in my thoughts.

Love

Gran x

Alasdair was rummaging in the drawer of his desk. 'Here's the keys. I know we should really wait until consolidation of the will is complete but, what the hell...eh?'

Finn didn't know what to say. It was the last thing he'd expected. When he thought about it, he realised that she had no one else to leave the house to. She had no other children other than his mother. And none of her brothers or sisters were still alive. He was her sole heir. He was quite taken aback. She could, he thought, have just left it all to a cat and dog home. That reminded him of her dog. Maybe he really could move into the old house and keep the dog for company? Humour her wishes. Wait a minute, he told himself, what are you thinking of?

'Ok, thanks,' said Finn, taking the keys. 'I'll go round and have a look at the place.'

'If you decide that you want to sell the property, I could, of course, arrange the conveyancing for you. I also know a good estate agent.'

'OK, thanks. I'll think about that.'

'So, Finn, do you think you'll stick around here for a while?'

'As a matter of fact, I'm here working. I'm looking into what happened to Jeremy Powell. The writer who died over at Yeswick. You wouldn't have been his solicitor by any chance?'

Alasdair shook his head. 'No, sorry. I didn't

really know him. But you should have a word with Murdo.'

'Murdo?'

'You remember Murdo Scrimgeour? At school?'

'Oh aye, Murdo. What's he doing now?'

'He's a polis! A detective sergeant. Here, on the isles.'

After he left Alasdair's office, Finn went round to the police station and asked to speak to Murdo Scrimgeour. But he wasn't there. The desk sergeant told him he had a day off today and asked what it was about. Finn explained that he was an old school friend of his.

'He'll likely be down at the boatyard, in his boatshed, mucking about with his boat,' the sergeant said. 'That's what he likes to do on his days off.'

When he got to the boatyard, he looked around the various sheds and then he immediately spotted Murdo. It wasn't difficult. Six-foot six and with a mop of bright red hair. He was as distinctive now as he had been at school when he had been pilloried for being a lanky ginger guy who wouldn't fight back. He wasn't a close friend of Finn's but they had known each other since starting primary school together. He was wearing overalls and cleaning the hull of a boat which was resting on huge wooden blocks.

'Murdo!' Finn said.

Murdo turned round. 'Hey, Finn, how are you?' he said, putting his cloth into a bucket. 'My desk sergeant phoned to tell me you might be on your way. How's it going?'

'Not bad. You?'

'Aye, OK. I was just doing a bit of maintenance here. That can wait.'

Murdo walked over towards Finn, wiping his hands on his overalls, and they shook hands. 'So good to see you, Finn. I heard about your gran. My condolences.'

'Thanks.'

'God, it's a long time! You are a blast from the past. Where are you staying?'

'At the Marine Hotel.'

'Ah, good place to stay. So, what are you up to these days? As far as I know, you've not been back here for a long time.'

'Well, I didn't expect to be still hanging around after the funeral but I'm a journalist and my editor insisted I look into the death of Jeremy

Powell. That's what I wanted to speak to you about, you being a detective. By the way, how did that come about? Last time I saw you was at the end of school at the prom. I was blootered but I think I remember you saying you couldn't wait to get away from Orkney. Weren't you going to join the navy or something?'

Murdo laughed. 'Aye, that's right. Well, there was a change of plan. I did go away but only as far as Glasgow and joined the police. Then moved into CID. When a post came up here as a DS I applied. Guess they liked the idea of a local lad. That was five years ago. I came back here and settled. I even met my partner, Sheila. We got married last year. She's a doctor at the hospital here in Kirkwall.'

'Congratulations,' said Finn.

'What about you? Married?'

Finn shook his head. 'No. Though I came close.'

'Oh well, there's always the future. I'm sure you'll meet the right person one day.'

'Maybe,' said Finn.

'So, what can you tell me about Powell's death? That I don't already know. His widow thinks it wasn't an accident.'

'His widow? Oh aye, she's convinced it

was murder, isn't she? The mystery of the disappearing dog and all that. Well, there's nothing to back up that theory, I'm afraid. We considered that it might be all about dog theft. We spoke to dog walkers, grooming salons, ferry crew and passengers. But no one remembers seeing the dog again after the event. It was quite distinctive. A white labradoodle. Most likely it was an accident. That stretch of coastline can be very hazardous, especially in windy and wet conditions. He could just have not been paying attention and slipped on a wet rock, eh? Maybe too busy looking at his phone? Unfortunately, we couldn't find it.'

'I heard there was a dog stolen here the other day. And another one disappeared a couple of months ago over in Stromness. I'm wondering, don't you think there might be a connection to what happened to Powell and his dog?'

Murdo sucked air into his lungs and then blew out again slowly. 'Oh… I don't know, Finn,' he said, scratching his head. 'That theft the other night has made us consider the possibility. But equally, it could just be a coincidence. That dog of Powell's was very attached to him. It would go anywhere after him, following him about, from what I've heard. It'd likely follow him into the sea, if that's where he ended up.'

'Laura says she saw someone. Just after he

left the house. Going in the same direction as her husband.'

Murdo sighed. 'Aye, that's right. The mysterious stranger.' He shook his head. 'We spent a lot of time trying to find this person. But we drew a blank, I'm afraid.'

'It's odd, though, isn't it. You'll have to admit that?'

'If she did see someone.'

'What do you mean?'

'I mean she was maybe confused, that's all. OK there may have been somebody. But we haven't been able to trace who it was.'

'What about the neighbour? Could his wife, Maria, and Powell have been having an affair and he found out, do you think?'

'Now you are letting your imagination get away with you, Finn. He couldn't have been the killer.'

'Oh? Why not?'

'We checked him out. He was away working in Dubai at the time.'

'OK, What about Maria? She could have been angry because he dumped her, ended the affair.'

Murdo shook his head. 'Listen, Finn, you're

getting carried away with this. There's nothing to indicate either of them had anything to do with it.'

'But if her husband was away, I guess she didn't have an alibi, eh?'

'It was probably just an accident. Drop it.'

'What about this builder, David Laing? Laura says he and Powell had a falling out. Laing told Powell he was owed money. Is that right? I assume you spoke to him about it?'

'We know how to run an inquiry, Finn. Of course, we did.'

'And?'

'Do you expect me to disclose details of the investigation to a civilian?'

'Come on, Murdo. I'm only trying to help Laura find out the truth.'

'And get a juicy story for your newspaper, of course.'

'Well, yes, and that. Tell me something. Go on. For old times' sake, Murdo.'

'OK. We brought Laing in. He admitted there had been a dispute with Powell about money. But he denied having anything to do with what happened to him. And he had an alibi.'

'Let me guess. At home with his wife.

Correct?'

'I can't possibly say, Finn.'

'Was it his wife? Come on.'

Murdo sighed. 'OK, yes, it was his wife. She confirmed he was at home, working, when the incident in Yeswick happened. David Laing had nothing to do with what happened to Jeremy Powell. And I doubt that anybody did.'

'I've heard stories about Laing.'

'Oh, aye? What kinds of stories?'

'Corruption.'

'I wouldn't know about that.'

'No? Well, I might have to do some digging. I don't like the sound of him.'

'You're the journalist. I won't tell you how to do your job if you don't tell me. Eh? Well, Finn, I better get back to my cleaning. See you around, eh?'

FIFTEEN

After meeting Murdo, Finn walked round to his gran's house clutching the set of keys in his hand. It was one of the oldest houses in Kirkwall facing out over the sea, but well looked after, with whitewashed outside walls and a well-maintained roof, unlike a few others he'd passed on the way. At least that was one thing.

He turned the key in the lock and went in. A strong musty smell hit him. Of course, she'd not been living here for a while. At the funeral he'd heard that for the last few months she had been in a hospice. The place needed fresh air.

He walked around the rooms. It felt very strange being back in his gran's house, the house he'd spent his childhood in. Nothing much had changed. Only one or two things. Like a new three-piece suite. A different carpet in the living room. Apart from that, everything was just as he remembered it: the kitchen with its tall oak dresser; the display cabinet with its hoard of tea sets; and the oil painting of boats in the harbour that his grandfather had painted was still on the wall above the fireplace.

He climbed the stairs to his old room. When he opened the door, he couldn't believe it. It was like going back in time. It was exactly as it was when he left. The posters of bands he'd followed at the time like The Strokes and Radiohead. On a bookshelf, were his well-thumbed copies of The Lord of the Rings and The Hobbit. He couldn't remember how many times he'd read them both. There was even, sitting on the bed, his old teddy bear, with one eye missing.

Suddenly, he was back in his teenage years. To begin with after his mum's death, he had seemingly coped. But at the age of fifteen, he felt that he couldn't handle things that had happened. He had daymares, night terrors, shaking fits, often felt generally anxious and afraid.

His grandmother had taken him to the local GP who arranged an appointment at the hospital one day with a consultant psychiatrist. He was middle-aged, and had silver hair and spectacles, which sat on the edge of his nose as he peered over them and asked him to talk. He didn't say much himself but Finn remembered the words just pouring out of him like a dam that had burst the first time he went to see him. And every time after that. He realised that he hadn't been able to talk about his feelings of his mum until then. It had all just boiled up inside of him like a pressure cooker ready to explode.

Talking therapy, he now knew. Along with a course of diazepam. It worked. After two months of seeing him every week he was able to sleep and go out places with people instead of just shutting himself up in his room alone as he had done previously. The trouble was that going out places meant going out drinking.

That was just the start of a different sort of troubles. And a different sort of medication.

His mobile rang. It was Laura. She wanted to see him urgently. Something had come up, she said, and she wanted to talk to him about it. He also wanted to speak to her about her husband's wandering hands that Amy had told him about. Was he a serial philanderer? It didn't match her earlier description of him.

SIXTEEN

Finn took a taxi over to Yeswick. It cost him fifty quid and would be the same on the return journey but the paper would refund him as long as he didn't lose the receipts. Laura answered the door in a white dressing gown, her hair hanging loose and wet. She'd obviously just had a shower. 'I was just working out in the basement gym,' she said. 'Go in and make yourself comfortable. I'll throw some clothes on.'

She pointed to the living room and disappeared up the stairs.

There were several cardboard boxes filled with objects wrapped in bubble-wrap. He sat down on one of the cream leather sofas and looked around noticing things he hadn't the first time he was here. Like the many vinyl LPs stacked on shelves beside the hi-fi. He went over and examined them. They were mostly jazz and blues with some classical. No pop or rock music at all.

When she returned, she was wearing a

white silk blouse and jeans. Her hair was still damp and she had tied it back in a ponytail. She looked stunning.

'I see you like jazz,' he said.

'Oh no, I can't stand it,' she said. 'All those were Jeremy's. He loved jazz. Hence, Charlie. He named our dog after the jazz musician, Charlie Parker.'

'Right. Of course. And these boxes? Are you packing up?

'Yes. I've decided to sell up. I'm going to clear out the house and sell it. To be honest, I get worried sometimes.'

Worried?'

'Yes, of course. Someone must have killed Jeremy. They might be after me next.'

'Where will you go?'

'Back to London. It's too painful here. Too many memories. And it's lonely without Jeremy.'

'I'm sorry. I don't suppose all the abuse on Twitter helps? All the trolls.'

She shook her head. 'I just ignore all that.'

'There was an awkward silence between them.

'I wanted to ask you something, actually. Your next-door neighbour, Maria. How well do you know her and her husband?'

'Not that well. Why?'

'I was told today, by someone who visited here to meet Jeremy, that Maria came to the door once to speak to him. Do you think that perhaps he knew her better than you think?'

'Do you mean, do I think they were lovers?'

'Yes.'

'No. I'm sure I would have known.'

'What's her husband like?'

She sighed. The police asked all this. He's nice. Friendly.'

'OK. You said on the phone you had something to tell me.'

'I found this today.' She held out a business card. 'It was in the inside pocket of Jeremy's suit jacket, the one he wore when he went to Cambridge. That's the last time he wore it. I was clearing out some of his stuff to give to a charity shop when I looked in the pockets and found it.'

'Can I see it?'

'Yes. Of course.'

She handed it over to him. The name on the card was Brian Clark, Cambridge Mercury. 'Brian Clark?'

Laura said, 'Yes, I remembered when I found it that he was the journalist who interviewed Jeremy when he was in Cambridge. He mentioned something about it when he came home. I thought maybe Jeremy might have mentioned something to him when they met that was important so I tried calling the number on the card but it didn't connect. Out of service. I then googled Brian Clark. Turns out he was murdered two days before Jeremy disappeared.'

'Bloody hell! Are you serious?' said Finn.

'Absolutely. Check it yourself.'

'How was he killed?'

'He was shot dead, apparently. Two gunshots fired through his kitchen window by an unknown assailant. In the afternoon. The local newspaper reported that the police investigation concluded that it was probably a case of mistaken identity in some sort of a gangland dispute. About drugs. But it can't be a coincidence, can it? I think it's somehow linked to what happened to Jeremy. Don't you?'

'I don't know. It *could* just be a coincidence but you are right, it all sounds mighty suspicious.'

'Maybe you can help find out the truth about what really happened to Jeremy. I'll pay you. I did a bit of research on you. I still know a few people in London. They vouched for you. I hope I can trust you.'

'There's no need for you to pay me. The newspaper has asked me to investigate so I'll do that. But I'll keep you informed. I might have to go to Cambridge to find out more about this and see if there's a possible connection. Can you remember who he met up with when he went to London after he'd been to Cambridge? I think you said he caught up with a friend there along with seeing his parents.'

'Yes. He said he met James Scott, he's an old friend of Jeremy's from his newspaper days.'

'Would you be able to text me his number if you have it. And that of his parents. I'd like to get in touch with them and see if Jeremy told them anything useful.'

'I can but there's no point. I've already asked them. They couldn't tell me anything. I think they all think I'm crazy for being so suspicious. But now that I've discovered this link to someone else who's been murdered ...'

'OK. Thanks for sharing this with me. And, for the moment, I wouldn't tell the police anything about what you've found out. I have a strange feeling about all of this. First, this journalist who interviewed Jeremy is gunned down in his home and it's dismissed as mistaken identity. Then your husband dies in circumstances that could be suspicious but it's also assumed to be an accident.'

I know. It's scary.' Laura ran her hands through her hair. 'God, it's awful. It makes me feel nervous. What if they come after me?'

She looked so fragile. Finn wanted to give her a hug but was worried it would be misinterpreted.

'It's just so isolated out here. I haven't slept a proper night since Jeremy died. I need to get away from here. Now.'

'I'm sorry.'

She seemed to pull herself together. 'Listen, you don't need to rush off, do you? Would you like a coffee? Or a drink?'

She offered him a glass of sauvignon blanc from a bottle which was already open.

'No thanks. I'd love to. But …' He hesitated, tried to think of an excuse, but then decided just to opt for the truth. 'I'm actually a recovering alcoholic. I don't drink. But please don't let that stop you.'

'Oh, I'm terribly sorry.'

'There's actually something I wanted to ask you about.' Finn then told her about what Amy had told him, the way Jeremy had sexually harassed her. He expected Laura to be shocked, angry even, but she wasn't. She just looked sad. 'I never suspected he would do anything like that,' she said. 'It makes me wonder how well I really knew him.'

'I'm sorry but it made me think ...'

'What?'

'Could he could have tried it on with someone else, you know, and it might have led to someone attacking him?'

'You mean a jealous partner?'

'Yes. That's why I mentioned your neighbour, Maria. The police say her husband was out of the country at the time but he could have hired a hit-man.'

'God! I hope not. The idea of living near to someone who got my husband killed!'

'There may be nothing in it, though. The police looked at it. I expect they thought of that. By the way, did Jeremy ever speak to you about his time in Beirut? According to Callum Maclean, something happened then that upset him. It concerned the death of a woman he was close to.'

Laura shook her head. 'No. He wouldn't speak about those days. I know the story, of course. It's the plot of his first book. I edited it. But I assumed it was all made up. Do you think some of it is true?'

'I don't know. Perhaps.'

'Could it have anything to do with his death, do you think?'

He shrugged. 'I really don't know.'

'You don't have to go,' she said, as he went to put on his coat.

'I do. I've got an invite to dinner. Sorry.'

In the taxi on the way back to Kirkwall, he wondered about Laura. Was she just lonely and wanting company? Or did she have other intentions towards him? And what would he have done if he hadn't been expected at Amy's? he wondered.

SEVENTEEN

Amy's flat was small, just a living room and bedroom with a small kitchen built into the living-room alcove. There was a shower room off the hall. A dining table sat in front of the living room window and there was a wood-burning stove in the fireplace throwing out enormous heat. There was just room for a sofa and a bookcase. A large framed print of a Georgia O'Keeffe painting hung in a prominent place on the wall above the mantelpiece: a swirl of bold colours, bright blues and reds. Finn's eye immediately scanned the bookcase to see what kind of books she liked. Plenty of literary novels, contemporary and classics from the nineteenth and twentieth century; a few books of poetry; books on nature and art; and several volumes of feminist theory.

She stirred a pot and told Finn to have a seat. 'Hope you like carbonara.'

'Love it!'

Soon, they were seated at the table, Amy with a glass of wine and Finn on mineral water.

'Is it difficult being with others who are drinking?' she asked.

'It's not got easier but I know it's the right thing for me. I don't feel as if I've got a choice.'

'Was it really bad? It must have been.'

'Aye, I was a mess. I had to sort myself out. It was either that or ending up in the gutter. Don't think I could have kept working for much longer. Maybe not even living for much longer.'

'Well, it's great that you've got your life back on track, Finn.'

'Think it was in my genes. Don't really know. I just know that I couldn't moderate my drinking. It was either one thing or the other. Binge-drinking or sobriety.'

'How did you stop?'

'The person I was living with left me. She couldn't take it anymore. That just made things worse to begin with. It got so bad I couldn't work. I was facing being sacked. I went to the GP and he recommended a clinic. Blew all my savings on it but it's the best thing I ever did. That was almost a year ago.'

'Congratulations. How did you get on with Alasdair this afternoon?'

'He shocked me. Apparently, my gran left me everything in her will, the house, her estate and so on.'

'Wow! That's great. What will you do with the house?'

'I don't know. Sell it, I suppose.'

She looked disappointed.

They finished the meal and moved to the sofa for coffee.

Amy said, 'Oh, I almost forgot. When I went back to the shop this afternoon I was thinking about Jeremy Powell as we'd been talking about him and I remembered that he had ordered a book just before he died. In fact, he never came to collect it and I've put it on the bookshelves.'

'What was it?'

'A historical novel set in Tudor times. It's called *A Tale for the Telling* by Rebecca Rossetti. It's a pen name of Olivia Andrews.'

'Never heard of her. Any good?'

'Well, it's a hardback costing twenty quid and been sitting on the shelf for a month so she's not exactly massively popular here.'

'Doesn't sound like Powell's kind of book. But thanks for letting me know. By the way, do you know of a builder called David Laing?'

'Yes. Horrible man. He's supposed to beat

up his wife, Janice.'

'How do you know that?'

'She turned up my Pilates class at the gym one evening with a black eye. Said she hit it with a cupboard door. Nobody believed her. She looked like she had been crying. Why are you interested in him?'

'His name came up in connection with Powell. They had a disagreement. He was a suspect but has an alibi, apparently, according to Murdo.'

'Ah, yes, Detective Scrimgeour. Who'd have thought at school that he would turn out to be a copper. He was so shy.'

'I know. Grace says Laing is well in with the authorities here. Probably with the polis, too. Sounds a right shady character. I wonder how hard they tried to investigate him.'

'You better watch out for him. He sounds dangerous. Poor Janice. You'll remember her from school. Janice McKinnon, as was. The blonde bombshell in fourth-year, when we were in sixth-year.'

'Ah, *that* Janice!'

She laughed. 'Oh, I see you remember her now. Thought you would have!'

'And she's married to Laing. I guess he's

loaded.'

'Undoubtedly. Anyway, how are you getting on with trying to find out what happened to Powell?'

'There's a possible connection to someone who was murdered in Cambridge. I'm thinking of heading down there to follow it up.' He told her about Brian Clark.

She said, 'This is turning out to be a real mystery, right enough. Maybe this Brian Clark guy had found out about some organised crime thing going on there that Powell was interested in? You know, for one of his stories? Perhaps it's a gangland thing that he got too close to down there and the gang found out and bumped him off?'

'I think you've been reading too many of the thrillers in your shop, Amy!'

'Ha, ha! I'm serious. They say truth is stranger than fiction.'

'True enough.'

When it got to eleven o' clock he said his goodbyes and left and made his way back towards his hotel. As he turned into Harbour Street, a man in a dark leather jacket suddenly leapt out of a black Range Rover. He was about the same height as Finn but broad and barrel-chested. Built like a brick shithouse was the expression which popped into Finn's head. He looked to be about forty, with a shaved head and a thick black beard. 'I hear you've been asking questions about me?' he said, squaring up to Finn.

'I don't know who you are.'

'Don't you? You should. I'm David Laing. Now, fuck off back to London, Morrison. We don't need your sort round here.' With that Finn got a hefty punch in the face and staggered backwards. 'And if you write anything about me, anything mind you, I'll fucking sue you.'

Laing jumped back into his car and sped off. The street was deserted. No witnesses. Laing had chosen his time and place well. How did he know how to find him? Finn wondered.

Once back in his hotel room, he inspected his face in the bathroom mirror. His cheekbone was swollen and bruised on the left side. His face looked a bit of a mess but on the whole, he thought he didn't look too bad, considering the life he had led. It wasn't a bad face: green eyes that looked a hell of a lot better than when he was on the booze and they had been red-rimmed most of the time; clear, healthy skin; and a full head of dark hair.

He phoned room service and asked for a bag of ice. When it arrived, he lay down on the bed for a bit nursing his swollen cheek. That eased the pain. Or, at least, numbed it.

He thought about what had happened. Had Murdo contacted Laing to tell him he knew about him? He'd told Murdo where he was staying. That would explain how Laing had found him. He couldn't think of any other way he would have known.

Was Laing warning him off because he was the killer? He drove a black Range Rover, after all and a witness had seen a large dark car speeding away from the village that day. Or was it just because he didn't want any probing questions to be asked about his relationship with the authorities?

Or was the killer, in fact, Laura, after all? Was all of this just a wild goose chase, directed by her to lead suspicion away from her as the real murderer? A deception.

Or could it be Maria, the Spanish neighbour, in a fit of temper after being jilted? Or her husband's hired contract killer?

Or, more prosaically, was it all simply about a dog theft? Maybe Powell had put up a fight with the dog thief, who had knocked him over the head and pushed him off the cliff?

Or maybe nobody killed him. In a fit of despair, he jumped off the cliff into the sea with the dog in his arms.

His thoughts were spiralling. He thought again about what might have happened between them if he had stayed longer at Laura's.

Then there was Amy. She had looked disappointed when he had told her he'd sell his gran's house. Did they have a future together? Until a few days ago, he'd thought not. He didn't think he'd ever see her again. But now? He wasn't sure. There still was an attraction.

He took out his phone and googled the name of the author that Amy had mentioned Powell had ordered a book of: Olivia Andrews. It was incredible how much you could find out about a person with just a few clicks on the internet and accessing their social media accounts. She had open access on Instagram, Twitter and Facebook. Within minutes he had her date and place of birth, knew what schools she had attended and found out that she had been at Cambridge University around the same time as Powell. In fact, she still appeared to live there, working as a lecturer in history at the university. Her spouse was listed as Stephen Moore.

Her Wikipedia entry listed her as a novelist specialising in historical fiction, mainly of the Elizabethan period, publishing her first novel five years ago under the pen name of

Rebecca Rossetti. Since then, two more in the series had followed. He then had a scan through the alumni photos on the university website for the years that she and Powell had been undergraduates together. Sure enough, he found one of Powell with members of the debating society. The young woman standing next to him had been tagged as Olivia Andrews and the man on his other side was Stephen Moore. Another online search revealed her to have got a first-class degree in history, graduating the same year as Powell. He decided to risk trying to contact her. Perhaps she had been in touch with Powell? At the very least, she'd surely have something she could tell him about Powell which would be of interest.

Had Jeremy possibly met her as well as Brian Clark when he went to Cambridge shortly before his death? Laura had told him that Clark and Powell had died two days apart from each other. He then did a search for *Brian Clark murder.* What Laura had told him was correct. Mistaken identity was the likely reason, police had said. He was just unlucky, it seemed. But was that all there was to it? Finn wondered. It had to be more than a coincidence that both Clark and Powell had died so soon after each other, surely?

He looked up the Cambridge Mercury newspaper site and found the interview that Clark had done with Powell. It was mostly about how he became a writer, his experiences at Cambridge, the authors who had influenced him and so on. One question did interest him, though:

BC: The main character in your novels is a journalist, a foreign correspondent working abroad in various hot-spots around the globe. How much have you used your own experiences of working in that role in your fiction?

JP: I do use my own experiences to a certain extent but I also use my imagination. So, for example, I might start off by basing something on an event that happened to me, or around me, when I worked as a journalist, especially things that upset me. I have a strong sense of justice and fairness. I saw lots of unfair things happening. I do try in my fiction to feature some of these, but I will also significantly change things to create dramatic tension and excitement. I do want to entertain the reader at the end of the day.

Was there something in this? It was an interesting response, especially the line about "things that upset me" and the reference to "fairness and justice". But there wasn't anything that jumped out at him that might signify why they were both dead.

Powell also made a few other interesting comments. In answer to Clark's question, 'Does living somewhere remote help you?' Powell replied: *'The thing I like most about living where I do is the peace and tranquillity. It's inspiring, though writing about violence in a place where there isn't any means I have to rely on my imagination! I get ideas walking the dog every day along the coastal path. I'm just down here in England for a couple of days and can't wait to get back home on Sunday.'*

Had something happened in Cambridge? he wondered. Was there a connection between the two men's deaths? He was going to have to go there and find out.

He then googled Olivia's husband, Stephen Moore. He was forty-five and graduated from Cambridge University in Arabic and politics at the same time as Powell. The Facebook page for Cambridge University alumni included a photo of the young Jeremy Powell and Stephen Moore, both members of the tennis club. They had won a match as part of a team in a double's competition against another Cambridge college. Moore was now a businessman, the proprietor of a company, SM Political Intelligence, which described itself on its website as a political consultancy. His father was a former top civil servant in Whitehall and his mother had been a classical musician. He had attended one of the top boarding schools in England. It might be worth speaking to him as well. See if he could shed any light on Powell's death.

Finn opened the copy of Powell's book, *The Beirut Affair*. He just had the final few chapters to read so he might as well finish it. He learned that Frost has an affair with the wife of a prominent Hezbollah politician. But she is blackmailed by Mossad, the Israeli security service, who want her to spy on her husband or else they would reveal her clandestine affair to said husband. She refuses, her husband consequently finds out about the affair and she is murdered. Frost then tracks down the Mossad agent who blackmailed her and kills him in a dramatic fight on the roof of a building.

In its setting, it appeared to have a few similarities to Powell's life. But did it shed any light on why he was now dead? Maybe the answer lay in Cambridge. Hopefully, he would find out.

THURSDAY

EIGHTEEN

Finn was woken early by the sound of loud hammering on his hotel room door. He had been having a dream before he was abruptly snapped out of it, a dream of being back at school about to sit his Higher French exam, realizing that he hadn't done any studying for it and was in a panic. It wasn't the first time he'd had that dream, though he hadn't had it for a while. He was about to enter the exam hall, knowing that he was going to wing it and hope for the best, when the banging summoned him back to consciousness.

He looked at his phone and saw it was just after 6.30 a.m. Why would someone be knocking so loudly on his door at this time? He felt confused and annoyed. 'OK, hold on,' he shouted, getting out of bed and switching on the light. He staggered to the door, eyes still half closed and opened the door to see Murdo Scrimgeour standing there. His hair was wet and he looked unshaven. He had on a black Berghaus jacket and water proof trousers.

'Sorry, Finn,' said Murdo. 'I need to speak to you.'

'OK. Come in.' He stood aside to let Murdo in and then closed the door, suddenly aware that he was standing there only in a pair of boxers. He closed the door and told Murdo to have a seat. 'I'd better put some clothes on.' He grabbed his jeans that were draped across a chair and pulled them on, then threw on his jumper.

'What the fuck happened to your face? You look like you've been in a fight. Never mind that just now. What the fuck do you want at this time of the morning, Murdo?'

'I need to ask you what you were doing last night.'

'Why?'

'Never mind. Just tell me.'

'I was with Amy Simpson. At her house. We had dinner then I came back here.'

'When were you there until?'

'Until about eleven. Look, what the fuck's this about?'

'Last night there was an incident. A man is dead. Your name has come up in the investigation.'

'Who is it? The dead man.'

'Callum Maclean. Your business card was found at his house. That's why I'm here.'

'That's right. I left it with him when I went to see him two days ago. He's dead? Jesus! What the fuck! He seemed a really nice guy. What happened to him?'

'His body was found by a passer-by in the harbour in Stromness.'

Finn thought of the bottle of whisky he'd brought him. Was he responsible? 'I'm sorry to hear that. I know Callum liked a drink. Did he fall in drunk?'

Murdo shook his head. 'I can't tell you any more about the circumstances. There'll be a press conference later today. You can attend that if you like.'

'So, I guess it's a suspicious death then? Fuck! I can't believe it. I only saw him the other day.'

Murdo stroked his chin and nodded. 'Aye, I know. Bloody awful.'

'That's just terrible. But I don't know how I can help you.'

'What did you talk to Callum about?'

'He was a good friend of Jeremy Powell's. His widow told me that. That's why I went to see him. I wanted to know if he had any idea why

Powell might have been killed.'

'And did he?'

'Not really. Though he did tell me about something that happened in Powell's past that disturbed him and I thought I'd follow that up. It was a useful chat.'

'I didn't know him myself. I believe he was a writer.'

'That's right. A poet. He and Powell met once a month to play chess together.'

Murdo nodded and stood up. 'OK. So that's all, thanks. I'll speak to Amy and ask her to confirm your whereabouts last night.'

'Fuck, you don't think I had anything to do with this, Murdo, do you?'

'No, Finn. It's a formality. That's all. We just need to rule out anybody that saw him recently. Oh, by the way, back to your face. What happened?'

'Your pal David Laing, that's what happened. He warned me off asking questions about him. I wonder how he knew I was staying here, eh?'

'Wait a minute, Finn. You don't think I had anything to do with that, do you?'

'I don't know. Did you?'

'Of course not. Fuck's sake, Finn, what do you take me for?'

'Well, I spoke to you yesterday about him and you knew I was staying here. It's a bit of a coincidence. How else did he know I was interested in him?'

'I don't know. This is a small place. You know that. Word gets around.'

Finn thought about this. It could have been Murdo. Or it could have been Peter Nicolson. It was possible that Grace might have spoken to Peter about the meeting with Laura in Yeswick and their conversation about Laing. He'd need to ask her.

'Do you want to report it?' asked Murdo.

'There's no point. No witnesses. No CCTV. He'd just deny it. Forget it.'

'What time did it happen?'

'Just after eleven p.m.'

'Hmm. OK. If you change your mind, let me know. Here's my card.' He placed a business card on the table. 'Good talking to you, Finn. See you.'

NINETEEN

'*Have you heard the news about Callum Maclean?*' asked Grace, as soon as Finn entered the newspaper office. Then she looked more closely at him '*What the fuck happened to your face?*'

It was the second time that morning he had been asked the same question. 'Why? Has something happened to my face?'

'Very funny!'

'In answer to your first question, yes, I know about Callum. Bloody awful. Such a gentle guy. Who would want to kill such a harmless old man?'

'I know. It's terrible. We've posted an item online about it. There's been a brief police press release and there's going to be a press conference at four o' clock in the town hall. We should get more details then. How did you hear about it?'

'I was rudely awakened at half-six this

morning by PC Plod wanting to know why my business card was found in Callum's house.'

'Who was the copper?'

'DS Murdo Scrimgeour. Do you know him?'

'Vaguely. I know his name more than him personally. Tall guy with red hair?'

Finn nodded. 'That's him. We were at school together.'

'What did he say?'

'He wanted to know where I was last night.'

'So, he had you down as a suspect. Why would he think you had anything to do with it?'

'Who knows? I don't trust him. He's probably a friend of Laing's.'

'Hope you have an alibi.'

Finn nodded again.

Grace smiled. 'Ah, let me see. Who could you possibly have been with last night? I can't think. Unless it was that woman you spent the night with the other night. And you said nothing happened.'

'It didn't.'

'So, you were with Amy last night?'

'She invited me to dinner. That's all. I left

about eleven.'

'Oh, yeah? So you say!'

'I did. I even have a witness.'

'Oh, yes? Who?'

'The guy who gave me this.' Finn pointed to his bruised left cheek.

'So, you were in a fight? What happened?'

Finn sat down at a desk in the main office and opened up the laptop he'd been given to use. 'You should see the other guy,' he said.

She smiled. 'Ha, ha very funny. Who do you think you are? Philip Marlowe?'

'I see you're a fan of Chandler.'

'I prefer Phoebe.'

'Phoebe?'

'I see you're not a fan of Friends.'

'You're very witty today.'

'You mean, I'm not witty every day? Anyway, seriously, what *did* happen to your face? Who did it?'

'David Laing.'

'Laing? Ah. That makes sense. He's a very dangerous man.'

'I found that out.'

'Coffee?'

'Yes, please.'

She filled the kettle and switched it on then went over to the cupboard and got out a couple of mugs. She spooned coffee into the cafetiere. 'So, what happened?' she asked, sitting down opposite him while waiting for the kettle to boil.

'He caught me on my way back to the hotel last night. It was late. No one about. He chose his time well.'

'How did he know where to find you?'

'I have my suspicions. Word travels fast in these parts, as you know. Tell me, you didn't happen to mention to Peter about what Laura told us about Laing?'

'Well, he asked me how the meeting with her went. I might have mentioned we talked about Laura thinking Laing was a possible suspect. Why?'

'Because Laing knew that I was interested in him. He might have found that out from Peter, as well as where I was staying. He was lying in wait for me.'

'I'm sorry if I put my foot in it.'

'It doesn't matter. I'm sure he could have heard in any manner of ways. Perhaps from Murdo, for example. I spoke to him about Laing yesterday.'

The kettle boiled and she poured the water into the jug and gave it a stir before plunging it and then pouring it into the mugs.

'I thought you were supposed to wait a bit for it to percolate,' he said.

'I don't believe in waiting,' she said, handing him the steaming mug. 'Help yourself to milk.'

'Thanks.'

'So?'

'So?'

'Did he say anything or just lamp you?'

'Just the obvious. Told me to fuck off. Oh, and threatened to sue me if I printed anything about him. Then hopped back into his Range Rover and fucked off. Leaving me bruised and battered.'

'Have you told the police?'

He raised his eyebrows. 'Well, I told Murdo when he popped round for his early morning chat, but there's no point pressing charges. Laing would just deny it. And I suspect the police wouldn't be too interested in pursuing it.'

'I did tell you he was well in with the authorities.'

'I should have listened. I should be thankful for that. I hear Laing is quite useful with his fists. Even his wife gets the treatment.'

'Who told you that?'

'Amy.'

'That's awful. What a bastard!'

'Indeed. I'm wondering if he might be our man, the killer of Jeremy Powell? He's certainly got a violent temper, so I wouldn't put it past him being the one who shoved him off the cliff and did likewise with his pooch.'

'Doesn't sound like the police are falling over themselves trying to catch anyone anyway.'

'He has an alibi.'

'Let me guess. His wife?'

'Yes.'

'Typical! Even though he beats her up. That's just sick. Poor woman. Sounds like a clear case of coercive control.'

'Isn't it! But for the time being I have another lead. Cambridge. I saw Laura again yesterday and she told me she'd found the business card of someone Jeremy met when he went to there last month. A reporter for the local paper. Who was killed shortly after he met Jeremy.'

'What? That's got to be more than a coincidence, right?'

He filled her in about the Brian Clark murder and Powell's connection to him. And about Powell's old university friends, still based in Cambridge. 'So, I need to go to Cambridge to follow this up and speak to a few people who might shed some light on whether it's a coincidence or not.'

Finn started making a few phone calls then booked a flight to London for the following day. He managed to track down the girlfriend of Brian Clark. Julie Sinclair had been mentioned in local newspaper reports which Finn found online. He found her on social media and managed to message her. Having told her who he was, he mentioned the connection between Clark and Powell, and said he was trying to find out more about Clark's death and how it might be connected to that of Powell's. Julie agreed to meet him and they arranged a time and place for the next day in Cambridge.

He then spoke to Olivia Andrews at her university office and told her a bit about himself; that he was researching Jeremy Powell and wanted to speak to people who knew him. She was very interested to hear that he had met Jeremy's widow, Laura. She agreed to meet him at 9 p.m. in a wine bar in Cambridge the next evening.

He had less luck trying to get hold of Stephen Moore. He got through to his PA and told her he was a journalist and asked to speak to Moore. She put him on hold but then came back and said he was sorry but he was too busy at the moment and hung up.

When he was finished with the arrangements, he phoned Amy to tell her what had happened after he left her place and his encounter with David Laing. As he spoke to her, he glanced at Grace. She rolled her eyes in his general direction.

'That's totally fucked-up,' Amy said.

'You did warn me about him. There wasn't much I could do about it, though. He sort of took me by surprise. Just appeared out of his black Range Rover and jumped me.'

'Oh, Finn, poor you! I don't know how Janice can stand living with him. He's obviously a complete monster. I think I might try speaking to her. My Pilates class is tomorrow. She's usually there.'

'OK. But, watch out. I don't think he'll worry too much about giving you a black eye either.'

'By the way, I just heard about Callum

Maclean from a customer. It's so sad.'

'I know. Murdo woke me up at six-thirty this morning to tell me about it.'

'Really? Why? Did he think you had something to do with it?'

'I don't know, but he will want to speak to you to confirm I was at your place last night. He found my card in Callum's house which I left when I went to see him the other day. There's a press conference later about it. Hopefully, we'll find out more.'

'Maybe he was just in the wrong place at the wrong time. But, something like that happening in Stromness, of all places. I can't believe it.'

'I know. Oh, and I am going to Cambridge tomorrow. I've got to follow up something to do with Powell there. Not sure when I'll be back here, Amy, but it's been nice seeing you again and thanks for the dinner last night.'

'Lovely seeing you, too, Finn. I'll let you know how my meeting with Janice goes. Take care.'

That afternoon, Finn called Hamish Anderson, the man who was boarding his gran's dog, left the office and got a taxi to Anderson's house. He thought he should at least set eyes on the dog before dismissing the idea of taking it.

Hamish Anderson answered the door. He was a bear-like man in his mid-forties, wearing a tent-sized red lumberjack shirt, with a large bushy brown beard and thick brown hair. He also had a wide grin. 'Come in, Finn. Good to see you. You're here to see Kiki then? Follow me.'

They went through the house and out to the courtyard at the back where Hamish had some outbuildings converted into kennels, the sound of loud barking coming from them as they approached.

'How many dogs do you have here?' Finn asked.

'Half a dozen. Apart from Kiki, they're all just for a week or two while their owners are away on holiday. In winter and early spring, it's skiing trips. Never seen the point of that, myself. Spending all that money just to slide down a mountain then queue to get towed back up! People are now getting away for the sunshine. The luck of some, eh? I'd like that. Being able to escape from this weather and head off to Spain or Greece!'

He did like to chat, thought Finn. 'You do know I live in a flat in London. I'm not sure I'll be able to take her but I thought I'd like to see her, seeing she was my gran's dog.'

'Och, she's a lovely wee dog, so she is,' said Hamish as he opened the door to one of the outbuildings. They walked past several doorways separated from the corridor by a gate, inside which Finn could see dogs of all shapes and sizes, some barking, some jumping up excitedly. They came to the last of the doorways. 'She's no bother at all. She's in here.'

Finn looked at the dog, a small dark brown cockapoo who jumped up and down at the gate. Hamish opened the gate and they went in. The dog started running around them and leaping about. Finn bent down to stroke her coat and she started licking his hand.

'She's gorgeous,' said Finn. 'Quite a lively wee thing.'

'I can tell she likes you. I knew you'd fall in love with her,' said Hamish.

TWENTY

That afternoon at 4 p.m., Grace was seated at the hastily-arranged police press conference in a room in the town hall. A few rows of chairs had been put out to accommodate the journalists, some of whom had flown into the isles, having heard the news of a murder early that morning. Camera crews from BBC Scotland and STV were set up to record and televise the proceedings live on air and print journalists, if that term could still be applied in a digital age, were ready, tablets and recording devices in hand. Reporters from radio stations clutched microphones.

Grace had got there in time to get a seat in the front row and sat sandwiched between a man from the *Scotsman* and a woman from BBC Scotland. She knew the woman, vaguely, from the Powell story. She was called Angela Chalmers, a friendly tall blonde in her late thirties with bright red lipstick and fingernails to match. The man she hadn't met before but he introduced himself as Ruraidh Maxwell, suited and booted and sounding every inch the ex-Edinburgh public school type, who made it obvious that he regarded Grace as an inferior sort of journalist, her paper only a local rag, not a national and therefore he was more interested in chatting to the man to his right, a reporter from the *Herald*.

By contrast with Maxwell, Angela was charm personified, asking Grace if there had been any developments in the Powell story. She was fascinated to learn about the *Chronicle's* interest and that Finn Morrison was in Kirkwall to cover it but Grace held back from revealing anything more.

Then the senior police officers, two men and a woman, entered the room and took up their places at the table in front, behind which three chairs had been placed with their names and ranks written on cards in front of them: Superintendent Keith Fleming, the only one in uniform, Detective Inspector Catriona Walker, in a light grey trouser suit and Detective Sergeant Murdo Scrimgeour, Finn's erstwhile school colleague, in a dark blue suit.

'Good afternoon, everyone,' said Fleming, who Grace thought was probably around fifty but gave the impression of being much older. He had a weary expression on his bespectacled face as he peered through his glasses as the assembled audience. 'Thank you for attending this press conference which I hope will assist in helping to catch the killer of a popular local man.

'Callum Maclean was violently attacked and killed just after eleven p.m. last night. This was a particularly brutal murder of an elderly man. We would like to appeal for anyone who was in Stromness yesterday evening who may have seen anything unusual to get in touch. Also, any photographs or dashcam footage taken there yesterday would be of interest as we conduct an investigation into what happened. Detective Inspector Walker will be leading the investigation and I'll now hand over to her and she will provide more details.'

Walker began by describing Maclean. 'For those who didn't know him, Mr Maclean was a well-liked man in the community. He was seventy-four and had lived all his life in Orkney. He lived alone. He was a celebrated poet who had received widespread acclaim and awards for his poetry which focused on the landscape of Orkney.

'I personally had the privilege to meet him on several occasions at local events when he was a guest speaker. He lit up the room with his anecdotes. He was a gentle man who, according to those who knew him well, wouldn't harm a soul. So, it is very sad for our community to learn of his death in such a violent and sudden way.'

Grace was impressed by such a moving tribute to Callum. She hadn't known the man herself but clearly he had made a powerful impression on the senior police officer, who looked both sad and angry at the same time.

Walker continued. 'What we know of Mr Maclean's movements yesterday evening is that he went to The Ship pub in Stromness around nine o' clock and met some acquaintances there. He stayed until about eleven p.m. when he left the pub alone to make his way home. The pub is situated near the harbour and Mr Maclean would most likely have passed that way on his way to his house which is about a twenty-minute walk away.

'We do not know exactly what happened but clearly there was some sort of incident there that led to his death, possibly a mugging as Mr Maclean's wallet is missing. A witness heard a splash and saw a body in the water and a figure running from the scene. He attempted a rescue, risking his life by going into the water and bringing Mr Maclean back to land. He then called the emergency services and an ambulance arrived and resuscitation was attempted but, sadly, it was unsuccessful and Mr Maclean was pronounced dead at the scene. A post-mortem examination today has revealed that the cause of death was a single stab wound to the chest.

'We would like to speak to anyone who

was in The Ship pub, or out and about in Stromness, last night. They may have seen or heard something which may prove useful to the investigation. This was a tragic death of a local character and I'd like to appeal to anyone who knows anything about what happened to come forward. Unfortunately, we do not have a clear description of the figure who was seen leaving the area as Mr Maclean entered the water. Only that he is described as male and of stocky build, wearing dark clothes and a black beanie hat. We would like this person to come forward. Thank you, I'll now take questions.'

'Callum Maclean was a close friend of Jeremy Powell's,' asked Finn, seated at the back of the room. 'They were both writers. Could there be a connection between the two deaths?' Every head in the room turned to look at him. He had told Grace to head over to the hall before him and he would join her there as he wanted to go and see Hamish Anderson but by the time he arrived there were no seats left near her and he had to sit at the back.

DS Scrimgeour gave him a look as if to say "Didn't I tell you to drop this!" Then he turned and looked at Walker and Fleming. Fleming whispered something to Walker and she nodded. Walker said, 'Mr Powell's death was likely to have been a tragic accident. There was no evidence of a foul play and it is not considered as a suspicious death. Mr Maclean, however, clearly suffered a violent assault. The fact that they may have known each other is therefore not significant.'

There followed some other questions from reporters. Grace wanted to know who the person was who had attempted to rescue Callum. Walker said they did not wish their identity to be revealed at the moment. The journalist from the *Daily Record* wanted to know if the murder weapon had been found. Walker said no, but that a search of the crime scene was still being conducted including within the harbour using police divers.

After a few more questions, which elicited little information because of what Walker described as "operational reasons", Fleming announced the press conference was at an end and the three officers departed.

Finn met Grace outside the hall. 'Do you really think there could be a connection between Powell's and Maclean's deaths? she said.

'I've no idea,' said Finn. 'But I wanted to see Murdo's face when I asked the question.'

Grace laughed.

'He definitely tried to steer me away from considering Powell's death was anything other than an accident.'

'DI Walker said the same thing.'

'Yes. But there is one thing. Callum did tell me he he'd also had some dealings with Laing and disliked him when I told him what Laura said about the builder. I wish now that I'd asked him more about that. But it couldn't have been Laing who killed Callum. He was too busy battering me at the time.'

'So, you're his alibi. Maybe the timing was intentional. He beats you up at the same time someone kills Callum. He could have had an accomplice.'

'He couldn't have known I would be there at that exact time. But he was clearly waiting for me to come back to the hotel. He must have been tipped off that I was staying at the hotel and that I had gone out. Maybe from someone working there. But why would he want Callum dead? Maybe you could follow it up and see what you can find out. I've got my hands full with the Powell investigation.'

'OK, I'll see if I can dig up anything that connects Callum with Laing. Good luck in Cambridge. Let me know if you find out anything useful. I'll do likewise.'

'Will do. Thanks, Grace. I'll keep in touch.'

FRIDAY

TWENTY-ONE

Finn flew into London, got the train and Tube to his flat, then drove to Cambridge. He booked into a travel lodge in the city centre. He had arranged to meet Brian Clark's girlfriend, Julie, in a pub, The King's Head, at six pm. after she finished work. He'd found out that she worked in a science laboratory as a technician on a science park in the outskirts of the city.

He arrived at the King's Head early. The pub was busy with office workers and part of a chain. It was the kind of nondescript pub you find in every city centre. What it lacked in character was made up for in its prices. The booze was cheap. Finn was well acquainted with that fact. He bought a mineral water, found a table in a corner and had a seat. He spent the time waiting for her googling for more information about the murder of Brian Clark on his phone.

When Julie arrived, he got her a drink, a white wine. She was small and slight and looked like a breath of wind might knock her over. She was pretty, though, thought Finn, with fine, delicate features and blue eyes that drew your attention to them. She looked sad, though. Understandably, he thought. He offered his condolences and asked if they could talk about the day Brian died.

Julie described what had happened that day. She told him that she had been due to meet Brian in a pub in the city centre that evening. But he hadn't shown up as they'd arranged. That was odd. He was usually very punctual. She had tried calling him on her mobile but got no answer. In the corner of the pub, the TV was reporting an incident in the suburb of Eastlands. Police, fire and ambulance crews were on the scene. There were images of what was happening. She recognised it as Brian's street.

In a state of panic, she had left her glass of wine on the table and sprinted to the nearest taxi rank. About fifteen minutes later she was in his street. There were police cars, fire engines and ambulances everywhere and a strip of blue and white police tape was draped across the road, guarded by two uniformed officers. Smoke billowed from the building where Brian's flat was located, fire hoses dousing the building with water.

Uniformed police officers, on the other

side of the crime scene tape, wouldn't let her get near the flat. Instead, she stood there, pacing back and forth. What looked like plain-clothed CID officers stood chatting. One even laughed, as if in response to a joke. How dare they? she thought. She wanted to storm past the tape and charge up the lane and give them a piece of her mind.

The TV report had said that there had been an incident, nothing more. What on earth had happened? Was it a gas explosion? She gave her name to one of the officers and told them who she was, that she knew Brian Clark, who lived in the street. Someone would speak to her, was all she was told.

Eventually, a detective came out and asked if she was Julie Sinclair. The detective introduced herself as Detective Inspector Richardson. She asked Julie to come to her car.

The detective broke the news to her. A man who was in that flat was dead. A firearm and a petrol bomb had been used in the attack. That was all she would tell her. Julie broke down in tears.

The DI then drove Julie to a police station near the centre of the city where she was given a cup of tea. When she appeared to be more composed, the detective started asking her questions. Julie told her how she'd first met Brian, that it was through a dating app and that they'd been seeing each other for a short while. She told her how often she stayed over with him, what she knew about him, his studies, his friends, his family and so on.

Then the police officer quizzed her about her own background, her family, her previous relationships. She seemed very interested in the fact that Julie was separated from her husband, Paul Wilson. The detective asked more about her ex. Who was he? Did he have any previous? Julie sighed. Her husband had a history of violence. That was one of the reasons she had left him. 'I told her she'd find out soon enough. He'd been inside. Before I knew him, though.'

'What was Brian like?' Finn asked.

Julie said, 'Lovely. Brian was passionate about his work on the newspaper. I told the police that. They were very interested in what stories Brian was working on, but I couldn't tell them anything about that.'

'What do you think of the mistaken identity theory? Do you really think that he was just unlucky, mistaken for somebody else, as the police concluded?'

Julie didn't answer right away. She seemed to take a few moments to think about this and sipped her drink. She looked on the verge of tears. Finn felt bad about putting her through this, even though he had done it countless times before with relatives of the deceased.

At last, she spoke. 'I think it must have been. I really can't think of any other explanation. I don't think it could have been Paul. And the police said he had an alibi anyway.'

They carried on chatting for a bit longer but there wasn't anything else that Julie was able to tell Finn that seemed significant.

Finn decided to go for something to eat before he met his next meeting. He chose an Indian restaurant near the pub. He thought the food would be more enticing than that offered in the budget pub. At the table, he got out his phone and looked up the local paper that Brian had worked for, the Cambridge Mercury. He found a phone number for the newspaper's office. He got hold of a woman called Claire Ferguson, who said she was a reporter. He explained who he was and what he wanted to know. She said she would speak to the editor. He gave her his phone number and thanked her.

A woman called Sharon Fisher then called him back. She said was the editor.

Finn explained that he was a journalist investigating the murder of Brian Clark.

'Such a shame,' said Fisher. 'Brian was a very talented reporter. And a nice guy. It was a terrible thing that happened to him.'

'Did Brian ever tell you what he was working on before he died?'

'He rang me up and told me it was going to be something big. But he wouldn't share what it was with me. He said he'd send me the piece. It would be a front-page splash, was all he said. But the next thing I knew, he was dead. I told the police all that.'

TWENTY-TWO

Amy approached Janice after the Pilates class that evening, as they were leaving the gym. 'Fancy a drink?' she asked.

Janice was a couple of years younger than Amy. She still looked like that girl from school all the Sixth-Year boys fancied, drawing attention to herself in her pastel-shaded, designer-brand leggings and box-fresh trainers. Amy had spoken to her a couple of times after the session but they had always then gone their separate ways. Janice lived on the other side of the town from her, she knew, on a modern housing development which her husband had built, choosing the prime site for himself, of course.

'What, just now?' Janice said, looking surprised.

'Well, yes, if that's OK. Or, if not, we could meet up another night. I just thought it would be good for us to get to know each other better. We see each other every week.'

Janice smiled. 'Yes, good idea. But I'd really like to go home first and shower and change. I could meet you somewhere in an hour. Would that be OK?'

Amy checked her watch. It was just after seven. 'How about we grab something to eat as well, just pub food? Or, were you planning to have dinner with your husband?'

Janice shook her head and laughed. 'With David? No. I can't remember the last time we sat down and ate together. He's usually home late. He's out tonight anyway with his mates, watching some football game in the Red Lion. Yes, that sounds good. Where do you want to go?'

'How about the Anchor? They have a pretty good menu there. And decent wine.'

'I like the sound of that. See you in an hour then. At eight.' Janice waved and headed for her car, a white Porsche Cayenne. Amy remembered what Finn had said about her husband appearing suddenly from his black Range Rover. What was it about these big fancy cars? she thought. It was definitely a status thing to have one amongst the elite, even on a tiny place like Orkney where there was nowhere to go, but the whole thing seemed stupid to her. Amy was quite happy with her bike.

Amy had also showered and changed and was wearing her best skinny jeans and lilac silk blouse, and trainers, though she had had to put her thick padded jacket on to brave the chilly wind coming from the north. At least it was dry, though, and only a short walk from her place to the pub.

The Anchor was one of the oldest pubs in Kirkwall, in a narrow wynd just back from the harbour. Its décor hadn't changes in decades, a traditional old pub with a stone floor, timber-panelled walls and oak beams. A log fire roared in the corner. It was a cosy place and with no TV or music, the ideal place for a chat, Amy had thought. It was reasonably quiet, too; perfect Amy thought, picking a corner table away from anyone else and sitting down to wait on Janice.

Janice arrived fifteen minutes late, looking stunning, as Amy expected she would. She was wearing a red leather jacket, a white lace top with a black bra underneath and a pair of tight-fitting black leather trousers with killer heels, the ensemble all, no doubt, thought Amy, from high-end designer brands. Her make-up was immaculate. Amy immediately felt underdressed.

'Sorry I'm a bit late. I ordered a taxi to get here but it didn't come on time and I had to wait. There's no way I was walking here in these heels!'

Janice said.

Amy said, 'You look fabulous.'

'Thanks. You're looking pretty good yourself.'

Amy shrugged and looked down at her clothes. 'It's nice to do something special, so why not, eh?'

There were a couple of menus on the table. 'I recommend the Marlborough, if you like white wine,' said Amy.

'Why don't we get a bottle, then,' said Janice.

Janice looked a little nervous, Amy thought. She kept twiddling with the gold bracelets she wore and fidgeting with her many rings. They talked about the Pilates class and how much they each enjoyed it and what else they did. Amy told her about the bookshop and Janice confessed that she had never been in it, hadn't read a book since she was at school.

As they drank and ate, Janice appeared to relax and spoke more about herself. She had left school at sixteen and, had tried modelling as a career for a while, moving to London. But she didn't like the constant travelling and got tired of how every agent attempted to get her into bed with them. 'I got sick of all the perverts. All I was getting offered was sex work, like chatlines and adult TV work so I gave it up and came back here to work as a barmaid in a pub. The Red Lion, in fact, where David is tonight,' she said. 'If that's where he really is!' That's how she had met David, she said. It was his local. He asked her out and wined and dined her. That had been five years ago. They got married six months after they started going out. She then got pregnant and had the twins, who were now three. They had a nanny who lived with them, who was looking after the children tonight.

Amy noticed that Janice was drinking much, much faster than she was, and Janice was now showing the tell-tale signs of intoxication which Amy knew only too well, thinking back to the other night at Finn's hotel. Amy had determined not to get have more than a glass or two, remembering the hangover and how she had had to endure the next day at work until she had to leave early for home. That was not to be repeated, she told herself.

'Actually, a friend of mine had a run-in with your husband last night,' Amy said.'

'Oh? Who was that?'

'Finn Morrison. You probably won't remember him. We went out together when we were in Sixth Year. He's now a journalist and lives in London but he came back here for his gran's funeral.'

'Oh, I remember Finn. All the girls in my year fancied him.'

'Really? Oh, well. Anyway, as I said, apparently David, your husband, punched him and warned him not to think about doing any stories about him'

Janice shrugged. 'That sounds like David, right enough.'

'I heard that David got questioned about the death of Jeremy Powell.'

'Yes. I had to say he was at home with me that afternoon.'

'Was he?'

'No.'

'Where was he?'

'I have no idea. Probably shagging his secretary at her house while her husband was at work. I've got my suspicions on that front, given the number of times he works late. She's married and wouldn't want the local fuzz asking her awkward questions, I guess. Anyway, he told me to say he was at home working on paperwork.'

'Why would you say he was with you when he wasn't?'

'He said it was important. He phoned me just after the police had spoken to him at his office and asked if I would cover for him. He said he had been busy that day doing something he'd rather the police didn't know about.'

'What?'

'Oh, he's involved in some shady stuff. It may well have been that and not his secretary. Anyway, with David, I've learned that it's better just to do as he asks.'

'That's awful. I couldn't help wondering,' Amy said. 'As David is handy with his fists, I was thinking. That time you showed up with a black eye. Was it really a cupboard door?'

By now, the mains were finished, the plates cleared away and they were waiting for the dessert to arrive, tiramisu for Amy and chocolate gateau for Janice. Janice suddenly looked tearful. She closed her eyes and sighed. Then opened them and stared at Amy and shook her head. 'No,' she said. 'It was David. He completely lost it. I hadn't cleaned the bathroom and he is obsessive about cleanliness. He started throwing things around and a deodorant can hit me in the face.'

'Fuck, that's terrible,' said Amy.

'I know. He said he was sorry, that he didn't mean it, but it's not the first time he's done something like that. He scares me sometimes.'

She took a large gulp of wine and reached for the bottle but it was empty. She turned to a waiter. 'Can we get another one of these, please?' she said, loudly enough for people to turn and stare.

'Why don't you just leave him?' asked Amy.

She shook her head. 'Where could I go? He'd find me. And he knows all sorts of people, lawyers and so on. They'd make out I was a bad mum and take the kids off me, I know he would.'

'How could he do that?'

'I have a drug history. It was when I was modelling. There was coke everywhere. I got addicted and spent time in rehab. He knows that. He'd use it against me.'

'But that's in the past, isn't it?'

She shook her head. 'I wish it was.'

'What do you mean?' Amy asked, lowering her voice. 'Do you still take drugs? Cocaine?'

'Only occasionally. I'm not addicted but David has a constant supply.'

'Really?'

'Yes. He imports it from Europe into Orkney amongst his building materials. It's in bags of sand or cement or something. He supplies most of the dealers here but ships most of it off to Aberdeen to dealers there. He makes a fortune out of it, too.'

TWENTY-THREE

*F*inn waved and stood up to greet Olivia Andrews as she arrived in the bar. She looked amazing and fitted the stereotyped image he had of a historical novelist: a flowery ankle-length dress and flowing, auburn Pre-Raphaelite hair. He ordered her drink, a small glass of pinot noir.

She had selected this wine bar in Cambridge as she reckoned it would be quiet but he also made sure that he got there early to nab a corner seat away from any prying ears. It was a step up from the chain pub he'd met Julie in earlier that evening. It was all bleached wooden floors and glass tables, with whitewashed stone walls. The windows looked out over the river. Jazz played on the sound system. John Coltrane, Finn recognised. The ambience was sophisticated and arty. This was definitely upmarket, catering for the professional and academic clientele rather than office workers. And its prices were to match. He got the receipts anyway but wasn't sure the finance office would approve them.

When she was seated, Olivia said, 'I did google your name to check you were genuine, not just some oddball. I don't normally meet strange men in pubs,' she said, sitting down.

Finn explained that he was looking into the possibility that Jeremy's death might not be an accident.

'Wait a moment. I thought the police concluded that his death *was* an accident.'

'Well, yes, that's what the police say, but his widow has her doubts.'

'You think it could be suspicious?'

'Yes, actually I do.'

'My God! Why?'

'I think it could be connected to another death, here in Cambridge. I'll tell you about that in a minute. When did you last see Jeremy?'

'Last month. When he was here to give a talk at St George's College. It wasn't long before he died, actually. That came as a terrible shock. I still can't take it in that he's gone. We hadn't seen each other for a long time, but he was a dear friend and it was so good catching up with him again. I had hoped that renewing our acquaintance meant we would stay in touch. Sadly, it wasn't to be.'

'How was he when you saw him?'

'In good form. He was enjoying being back in Cambridge. We reminisced quite a bit about the old days. We went out for a bit when we were undergraduates, you know. It was a lovely evening. I'm so sad that I'll never see him again. I still can't quite believe that he's gone.' She took a sip of her drink.

'Do you have any idea why anyone might want to harm him?'

'No. Absolutely not. Jeremy was a gentle soul.'

'Did anything unusual happen in Cambridge when you saw him? '

'No. We had a meal after his talk then a few drinks, that's all.'

'What did you talk about?'

'Oh, you know, the usual stuff. Careers. Marriage. His life in Orkney. His books. My own books. The pandemic. Politics. Bloody Brexit, of course! The narcissistic shit that's in number ten …'

'Have you heard of Brian Clark?'

'No, I don't think so, who is he?'

'He *was* a journalist in Cambridge. He was killed last month. Shot actually. In his home.'

'Oh, yes, now you mention it, I remember hearing about that. Terrible. Wasn't it some drug-related thing? Gangs? Mistaken identity.'

'That's what was reported, yes. Jeremy had Clark's business card. His wife found it in his belongings. That's what put me onto him. He had interviewed Jeremy when he was down here. Clark was shot soon after that. I wondered if there could be a connection between what happened to Clark and what happened to Jeremy. It seems odd both of them dying so soon after each other, don't you think? Brian Clark meets Jeremy. Clark is then shot and killed. Jeremy returns home to Orkney and dies soon after.'

'But what could Jeremy's death possibly have to do with this other man's murder? I don't understand. I don't think Jeremy would have got involved with gangs? Do you think he might have known who killed Clark and that made him a target?'

'Possibly. Well, I don't know.'

You're married to Stephen Moore, aren't you?' said Finn.

'Actually, we're now separated. Recently, in fact.'

'I believe Jeremy and Stephen were friends at university, is that right?'

'Yes. And they were in Beirut together.'

'Beirut? Really? I wanted to talk to your husband as he and Jeremy had been friends at one time and I thought he might have heard from him. But I'm having difficulty seeing him. I get the impression he doesn't want to speak to me.'

'Well, if he knows you're a journalist, I'm not surprised. He likes to keep a low profile.' She finished off her wine.

'Can you tell me where he lives? I'd like to speak to him about Jeremy.'

'Well you can try. He still lives in our house, or rather what was our house. It's his now, since I moved out. It's in Houghton.' She sighed and closed her eyes. 'Poor Jeremy.'

'You didn't hear from him again?'

'No.'

'Can you think of anything, anything at all, that you talked about that evening with Jeremy that he might have spoken to this journalist about?'

Her face went pale. 'Oh, fuck. Cerberus!' she said.

'Cerberus? What's that? Said Finn.

'Oh... never mind. Fuck. I can't say any more. I've got to go.' She suddenly stood up and put her coat on.

'Listen. Thanks for everything you've told me. I really appreciate it. It's been most helpful. Can I give you my card, in case there's anything else you think of which might help? My email address and mobile number are on there.' He fished a business card from his pocket and put it on the table. 'Oh, just in case. Let me write down the number of someone who's been helping me with this.' He scribbled a number down on the back of the card after checking it on his phone. 'She's called Grace. She's a journalist up in Scotland. Just in case you can't get hold of me and need to speak to someone in a hurry. I check in with her all the time.'

'Well...I'm sure that won't be necessary but I'll take it just in case, as you say.' She picked up his card and put it in her pocket and quickly disappeared out of the bar.

After she left, as Finn made his way back towards his hotel, he had a feeling that he was being followed. A man was walking about twenty paces behind him and turned into the same streets he turned into. But by the time he got to his hotel, he looked around and couldn't see anyone. Maybe he was simply being paranoid, he thought, after what had happened with being mugged by Laing in Kirkwall.

When he got back to his hotel, he started an online search on his laptop for anything about Cerberus. He was interrupted when his phone rang. It was Amy. She told him about her meeting with Janice Laing. 'His alibi is false', she said. 'His wife didn't know his whereabouts that afternoon.'

'I knew it!'

Then she told him about the cocaine.

'Fuck! He's supplying coke!' said Finn.

'Yes. I thought you'd like to know that.'

'And he's got the local cops in his pocket, by the sound of it, so no one is interested in investigating him. He might even have got away with murder. And the *Orkney Times* won't run any stories about him as he's a pal of the editor's. Obviously, though, there's no proof.'

'I've got an idea,' she said.

'What?'

'I'll let you know if it works!'

After she hung up, he phoned Grace and told her what Amy had told him about Laing and drugs.

'Wow!'

'You won't be able to print anything about it, though. For one, Peter wouldn't allow it. But, secondly, it's just hearsay at the moment. There's no actual proof. We'll see what Amy can come up with.'

'OK, I'll sit on it for the time being. I've also got some news you'll like to hear,' she said. 'I was just about to phone you.'

'What is it?' said Finn.

'Apparently, Laing had been purchasing land around where Callum lived, to build luxury homes on. Callum owned a field behind his house, and I'm told that Laing made several offers to buy the land from Callum but he refused to sell.'

'That's very interesting.'

'I know. That could be a motive for murder.'

'Indeed. If he could get Callum murdered, he could have Powell killed as well. But he'd need an accomplice. By the way, you know how I told you about that reporter, Brian Clark, who interviewed Powell and then was killed? Well, I met Clark's girlfriend and spoke to the editor of his newspaper. It appears that Clark was about to publish an article about something big. As you know, the police investigation concluded that the killing was most likely a case of mistaken identity, that he'd been murdered by gangsters carrying out a feud, who had mistaken him for someone else, but I'm working on the theory that whoever killed Clark, also killed Powell.'

'Are you sure?'

'Two days after Clark's murder, Powell disappears while out for a walk. Coincidence? I don't think so. Highly suspicious, I would say. I've just met Olivia Andrews, who knew Powell at university and met him on that trip to Cambridge before he died, and she let something slip. When I asked her if there was anything that Powell might have told Clark about, she said "Cerberus". Then she seemed to think the better of it and wouldn't say any more.'

'Cerberus? What's that?' asked Grace.

'That's the thing. I've googled it and there's nothing online that jumps out. I am wondering if this might be what Powell told Clark about. I need to speak to her ex, Stephen Moore. Maybe he knows something about it. I don't know, but it's worth a try. I haven't been able to get hold of him yet but I know where he lives and I'm going to doorstep him tomorrow morning.'

TWENTY-FOUR

Back in her apartment, Olivia thought about that night she'd brought Jeremy back to her flat. Jeremy's death had been reported as accidental, so she hadn't considered that anything she had done would have had anything to do with it until now. And she hadn't thought anything about him passing anything to Brian Clark. His death didn't even register with her. Until she'd met this journalist and made the connection. She tried to recall what had happened that night.

At his talk at St George's College, she had met Jeremy again. They had been students together and when she had found out that he was going to be delivering a talk, she had messaged him on Facebook to say she would be coming to hear it and would love to see him again. After the event, she met him at the door of the college's hall where the talk had been held, and they took a taxi into the city centre, to a favourite Italian restaurant that they used to frequent when they were students.

Olivia had flung her arms around him in the taxi and kissed him. 'It's so good to see you again, Jeremy. I loved your talk.'

'Thanks.'

'All those stupid questions, though, about where do you get your ideas from and how long does it take to write a book, honestly how unoriginal!'

He laughed. 'I suppose I'm used to it. I don't mind.'

The taxi pulled up on a cobbled street and they got out.

Inside the restaurant, they ordered a bottle of champagne and a waiter filled their glasses.

'Cheers!' said Jeremy, as they raised their glasses and clinked them together.

Olivia said, 'God, how long is it since I last saw you? Twenty-odd years? And you're still as handsome.'

'You haven't changed either, Olivia. Still gorgeous.'

'And you're even more famous now. How many books have you sold, Jeremy? It must be millions.'

'I suppose so,' he said.

'Always modest. I often wonder what it

would have been like if we had stayed a couple, Jeremy, don't you?'

'Sometimes. We were so young, though. It's a long time ago. So, tell me what you've been up to, Olivia. Are you still with Stephen? I follow you on Facebook, but you don't post much, like me.'

She took a gulp of champagne. 'No, actually, we're separated.'

'Why? What happened?'

'We just hadn't been getting on for ages. We've led very different lives for years. I don't know how I stood it for so long. You know what he's like. In December, I found out he was fucking one of his employees. He even took her to a conference in Istanbul. She's half his fucking age, would you believe!'

How did you find out?'

'I got an anonymous phone call telling me about it. And telling me he had put her up in a flat in the city at his own expense. I suspect it was some jilted lover of hers seeking revenge. Or someone who just hates his guts. Like I do, now. Anyway, that was the last straw. We will get a divorce and I am going to take him for all he's worth.'

'I'm sorry to hear that, Olivia. That must

have been terribly hard for you.'

'It was hell. I don't mind saying so. Someone you trust going behind your back like that. It made me think, did I really know who he was? What he was capable of? I did love him in the beginning and we were very happy for a long time, but over the past few years I suppose our relationship gradually deteriorated.'

'I'm sorry to hear that. And how's your daughter doing? Charlotte, isn't it?'

'You have been keeping a keen interest in me, Jeremy! I suppose you know about her from Facebook as well? Yes, she's nineteen now and studying politics and sociology at Edinburgh University. She's in a flat up there with a couple of other girls. Loves it, she says. Of course, Stephen isn't her father but he was fond of her. She took it hard when we split up but she's getting over it. Yes, it's been bloody awful but I'm now free and have my own place and I love it.' She refilled their glasses.

'Who was Charlotte's father?'

'Oh, this guy I shacked up with after I graduated. It was a terrible mistake. He was a musician. In an indie band. It was all hopelessly romantic for a while but then he was off touring and everything and we drifted apart and we split up when she was a baby. After that he hardly ever kept in touch. An occasional card and a present would appear for her, rather haphazardly. I don't think he could remember when her birthday was. He's dead now. Five years ago. Drug overdose. Classic live fast, die young rock mentality. I hope Charlotte doesn't inherit those genes.'

'Sorry to hear that.'

'Yes, well, that's life, isn't it? After he and I split, Stephen came on the scene and became a step-dad to little Charlotte. She was fond of him too, but since she's learned what he's done, she says she'll never speak to him again. Poor Charlotte.'

'Are you still teaching?'

'Yes, but only part-time. I got to a position of seniority but then thought: what's the point trying to climb up the greasy academic ladder to get a chair? The constant demands to publish and so on. So, like you, I decided to turn to fiction. Though nothing like as successful as you are. I don't have Netflix clamouring to turn my books in to TV thrillers!'

'I've read your books, Olivia. I've got the latest one ordered. They're bloody marvellous! I love all that cloak and dagger stuff in Elizabethan London. Sir Francis Walsingham and his spies. Political intrigue and so on. Religious schisms. You've done well. Don't put yourself down.'

'Well, for me it's a form of escapism, honestly. I love to just immerse myself in the past. God, what's the present like? We need to escape from it as much as possible. The world has gone mad!'

'I know. We do get the news in the Northern Isles, you know. Brexit, Trump and so on.'

'Do you remember how idealistic we were once, Jeremy? How we thought we could change the world, make it a better place? What happened?'

'We grew up. We can't change the world. I think when I realised that I started writing fiction. There, I can make a world as I like it.'

'Now that's the most interesting thing you've said on the subject of writing all evening. You know. I love all your books, Jeremy, but it's always been the first one that intrigued me.'

'*The Beirut Affair*?'

'Yes.'

'Why?'

'Well, you know that Stephen and I got together once he came back from Beirut, didn't you?'

'Yes, of course.'

'He came back to live in Cambridge. I, of course, never left. Straight into a master's, then a PhD. Then a fellowship in the history department. You and Stephen were good friends at university when I met you. The two of you were close. Then you and I went out for, what was it? Six months? After we graduated, we drifted apart, you off abroad and me to academia. Some years later you crossed paths again with Stephen in Beirut and something happened between you and you fell out and never spoke to each other again. In *The Beirut Affair*, the journalist is a lot like you and there's a character who is a bit like Stephen. How much of that was true?'

'Now, that would have made an interesting question at the college tonight.' He laughed. 'Well, as you know, Stephen had a post in the American University in Beirut, lecturing in politics and international relations, like the character in my book. So I did base a character on him.'

'I know that. But what about the plot in the book, about the politician being blackmailed, is any of that true? Did any of that really happen?'

'Not exactly, though there's an element of truth to it. I changed a few things. In real life, my girlfriend, Laila, was actually a businessman's daughter, not someone's wife. She was a student of Stephen's. She was active in politics, supporting the Palestinians. I was madly in love with her and we had clandestine meetings at my apartment so her parents didn't find out. I'll never forget her. Then it all changed. She told me that she had received a blackmail threat but she dismissed it and the next day she fell to her death from a tower block. I spoke to Stephen about it. After all, he was the one who introduced me to her. He reckoned it must have been Mossad who were behind it. Then he told me to forget her, that she wasn't worth bothering about. That she was nothing special. Said he could fix me up with some other student. I lost my temper with him. That's why we fell out.'

'I asked Stephen once how much of the book was based on what happened in Beirut, but he said he never read any of your books. In fact, I believe you gave him my phone number?'

'That's right. Then he stayed in England and quit academia, deciding to start his own business. Political consultancy, is that right?'

'Yes, though that's not all. He's always had a secret side to him, I realise now. Mistresses. That secret company on the side.'

'Secret company?'

'It's all very hush-hush. It's called Cerberus Security Services. You know, after the multi-headed dog that guards the underworld in Greek mythology. I took some of the company's documents, including contracts. As an insurance policy, in case he tried to cheat me out of my share of what he's worth in the divorce. The company is entirely separate from his Cambridge-based business. It's all tied up offshore. In Jersey. He wouldn't want the tax authorities to know about it.'

'Hmm. Sounds intriguing. What kind of company is it?'

'It's a private security group, like the Cambridge company. He told me it's to offer armed protection to VIPs threatened by terrorists. Bodyguards, that kind of thing. There's contracts with some African governments, like Mali, Niger and so on for work. Though the work is pretty obscure in the documents'

'Really?'

'Yes. Well, I'm not sure what it really all entails, but he's made a packet out of it.'

'Interesting! I just might have a character who is an Oxbridge businessman with a secret company in my next book!' He took a drink of champagne from his glass.

She laughed. 'That's a great idea. Stephen would go apeshit! Oh, it's so good to see you, Jeremy. I'm so glad I heard about your talk and we got back in touch. I might have missed it. I'm so out of the loop, immersed in my books.'

'I know the feeling.'

They talked a bit more about Jeremy and Olivia told him some more things he didn't know about him.

'Listen. Why don't we have another drink after this back at my place, eh? A little nightcap'

'Sounds a good idea,' he said.

Once inside her apartment, she poured them both a whisky and they sat on the sofa reminiscing about old times. She kissed him and then they were all over each other. He removed her dress and bra and caressed her breasts while she undid his zip and ran her hand down inside his trousers. Then she led him to the bed.

Stephen had come round soon after that and asked for the Cerberus papers back. He must have noticed they were missing and realised that she had taken them. She'd handed them back. At the time, she had no idea that the death of Jeremy would have had anything to do with Stephen or Cerberus but now she wasn't so sure. He'd died in an accident, she had believed.

But this journalist she'd met earlier had created a doubt in her mind. He'd told her about this other journalist, Clark, who had also died. Was it all connected to Cerberus? Had Jeremy told Clark about it? Why would he do that? But she hadn't told him that much detail, had she? Not that she could remember anyway.

She did an online search putting in *Brian Clark Cambridge death* and amongst the rows of results was the BBC report of the death of the journalist. He'd been killed by an anonymous gunman just two days before Jeremy had disappeared in his "accident". Shot through his kitchen window. Believed to be case of mistaken identity. The killer or killers had not been identified. There were no witnesses. It all confirmed what Finn had told her earlier.

Did this really have anything to do with Jeremy's death? Maybe it was all just a coincidence? Olivia felt a migraine coming on. She took a couple of painkillers and lay back on the sofa and switched on the TV to watch the news. An incident in France, near Calais, was being reported. Eight men had been found dead in their vehicles, victims of a violent attack. It wasn't clear yet what they had been doing there or why they had been killed.

SATURDAY

TWENTY-FIVE

On the Saturday morning, Finn went to doorstep Stephen Moore. As it was early, he suspected he might be at home, especially it being a Saturday. He had learned from Olivia that he had a house in the village of Houghton, just three miles outside Cambridge, and managed to locate the property through checking the electoral register online. He drove to the house and parked in the street outside.

It was a large Victorian detached two-storey house. He walked up the driveway and noticed that there was a Mercedes parked on the drive so Moore was, presumably, at home. Oddly, the front door was ajar. He rang the bell and shouted into the house. 'Hello! Mr Moore?'

There was no answer so he pushed the door open and entered the hall. There was a staircase leading to the upper floor and to the left and right were doors to the rooms at the front of the house.

'Hello! Anybody there?' he shouted.

He opened the door to the left. A living room. A corridor ran to the back of the house. He followed it and found the kitchen diner which ran into an extension with glass sliding doors leading out to the garden.

Finn went back to the hall. 'Hello. Mr Moore?' he called. But there was only silence. He climbed the staircase to the upper floor. In one of the bedrooms, in a bed, he found a body lying in blood-soaked bedding.

He went closer. It was definitely Moore. He recognised him from the photos of him he'd seen on the internet. And there was no doubt that he was definitely dead: there was a bullet wound to his skull. Blood and brains everywhere. Finn thought about what to do. Obviously, he should phone the emergency services. But could he explain what he was doing there sufficiently not to draw suspicion on himself? He thought of just making an exit, pretending he had been nowhere near the place. But he'd noticed a camera at the front door. It may have been linked to a central store somewhere remotely with his image already being scrutinised. If he was to now disappear that would be even more suspicious and put him in the frame for murder. Plus, his fingerprints and DNA would be everywhere by now. He made a decision. He got out his mobile and dialled 999.

'I've just found someone. I think he's dead,' he told the operator and gave the address. He was told that an ambulance would be there as soon as possible. He gave his name. Then rang off.

Finn didn't know how long it would take them to get there. Could be ten minutes, maybe longer. He had a look around but was careful not to touch anything. It didn't look like the place had been burgled. If that was the case, he would have expected to have seen the house ransacked with stuff scattered everywhere. Instead, everything appeared normal.

Then he heard a siren. It sounded like it was coming nearer. Quickly, he went back downstairs and went out into the doorway to greet the paramedics and police, who both arrived with blue lights flashing and sirens blaring.

TWENTY-SIX

When Detective Inspector Helen Richardson, who'd been assigned the role of SIO, arrived, it was already full of SOCOs, in their white suits, gloved and masked from head to foot. She also put on a protective suit as well as nitrile gloves, bootees and a face mask. She was immediately informed by a uniformed sergeant that the householder, Stephen Moore, had been found lying in a pool of blood in his bed upstairs. He'd been shot in the head, apparently. The crime scene had been secured.

'Who discovered the body?' she asked Detective Sergeant Nick Phillips, who'd arrived ahead of her. The DS looked at his notebook. 'A Finn Morrison, boss. A journalist. Says he came round early to doorstep the victim in connection with a story he was working on. Claims that the front door was open. Found the victim in bed and called it in. Uniform arrived and sealed the place off.'

'What have you done with him?'

'He's been taken to the station. He's being held there for questioning, and will have his fingerprints and a DNA sample taken.'

'Good work. I'll speak to him later. What's your thoughts on this, Nick?'

'Well, there doesn't appear to be anything taken, as far as I can see. As you'll see around you, there's plenty of things that could have been taken that haven't. There's a collection of luxury watches in a drawer in the bedroom, for a start, that would fetch a fair sum.'

Helen looked around the room they were in, a living room. It certainly appeared to be undisturbed. There were oil paintings on the walls, ceramics on shelves, a widescreen TV on a wall. 'Hmm. So, it's a targeted killing? An assassination.'

'Looks like it, boss.'

She went upstairs and saw the victim, whom she recognised as Stephen Moore, a local businessman. Helen had spoken to him once when his name had come up in another investigation. The duvet cover had been pulled back and he was lying on his back on blood-soaked sheets, wearing a T-shirt and shorts. The bullet wound was in the head, with the blood spatter across the bed and on the wall. It looked like whoever came into the room got close enough to discharge the weapon at close range. Death would have been instantaneous.

The pathologist was already there and had just finished her examination of the body.

'Any idea of approximate time of death?' she asked her.

'From the rectal temperature reading, I'd say he's been dead for between eight to ten hours.'

'So that puts his murder between two and four a.m. then.'

'Give or take an hour or two. It's difficult to be exact, but I'd say that's probably about right judging by the body temperature.'

'Not much doubt about the cause of death, though, eh?'

'No, though we'll carry out a full post-mortem, of course.'

Helen approached the man in charge of the SOCOs, James Stevens. 'Found anything of interest, James?'

He nodded. 'Yes. A very impressive job. Looks like they disabled the alarm system and got in by picking the lock. Either that or they had a key. It certainly doesn't look like it's been forced. The security camera above the front door has been tampered with. They've removed the

SD card and taken the NVR that also stored the footage. They obviously knew what they were doing.'

'Anything for the lab to examine?' she asked, already knowing what the answer was likely to be.

'We've dusted for fingerprints but they may just be the victim's or that chap who found the body. We'll have to cross-match. Whoever broke in here will have worn gloves, no doubt about that. These people were professionals. We did recover the bullet which made an exit wound in the back of the victim's skull and lodged in the mattress. Looks like a 9mm pistol was used. Ballistic tests on it should be able to identify the type of gun.'

Finn was seated in an interview room in the police station waiting to be interviewed by the SIO. Helen arrived, introduced herself and asked him to tell her a bit about himself. He explained that he lived in London, worked for the *Chronicle* as an investigative reporter, and was in Cambridge following a story.

'And this story, led you to Stephen Moore's house?' she said.

'Yes. I wanted to speak to him.'

'Did you see anyone when you arrived at

the property?' she asked him.

'No. The front door and it was ajar so I shouted Mr Moore's name and went in.'

'And you found him lying dead in bed?'

'Yes. Then I phoned for the emergency services.'

'What did you want to speak to him about?'

'It's a long story. I'm investigating the death of someone called Jeremy Powell.'

'Who's that?

'An author. He was found dead last month, apparently having fallen from a cliff path near his home in Orkney. He'd been out walking his dog. The dog was never found. The police regarded it as an accidental death. My paper wanted me to look into it, though. His widow thought he may have been the victim of an attack.'

'Killed, in other words?'

'Yes.'

'OK. Go on. What's Stephen Moore got to do with it?'

'He and Powell were once friends. Powell was in Cambridge shortly before his death for a talk. He met Moore's estranged wife then and I thought her husband might be able to shed some light on what happened to Powell. I wondered if they had been in contact when he was down here. Powell also did an interview with a journalist, who was later killed. I thought there might be a chance that the two things might be connected.'

'A journalist. You're talking about Brian Clark?'

'Yes.'

'And you think that those two deaths are connected?' she asked.

'They could be. I don't really know.' He told her about meeting Moore's wife, Olivia. 'She's separated from her husband. When I asked her if there was anything that she might have mentioned to Powell, which he then could have told Clark about, she said "Cerberus".'

'Cerberus? What's that?'

He shrugged. 'I don't know. Maybe you should ask Olivia about it?'

Helen nodded. 'Yes, I will. I'm told you've had your prints and a DNA sample taken already. So, we'll get a full statement from you written up and signed then you can go.' She gave him her business card. 'If you think of anything else useful, let me know.'

TWENTY-SEVEN

Helen was intrigued by the possible link to the murder of Brian Clark. He had lived on a housing estate on the outskirts of the city, an estate notorious for its poverty and low-level criminality. The tabloids liked to depict these kinds of places as the home of the feckless poor, easily stereotyped, though Helen knew there was much more to it than that. She had grown up somewhere similar. Still, it could be a tough place at times, there was no doubt about it. Clark had probably chosen to live there simply because the rent was cheap.

Clark's phone and laptop were destroyed in the blaze caused by the Molotov cocktail crashing through his kitchen window so there was a lack of digital material to work with and his phone records had produced nothing untoward. Eventually, his email and cloud storage account were accessed but there was nothing useful found in his emails and his cloud account was empty. Either he didn't back up his work or someone had hacked into his account and wiped it clean.

On the day after the killing, she spoke to Brian's friends and neighbours. Everyone who knew him described him as a quiet, polite young man who kept himself to himself. He had no apparent enemies. In other words, he wasn't someone whom you would automatically think could be the target of a hit-man or involved in organised crime. It had all the hallmarks of being a professional hit, after all.

Unless it had something to do with his girlfriend's ex, of course. Was he jealous of his former partner's new beau? Julie's ex, Paul Wilson, *did* have connections to the crime scene in Cambridge. He also lived on the estate and had a record for robbery and assault. But he had an alibi. Of sorts. He said he was drinking with them in someone's flat at the time of the shooting. His friends backed him up. But, of course, they would: his friends had records almost as long as Wilson's.

Or was the whole thing a case of mistaken identity? That's what her boss believed, anyway. Clark's rented flat was across the street from one belonging to Craig Young. Shortly after Clark's death, there had been an anonymous tip-off sent in to the police about Young. His flat was raided and a stash of cannabis found and Young was arrested for possession with intent to supply. Young was found to have previous convictions for dealing in Manchester where he'd lived for five years. He'd dealt everything there: cannabis, speed, ecstasy, ketamine, cocaine, you name it. Even heroin. Young, Helen thought, was perhaps trying to build a customer base in Cambridge. Originally from Cambridge, he had moved back to the city nine months ago from Manchester, where he had been a student before he dropped out of his course. His contacts in Manchester likely had contacts in Europe: the ports of Rotterdam, Marseille, Hamburg, Antwerp and so on, where drugs came into Europe in shipping containers. Sometimes, Europol managed to get information and seize a haul but the smugglers were clever, constantly shifting the cargoes and ports they originated from, went via, or were destined for, as well as the shipping companies they used, no doubt greasing the palms of various shipping agents around the globe to ensure anonymity and secrecy. Other drugs came overland across Europe, originating in Afghanistan or North Africa. It was a well-run operation. Getting the drugs into the UK ran along much the same lines: specially-designed trucks with hidden compartments were usually the main avenue of choice but containers on ships could also be used. Carefully sealed and disguised to evade even the most sensitive of sniffer dogs' nostrils.

Young's Manchester contacts could have been happy to supply him with regular amounts to shift. That, like the cocaine and speed themselves, would be bound to get up some people's noses. The kingpins of the Cambridge drug scene, who'd been around a long time, wouldn't take kindly to a new usurper. Was Craig Young the intended victim of a hit-man with a dodgy sense of geography? Young, of course, said he knew nothing about the attack and wasn't involved in drugs any more, working as a security guard. Any of Brian's other neighbours, though, who might have heard the shots and witnessed the attacker, also didn't appear to want to get involved in identifying any assailant who could be connected to one of Cambridge's crime syndicates in case they found themselves next on their hit list. There was an omerta surrounding the attack. Her superintendent and colleagues were of the view that this was definitely a case of mistaken identity; Brian Clark was just an unfortunate piece of collateral damage in Cambridge's drug wars. But was he? thought Helen.

A silver BMW was found burned out on the edge of the city but Forensics were unable to obtain anything useful from its burned-out shell. It had all the hallmarks of a gangland hit, as had been suggested by the proximity of his neighbour being a suspected drug dealer.

On the evening of Clark's death, she'd

contacted the Mercury's editor. She said she didn't know what he had been working on but Clark had told her it was big. Helen had always wondered if it was somehow connected to his murder. Was it an expose of Young, the drug dealer who lived across the road and news leaked out about his intentions? That would have been a risky strategy for Clark, writing about a neighbour. Maybe he had intended to anonymise it, publish an article without a by-line. That could still have been dangerous. Young was interviewed in connection to the murder but there was no forensic evidence linking him to the attack. Or had the intended target been Young himself? The theory that it was a gangland hit, possibly a case of mistaken identity, remained the most popular in the force. But Helen knew never to rush to any conclusions, no matter how obvious it seemed.

Now, here was an intriguing link to another murder. Clark's phone records had shown that he'd called Stephen Moore's office the day before the journalist had been shot dead. She'd visited Moore at his office to ask why, and Moore had told her that Clark had wanted his opinion on whether, at the next general election, the Tories might hold onto the Cambridgeshire parliamentary seats they currently held. Now Moore had been shot dead as well. Helen began to wonder if Moore had told her the truth.

TWENTY-EIGHT

Helen had buzzed and introduced herself on the intercom. At the door to the apartment, she showed Olivia her warrant card and asked if she could speak to her. Olivia looked confused. 'What's this about?' she asked.

'It's about your husband,' said Helen. 'I think it's best if we talk inside.'

Inside the apartment, Helen noticed that the windows had a view over a park opposite, sunshine dappling on the distant pond below a clear blue sky. A beautiful morning, in fact. But clouded by death. Several paintings hung on the walls, watercolours, mostly landscapes. A bookcase contained a large number of books on Renaissance history. Much to be expected, thought Helen. She'd googled the author and academic before the visit and found out about her specialism. A desk sat in front of one of the windows, its surface littered with pages of handwritten notes, the laptop open.

They sat down, Helen on a chair, Olivia on the sofa.

'I'm sorry to tell you that your husband, Stephen Moore, was found dead this morning,' said Helen.

Olivia appeared stunned by the news. 'What?' she said. 'Stephen's dead?'

'I'm very sorry,' said Helen.

Helen offered to make her a cup of tea or coffee. 'Or would you like a glass of water?' said Helen.

'No, nothing, thanks'

'I can arrange for a family liaison officer to come here, if you want?'

Olivia shook her head. 'That won't be necessary. Stephen and I had our troubles and weren't close any more but it still comes as a shock.' She took a deep breath. 'What happened?' she asked.

Helen explained the circumstances of her husband's death.

Olivia put her hand to her forehead. 'Shot? In his bed? Why?'

'We don't know, but there will be a full investigation.'

'Was it a robbery or something? Why was

he shot?'

'As I said, there will be an investigation. It doesn't appear to have been a robbery but we can't be sure as yet.'

'God, what's happening? First Jeremy, now Stephen. What a mess.'

'Jeremy? You mean Jeremy Powell?'

'Yes. How did you know that?'

'I've just been speaking to a journalist, Finn Morrison, whom I believe you met yesterday.'

'That's right. He told me he was investigating the circumstances that led to Jeremy's death. His widow believes he was murdered. When he told me that, I wasn't convinced, but now that Stephen has been killed…'

'Mr Morrison had gone to visit your husband this morning and actually was the one who found him dead.'

'Oh my God!'

'Do you have any idea why Stephen might have been targeted? Mr Morrison told me that you mentioned something called Cerberus to him. Is that right?'

'Yes, that's right. I did.'

'What is it?'

'Well, as well as his political consultancy business, SM Political Intelligence, Stephen ran another company called Cerberus Security Services. Maybe that has something to do with why he has been killed. You won't find any information about them online. It's a private security company, working mainly overseas, offering protective services for wealthy clients. For businessmen and politicians who may be the target of terrorists. Bodyguards and the like. I can give you something that might be useful. I took some of the company's documents for leverage in a divorce settlement before I left Stephen and scanned them onto a memory stick before he came to ask for them back.'

She went over to the desk and opened a drawer. She came back and handed Helen the stick.

'Thanks,' said Helen. 'Do you think this has anything to do with why Stephen has been killed?'

'I don't know. I told Jeremy about Cerberus and he is also dead. As is that journalist, Brian Clark, who interviewed Jeremy.'

'Yes, Mr Morrison told me that Jeremy Powell and Brian Clark knew each other. OK, Olivia, when you're feeling up to it, I'd like you to formally identify the body. I'll ask someone to contact you later. Is that OK?'

'Yes. Of course.'

'Can you think of anyone who would have reason to kill Stephen?'

Olivia shook her head. 'No. I left him when I discovered he was cheating on me. I guess that makes me a suspect, doesn't it?'

TWENTY-NINE

*B*y early Saturday evening, Finn was back home, on the first floor of a block of flats in Finsbury Park. After he finally had been released by the police in Cambridge, he had taken a taxi to Houghton to retrieve his car from outside Moore's house and driven back to London. His thoughts were all about what had happened earlier. He'd gone to Cambridge because there seemed to be a possible link between the deaths of Powell and Clark. Now Stephen Moore was also dead. But who had killed him and why?

When he had asked her what Powell could have passed onto Clark that got him killed, Olivia had said "Cerberus". Had Powell got hold of something related to Cerberus? Finn hadn't been able to find out what that was. Could this have triggered the murders of Clark, then Powell and now Moore? Clark's phone and laptop had, according to the police been, destroyed in the fire when he had been killed.

Finn had a shower, cooked some pasta with a jar of pesto sauce for dinner, then phoned his editor to update him on the story.

'Iain, you'll want to know that I am still pursuing the Powell story and I've made some progress.'

'I was wondering how you were getting on. Are you still in Orkney?'

'No. I'm at home, in London. I had to come down to Cambridge to speak to a few people. One of whom is now dead.'

'What?'

'Yes. You'll be aware of the death of Stephen Moore?'

'Yes. Shot. Is that right?'

'It was me who found his body.'

'What? The police are saying that a visitor discovered the body but aren't saying who it was.'

'Yes, it was me. I went to his house to doorstep him this morning as I wasn't getting anywhere with setting up a meeting with him. He and Powell are old buddies from way back. I thought it would be useful to speak to him, especially after speaking to his estranged wife. Anyway, to cut a long story short, when I got to the house, he was lying dead upstairs in his bed. Shot in the head.'

'Fucking hell, you're kidding me!'

'I've been with the police all day. Just got back home.'

'So, what's the story with him and Powell's death? Is there a connection?'

'I don't know. I found out that Powell had met a journalist in Cambridge last month, Brian Clark, who was shot and killed soon afterwards.'

'I remember that. Mistaken identity or something.'

'Well, there may be more to it than that. I think Powell may have told him something. Could you get the business section to see if anything under the name of Cerberus links to any of this? There's nothing on the web that stands out as significant.'

'Sure thing.'

'Anyway, I'm sure these things are all linked. I'll work on the story and send it to you in the next couple of days. There's a few more things I want to find out.'

'Sounds good, Finn. I knew I'd made the right decision telling you to look into the Powell story. Excellent work. This will make a great story. Write it up as soon as you can. A first-person account. Full personal angle. It'll be sensational.'

'OK, will do, Iain, cheers.'

As soon as he'd finished talking to his editor, his phone rang. It was Grace. She hadn't heard about the death of Stephen Moore and was shocked when Finn told her he had discovered the body. 'You were lucky,' she said. 'You could have walked in on the killer and been shot yourself.'

'I know.'

'How are you getting on with looking into what happened to Powell?'

'I think Powell was told something significant by Moore's wife, Olivia. She mentioned something called Cerberus. I'm not sure what that is yet but he may have told Clark about it and it's led to his death. Possibly both their deaths. I'm still working on it.'

'Sounds pretty mysterious. Anyway, I wanted to call you and give you some news. You know that dog that was kidnapped? The one belonging to June and Bill Lockhart.'

'Yes. What about it?'

'It's been found. Apparently someone saw a stray dog which looked like the Lockhart's dog, and they phoned the police. The Lockharts have identified it as their dog. But nobody knows where it's been or who took it. Presumably, the thieves decided it was just too risky to hold onto it and let it go.'

'I suppose so. Well, that clears that up. No sign of Powell's dog, though, I guess?'

'No, nor the one stolen from Stromness two months ago.'

SUNDAY

THIRTY

*H*elen had come into the station on Sunday morning to try to find out more about Stephen Moore's background and his offshore firm. There wasn't anything unusual about her working on a Sunday. It was a major investigation, after all, a murder, and she had been appointed as the senior investigating officer. She expected to have no days off for the first week, at least and to have to update her boss regularly on the investigation. She heard the news about Olivia Andrews just after 10.00 a.m. and went straight over to her apartment.

When she arrived, the pathologist was examining the body which lay flat out on the floor of the stairwell landing. It was the same pathologist she'd seen the previous day.

The PC on duty told Helen that Olivia Andrews had been found hanging from a rope tied to the banister of the staircase at the top of the stairwell in her apartment block. As most people used the lifts, she hadn't been discovered until just before 9 a.m. when a neighbour on the floor above had used the stairs to go for a Sunday morning run in the local park. He'd called the emergency services immediately. The paramedics who'd arrived along with police officers, hadn't been able to take her down so the Fire and Rescue Service had to be called to bring her down. She was then declared dead.

The corpse looked awful, as hanging cases do, the neck stretched and twisted, the eyes bulging, the mouth and tongue strangely disfigured. Helen thought Olivia looked almost unrecognisable from the refined, elegant woman she had met the previous day, although she was still wearing the same clothes she had seen her in yesterday: trainers, skinny jeans and a grey cashmere jumper.

Why had she taken her own life? She was clearly distressed by the death of her husband, but they were separated and Olivia said they weren't as close as they had been. It was, of course, impossible to know what really was going on in someone's head when they decided, on an instant, to take their own life. It was a sudden impulse to escape from the torments that they felt were insurmountable. What were Olivia Andrews's torments?

Had she really taken her own life, though? Could someone else have done this to her, or even strangled her then made it look like a hanging?

'I'd put time of death as sometime between nine and eleven p.m. last night,' said the pathologist.

'It's definitely death by hanging, Doctor?' said Helen. 'Not strangulation?'

'Difficult to be certain, Inspector. But, looking at the wound caused to the neck, I'd say it's more likely to be hanging that caused it. Looks like a broken neck. Though once we've got her on the slab back at the mortuary, I'll know for sure.'

So, she had been hanging there all night without anyone noticing, thought Helen. She supposed that probably nobody used the stairs as there was a lift. If that neighbour, this morning, had used the lift instead she could have been there for days.

Did she have any visitors after Helen saw her? There was a security camera, though, she'd noticed it on the way in. At the entrance. She'd get the footage from that checked and ask uniform to doorstep the neighbours and ask if they heard or saw anything unusual. There were sixteen flats in the block, two apartments on each floor. Maybe someone noticed something.

The landlord of the flat arrived with a spare set of keys for Moore's apartment. Helen put on a pair of nitrile gloves to explore the flat. Inside, everything appeared normal, just as it had done the day before when Helen had been there. There was no sign of a note anywhere. Wouldn't a writer have left a suicide note? Helen thought. Her desk was tidy, the laptop switched off and closed, the notepad beside it seemingly containing only jottings about the novel she had been currently working on.

Helen had a look around. It was a lovely apartment, full of beautiful things that Olivia had furnished the flat with – Persian rugs, stylish sofas and tables, watercolour paintings on the walls, ceramics and ornaments on shelves, masses of books, of course, and the odd antique. The landlord had told her that it was rented unfurnished. Helen supposed that Olivia must have wanted somewhere quickly when she had left her husband, so had just found somewhere unfurnished to rent before finding a place to buy, which she could easily have afforded but would take time. Now she had run out of time.

There was no sign of anything that would make this a suspicious death. The door hadn't been forced open, the windows and their locks were intact. Cupboards and shelves were organised and everything looked just as Helen had remembered it. She found a handbag and had a look inside. There was a purse with about thirty pounds in cash, bank cards, make-up, not much else.

Where did she get the rope from, though? wondered Helen. Did she buy it purposely, or did she have it already? There wasn't a receipt for a rop in the handbag but maybe she didn't get one. A check on her bank statements might show up something but, then again, she could have paid cash. Or, of course, it was possible it wasn't her rope, and she hadn't, in fact, taken her own life.

In the bedroom, the bed was made up. It hadn't been slept in. Whatever Helen had been doing before she decided to end her life, she hadn't left any traces of. There was no empty gin bottle or wine glass. In fact, the dishwasher in the kitchen had been programmed to run and had finished its cycle, a red light flashing to indicate it needed emptying. Who puts their dishwasher on before they take their own life? thought Helen. Maybe Olivia did. Maybe she was the type of person who was considerate and always thinking of others, not wanting to leave a mess or anything for anyone afterwards to have to clear up.

So, Olivia had, at some point last night made the decision that she wanted to kill herself. When she had spoken to her, Helen hadn't thought she seemed depressed or in the frame of mind to be thinking like that. Yes, she had been obviously shocked to learn that her husband had been murdered. But, once she got over the initial shock, she had appeared calm and coherent.

What could have driven her to it? Helen wondered. The empty apartment gave no clues. Had she, in fact, killed her husband? Gone there in the middle of the night, switched off the alarm and disabled the CCTV, and shot him? She had no alibi. She'd told Helen she'd spent the night at home after meeting Finn Morrison. Then, in a fit of guilt, done away with herself?

The neighbours weren't much help either. None of them had seen or heard anything unusual. It had been a quiet Saturday evening. One of them, though, had seen her on Saturday afternoon and spoken to her as they were going down in the lift. It must have been just after Helen's visit. The neighbour said she had appeared 'normal' and they had briefly chatted about the weather.

One of the last people to have seen her had been DS Nick Phillips who had accompanied her to the mortuary to identify the body of her late husband. That was at 6 p.m. Phillips told Helen that Olivia had appeared 'reserved and subdued', which wasn't surprising, under the circumstances.

In the afternoon, Helen got a phone call from the French police. A senior French police officer, Commandant Audrey Dupont, said she would like to speak to her.

'You are leading the investigation into the killing of Stephen Moore, I believe?' said Dupont.

'Yes, that's correct,' said Helen.

Dupont said that she was leading the investigation into the deaths of a group of men near Calais. Helen was vaguely aware of the incident from the news. Dupont was interested to hear what Helen had to tell her about the death of Stephen Moore.

'Can I ask why you want to know?' asked Helen.

'We recovered the satnavs from the men's vehicles and the location of their base was amongst the recent destinations. It is a large house that had been rented for a month by a company in Jersey, Cerberus Security Services.'

'The company belonged to Stephen Moore,' said Helen.

'Yes, we have been able to confirm that. I googled his name and found out that he had been killed yesterday. Suspicious, don't you agree?'

'Yes. It appeared to be a targeted assassination. Tell me more about this group of men. How did you identify them?'

'In their base, we found their passports, so

we were able to identify them from those. There were also weapons, changes of clothing and other vehicles. It looked like their plan was to split up after their mission and leave France, going their separate ways.'

'What do you think *was* their mission?'

'I'd say they were hired to take out a people-smuggling gang. The dead men in the van were wearing black military-style clothing. They all died in an attack from assault weapons and grenades. They would probably have been heavily armed themselves but no weapons were recovered at the scene. We suspect their assailants seized them for their own use. They would have been prepared for a major assault on a gang. But clearly, the people-smuggling gang got word of their intentions and ambushed them.'

'People-smuggling?'

'Yes, there are many people-smuggling gangs active in this part of France, all along the coast, especially around Calais. We've received intelligence reports that a group has been hunting for people smugglers.'

'Who would hire them to take on smugglers?'

'Maybe a rival gang. Other smugglers. These men were mercenaries. Trained to kill. If a gang can eliminate their rivals and take over a stretch of coast, there's millions of Euros to be made. We believe a single gang currently control this stretch of coast. Whoever, hired them, it's got to be more than a coincidence that this operation in France backfired and then the man whose company rented the base, Stephen Moore, is found dead, wouldn't you say?' said Dupont.

'Definitely,' said Helen.

'What do you know about this man Moore?' asked Dupont.

Helen told her about his Cambridge company and what she had learned about Cerberus Security Services.

Dupont was also interested in the death of another so-far unidentified man, found in a quarry in the area, who had been killed around the same time as the other men. She thought there might be a connection. The commandant's English was flawless and Helen felt embarrassed by her own inability to converse like that in another language. Helen told Dupont a little about the circumstances surrounding Stephen Moore's killing and they agreed to share information which they thought might be useful to each other's investigations.

After the call, Helen decided to look further into what had happened in France, and went on the internet to see what she could find out about it. The French police had released a statement online. The men killed near a remote farmhouse had been identified as British, Norwegian, Swedish, South African and American, all former Special Forces personnel. Mercenaries, in other words, just as Dupont had said. My God! thought Helen, this looked like a death squad. But why would they be operating against smuggling gangs in France?

She also looked up the details of the other, so-far unidentified, man who had been found dead, not far from the site of the other killings. And the times of death were only hours apart. Were the two events connected? she wondered. Dupont thought they might be. So did Helen.

Helen's phone rang again. It was the pathologist. 'Just finished the post-mortem on Olivia Andrews,' she said.

'Yes?' said Helen. 'I take it you have confirmed the cause of death?'

'Yes, she died from a fracture of the upper cervical vertebrae, the C2.'

'A broken neck, in other words, Doctor?'

'Yes. It's certainly consistent with falling from height with the rope around her neck.'

'Were there any signs that she could have

been forced in any way? You know, marks on her body, any other injuries? Defensive wounds, that sort of thing?'

'No. Nothing on the hands or arms, where you would expect to see bruising or marks if she had been attacked. No drugs or alcohol in her system. No signs of any sexual assault, either.'

'Definitely self-inflicted then?'

'Well, I only describe the cause not the method. It's impossible to say whether she had any assistance or not.'

Later she received the CCTV footage from the security camera at the entrance to the block of flats. Two figures, a man and a woman, had gained admittance to the block at 8.59 p.m. Their faces were obscured, though, as both were wearing FFP2 masks. They left at 9.27 p.m. She asked uniform to check the neighbours again to ask if anyone knew who they were. No one did.

MONDAY

THIRTY-ONE

On Monday morning, Helen was called in to see her boss, Superintendent Bairstow. Bairstow was a heavily-built bald man, with large round spectacles, in his late fifties; a man whose presence could be intimidating. He looked like he should be doing something more physical like weightlifting or manual labour rather than being behind a desk, though the effort would probably kill him. Helen, though, never felt intimidated by him and found that, contrary to his appearance, he was usually amenable to persuasion. He was actually a good listener and she found him someone she could often talk to if she had a problem with anything.

As she sat down opposite his desk, Bairstow said, 'Helen, I'll come straight to the point. We are handing over the Moore case to a specialist counter-terrorism branch of the Met, SO15.'

'What? But, sir ...'

'I know you won't like it but there's

nothing we can do about it. Instructions from on high and all that. You'll need to hand over everything you've got on the case to me immediately, to pass on to them.'

'But, sir. Why?'

'There's no point in arguing. I've been told that it's because the case touches on issues of national security. All highly sensitive and confidential. They clearly don't want us poking our noses into it. Whoever has killed him may be linked to extremists.'

'But, sir, I think we can handle this ourselves without involving the Met. And there's a possible link to another case. The Clark murder.' She explained about the phone call from Clark to Moore.

'That could be entirely coincidental. But, as I said at the start of our conversation, we're handing all of this over to the Met. Let them deal with it. Frankly, we've got enough other cases on our hands to be going on with.'

'But there's more, sir. You'll be aware of the men massacred in that shooting in France? Mercenaries. According to the French police, Moore, through his company, Cerberus Security Services, may have organised an operation using mercenaries against a gang of people smugglers. It somehow went badly wrong and they were all killed. The house that the mercenaries used as a base was rented by Moore's company. But who were the Cerberus team working for, that's what I ask myself? Who hired them? I've requested Moore's bank statements, phone records and access to his emails from his internet service provider. I expect them later today.'

'Drop it. Don't go there. Let SOI5 handle it.'

'What?'

'If you know what's good for your career, don't go there. SOI5 are taking over the case. National security has been cited, and we can't interfere or question that. Moore may have been killed by the people smugglers who were the intended target, seeking revenge. They may have been able to trace that Moore was behind the operation in France. That's probably what SOI5 are working on. It's not unusual for smugglers and terrorists to be the same people. They raise funds from smuggling and use it to purchase weapons. The French know that as do we in this country.'

'But sir, there's also something strange about Moore's wife, Olivia Andrews, hanging herself,' said Helen. 'She just didn't strike me when I saw her as someone about to do that. Could she, in fact, have been murdered, sir? There were two unidentified visitors to the block around the time of her death. Both wearing masks. There's definitely grounds for suspicion.'

'I've told you, Helen. Drop it. Let SOI5 deal with it. They'll look into it. If there's grounds for suspicion about the Andrews death and any connection to her husband's murder, they will find it. Frankly, we have enough other cases on our plate to be going on with, as I've said already. Transfer your files on the case to me and if anything else arrives, ignore it. That's an order.'

'Is that what you've been told to tell me, sir?'

'That's all I have to say on the matter, DI Richardson. Now, I've got a meeting with the Chief Constable in five minutes so I'll have to go. You're a damn good officer. Just move on to the next case and forget all this. That's the last word I'll say about it.'

THIRTY-TWO

Helen reluctantly did as she was told and transferred the files to the superintendent, but in the afternoon, she received several emails with material which she had requested on the case and, despite Bairstow's order, decided not to ignore them. Her curiosity was piqued.

Firstly, she got details of Moore's various bank accounts, both personal and business. They made for interesting reading. He had a personal HSBC account, a Barclays account for the political consultancy business and a Bank of Jersey one for Cerberus Security Services, the firm for which he was the sole company director. She had paused after her instructions from Bairstow, but events and number of deaths on her patch nagged at her, especially that of Olivia Andrews.

She didn't yet have access to his emails, which was taking longer to be authorised, but thought they might show little that was useful, anyway. He probably had several email addresses and would undoubtedly have had another way of communicating with his clients, possibly using the dark web, she thought, or encrypted mobile methods. He would want to keep that information as discreet as possible. He would also have used a different phone to contact personnel he employed to do anything illegal, she was sure.

Then she also received Stephen Moore's personal mobile phone records, and traced the numbers he'd called or been called from to their owners. One number belonged to someone called Simon Parkinson. Further digging revealed that he had attended the same exclusive private school as Stephen Moore, but more than that, he worked as a special advisor for the Home Secretary. Helen was well aware of recent speeches by the Home Secretary. Her obsession was in stopping the small boats transporting refugees and asylum seekers across the Channel. She had announced various punitive strategies and deterrents including deporting them to Africa and housing them on barges or former MOD facilities which critics, including UN agencies, said were entirely unsuitable for the purpose. But the number of boats stubbornly refused to decline.

Was the operation, then, some sort of covert activity by the government aimed at striking at the people smugglers in an attempt to disarm them of their ability to supply the boats? It would have been a drastic step. Highly irregular and, of course, illegal. No wonder the need for secrecy. If her suspicions were correct, this was a conspiracy that led right to the heart of government.

But there was no point telling the Superintendent about any of this. He'd made it clear everything had to be handed over to SOI5. He'd no doubt been ordered to do that by the Chief Constable and wouldn't question such an order. She'd also been ordered. But, unlike Bairstow, this was one time she wouldn't obey.

She phoned Finn from her personal mobile. 'Can I meet you in London tomorrow?' she said. 'I may have some information for you, entirely confidential, you understand?'

'Of course.'

He sounded surprised but she didn't want to say any more over the phone. They agreed to meet at the café in the National Gallery in Trafalgar Square at twelve o'clock the next day.

THIRTY-THREE

*F*inn received an email from Sarah who worked in the business section of the Chronicle. She told him that Cerberus Security Services was a company registered in Jersey with its sole director named as Stephen Moore. Unfortunately, the nature of the business was obscure, and she hadn't been able to obtain any details about the services it offered. There was no website or contact details for it.

So, that's what Powell had discovered about Moore, and told Clark about, thought Finn. Moore ran an offshore security company cloaked in secrecy in addition to his political consultancy. But so what? Why would that be such a big secret? Big enough to lead to murder. And why would Powell be so keen to spill the beans about something related to an old university chum to a journalist?

Around seven o' clock he crossed the room to close the curtains when suddenly there was a blast and glass flew everywhere. 'Fuck!' said

Finn. Then there another bang. He hit the floor and crawled across the room. 'Fucking hell!' He reached up and grabbed his phone off the table and, for the second time in three days, dialled 999.

'Someone is shooting at me,' he managed to say. He was told to stay where he was. He'd made sure his front door was securely locked and stayed on the floor and away from sight. When his buzzer went, he reached up to answer it and made sure they showed him their warrant cards on the video-screen before he pressed to allow them in.

A minute later, a pair of male detectives stood in his flat. One was in his mid-thirties, well over six feet tall, wearing jeans and a green bomber jacket. He had short dark hair and introduced himself as DS Clive Jones. He had a Welsh accent. The other one was about ten years older. He was shorter with blond hair and wore a brown leather jacket and jeans. He said his name was DI John Stevens. He had a London accent.

There were two bullet holes in the window and across the room in the wall opposite.

'You're lucky those shots missed you,' said Stevens. 'But there's no sign of anyone in the area. An armed response team was dispatched as soon as you phoned and scoured the area without success, unfortunately. We're sure they came from the hilly wooded area of the park opposite your flat. Most likely from a high-powered rifle. Have you any idea why you might have been targeted?'

'I'm an investigative journalist. I cover all sorts of stories, some involving organised crime. There are all kinds of reasons why some people might take a dislike to me or what I do. As I'm sure you can imagine.'

'Any reason why this happened tonight?' asked Jones.

'I've been following a story and found a body on Saturday morning in Cambridge. Stephen Moore. You'll have heard about it. He was shot in his home. I gave a statement to the Cambridge police about it and you can check that, if you like. I can't help thinking it's connected to that.' He told them a bit about being asked by his editor to look into the death of Jeremy Powell in Orkney. 'I wanted to speak to Stephen Moore as he was once a friend of Powell's. So, I went to his house. The door was open. Then I found him.'

As he spoke, he had the feeling they were thinking that there must be something else behind this, something he wasn't telling them. They were right. There was no way he was going to tell them everything. He didn't tell them about the Cerberus connection. They asked more questions but Finn didn't feel like going over it all. He kept his answers brief. He wasn't sure how much to trust them.

After the detectives left, Finn decided to move out. He didn't feel safe where he was. It was what the police had advised but he didn't tell them where he intended to go. A hotel would be an option but he felt vulnerable on his own. He phoned a colleague from the paper, Jack Roberts. 'Jack, something's happened. I've got a problem. Can I stay with you tonight?'

'Of course. No problem. Come on over. Are you OK?'

'Yes. I'll explain when I get there. Thanks.'

He phoned for an emergency glazier and they sent someone to fix the broken window. They arrived within an hour and made a temporary fix, boarding up the window, saying they would return at a convenient time to replace the glass. They'd phone him to arrange when suited. Once that was done, he packed a bag with some spare clothes, put his laptop in its case and locked up. He went down the stairs to the basement car park to his car, feeling anxious. Would they be tracking him, whoever it was that had tried to kill him? He had a look around and underneath the car but couldn't see anything suspicious like a tracking device, or even a bomb, fixed to the underside of the vehicle. He sighed with relief when the engine burst into life and nothing unusual happened. He drove across London to Blackheath, to Jack's house, all the way checking in his mirrors to see if he was being tailed. If they were tailing him, they were doing a bloody good job, he thought. There wasn't any obvious sign of a tail.

He arrived at Jack's house just after 10 p.m. It was a Victorian terrace house on a hill overlooking a large area of grass and trees. Jack answered the door with his black Labrador, Sooty. Finn hadn't been there for a while, but Sooty seemed to remember him, jumping up and down, excited to see him.

'Down, Sooty,' said Jack. 'Come on in, Finn. Make yourself at home.'

'Jack was from Gateshead, just a couple of years older than Finn, with a strong Geordie accent. He and Jack had often worked together on stories that required more than one pair of hands: complex economic crime cases, especially. Jack was very good with figures and money.

Jack brought Finn into the living room where his wife, Vicky, was sitting on the sofa. Vicky was a pretty blonde Glaswegian. She was a photographer and examples of her work adorned the walls of the room, moody black and white shots of people and places. 'Finn, nice to see you again,' said Vicky, 'I'm sorry to hear you're having a difficult time.'

'Thanks. I'm very grateful to you and Jack for having me. I hope it's not any bother.'

'Of course not. You're welcome.'

'Anyway, I'll leave you guys to chat. Goodnight, Finn. You're welcome to stay as long as you like.'

'Thanks, Vicky. I appreciate it. Hopefully it's just for a couple of nights.'

She left the room and he and Jack sat down. 'So, what's this all about?' asked Jack.

Finn explained that he'd got a call from the editor asking him to look into the death of the writer, Jeremy Powell, when he was at his gran's funeral in Kirkwall and everything that had happened up to being shot at in his home. 'So, I go to Cambridge and walk into a house to find a dead guy. Stephen Moore. Then it's me they're after. I better phone Iain and tell him what's happened.'

'Wow! Quite a chain of events,' said Jack. 'And now you're the target. Do you think it's connected to the story you've been looking into?'

'I suppose it could have to do with any number of the stories I've done over the past year or so but the fact that I find someone shot dead then I'm next for a bullet does make me think so.'

'So, why? What do you know makes someone want you silenced?'

'Maybe something called Cerberus,' said Finn.

'Cerberus?'

'Yes.'

'What's that?'

'A company that I think got Powell and a Cambridge journalist killed. As well as Stephen Moore, whose company it was.' Finn told Jack as much as he knew about it.

'This is a great story, Finn, but you look shattered. You should try to get some rest. There's a bed made up for you upstairs in the spare room.'

'Thanks. Yeah, I feel done in.'

After he went upstairs, Finn phoned Iain to tell him about the shooting but there was no answer. He left him a voicemail telling him what had happened and that he was OK and would phone again in the morning.

SEVERAL DAYS EARLIER

THIRTY-FOUR

When he arrived in France, Ibrahim headed for the migrant camp outside Calais, with a false name, cash, a rucksack, a tent, a sleeping bag and a backstory of how he'd fled persecution in Iran: by travelling overland through Europe towards a new life in Britain, after paying an agent from a gang ten thousand euros for transport across Europe to take him as far as the English Channel.

But Ibrahim Mahmoudi was the son of Iranian immigrants and hadn't been near Iran since his childhood. His office was in south London. As a private detective, he mostly spent his time tailing errant husbands and wives in the service of their distrustful spouses. A month earlier, a man had spoken to him on the phone and introduced himself as Michael Brown. Ibrahim didn't know if that was his real name. It probably wasn't. It didn't matter, though. In his line of work that wasn't too unusual. He offered a confidential service. Some people might not trust him entirely. If they wanted a job done, he would do it. For money. It was purely a transactional arrangement.

They agreed to meet. Not in his office in Southwark. On a park bench by the Thames on a Thursday afternoon. It was a pleasant day and the river flowed past at a leisurely pace. It wasn't too far from Ibrahim's office, either, so pretty convenient. He'd met clients in all sorts of places. Roofs of car parks, quiet pubs, parks and even, once, on the beachfront at Brighton.

Brown, or whoever he was, outlined what he wanted. There was a basic task for the assignment. He just had to obtain some information. His mission: to pose as a refugee, find out who the main smuggling gang was in the Calais area and where their base was, and pass the information to Brown. After that, he could disappear.

A week or two on the French coast was involved. He would have to slum it, though. It would be far from a holiday. He'd be camping in scruffy clothes, rather than staying in a swanky hotel. A fee was negotiated, more than Ibrahim could hope to earn normally. Half paid up front, the rest once the assignment was complete. He readily agreed.

Of course, Ibrahim knew that the man

wasn't really Michael Brown. He'd traced the mobile number he'd contacted him on and discovered that he was actually someone called Stephen Moore. He wasn't sure why Brown, or rather Stephen Moore, wanted the information, but didn't care. It was good money. And these gangs were ruthless. Exploiting and profiteering from people who were desperate for a better life, most of whom were genuinely in fear for their lives when they escaped from whatever hell-hole they had come from to make the long, expensive and perilous trip towards Britain. So, he'd do the job, get the hell out of there and take the money. It all seemed straightforward.

It had all gone well to begin with. He'd infiltrated the camp, posing as a migrant desperate to get to Britain to get away from the religious extremists running Iran. He said he had been an English teacher in Tehran. It helped that he had been brought up to be fluent in Farsi. In fact, Brown had asked about that when he'd first phoned him. He obviously wanted someone who would appear authentic. He befriended some other refugees and listened to their horror stories of relatives who had been killed back where they came from, as well as family members and friends who had perished on the long journey to the French coast. It was heartbreaking to hear. He couldn't help but feel like a fraud, inventing a fictitious legend about himself.

He quickly learned vital information from them about who the local gang of people smugglers were, including the names they went by when they visited the camp. They were a powerful Albanian gang who had recently taken over the people-smuggling operation in the area, having successfully displaced other smaller gangs through sheer will of force. He heard about several gunfights which had preceded their newfound dominance. The gang was, apparently, headed by someone known as Valmir.

Now, after a few days in the camp, Ibrahim had heard that the people smugglers were going to be arriving around midnight to collect a group to cross the Channel. Well before midnight, making sure no one was watching, he crossed over to where he had concealed a cheap secondhand moped on the hill overlooking the camp. He'd purchased it for cash in Calais when he'd arrived by ferry and hidden it in a heavily-wooded spot, buried beneath branches. He concealed himself in amongst the trees but with a view of the camp from a distance and got out his binoculars. Fortunately there was a full moon which made it easier to make out the camp below.

They arrived just after midnight in a truck, its headlights illuminating the entrance to the camp. Two large, muscular types, with shaved heads and tattoos and leather jackets got out of the compartment. These guys looked the real deal. He got out his phone and sent a short message:

Going to follow truck to base. Will send location

He then took the opportunity to make a quick call to his wife in London. 'This is just a short call. I'll be home soon,' he said.

'Where are you? I've been worried about you.' she asked.

'In France. I'm on a job. But I can't say any more. I'll see you soon. Promise.'

'Love you.'

'Love you too.' Then he rang off. It was a burner phone he had brought with him to France. There was no way he was going to use his own phone and get caught up in whatever shit came down if Brown, or whoever he was, got caught doing whatever he was doing, which was certainly not going to be anything legal. He couldn't wait to get away and back to England once his mission was completed. He would ride the moped back to Calais and then dump it before catching the first ferry back to Dover.

He watched as the refugees who had been told to be ready handed over their cash, which was counted and placed in a large holdall. They were then loaded into the truck. Then it set off. He followed at a distance, with the headlight on the moped switched off, as the truck drove along the coast until it stopped at a beach. Two other men with a van were waiting there. He made sure he was somewhere he wouldn't be seen and took out his binoculars and watched as everyone got out and were led to an inflatable boat with an outboard motor. The group consisted mostly of men but there were also a few women and children. Life jackets were thrown at the passengers as they crammed into the boat and the motor was started. Finally, off it went into the dark night, out through the waves which rolled against the shore.

Once the boat was far enough out to sea, the gang members moved to the truck and the van and headed off again, Ibrahim following at a distance. They eventually arrived at a large house in the countryside with a gated entrance and a surrounding wall. He stopped and watched as the gates swung open and the vehicles entered. He took out his binoculars. He could see through the gates to the house beyond. He watched as they parked in the driveway and the men got out. They approached the house to be warmly greeted at the door by a middle-aged bald man wearing a white shirt, presumably Valmir himself. One of the men handed over the bag of money and they all went inside.

Now Ibrahim knew where the centre of the operation was, he could relay the information back to his employer and hopefully that would be it. He would get the hell out of there and back to England. He couldn't wait.

He took his phone out to share the GPS coordinates from Google Maps with Brown. Just then, he heard a voice speaking English with a strong east European accent from behind him. 'Drop the phone on the ground. Then put your hands in the air.' He did as he was told then he felt something pushed into his back. It felt like a gun. 'Now, get off your motorbike and turn around slowly.'

He did as he was told. A man was holding a pistol, aimed at his chest.

The man said, 'Do exactly as I tell you. Or else I shoot. Understand?'

Ibrahim nodded.

'OK,' said the man. 'Stay still and don't move.' With one hand he held the gun. In the other he had a walkie-talkie, which he now spoke into in a language Ibrahim assumed was Albanian.

When he finished the conversation, the

man said. 'Now we wait.'

Ibrahim thought about running. He might have a chance if the guy was a poor shot. But it was too late. The gates opened again and two men approached from the house, each one carrying a machine gun.

When they got to him, one of them hit him hard in the face with the butt of the gun. Ibrahim's head ached like hell and his face streamed with blood from the blow. His lip felt swollen. A tooth felt loose.

'Who the fuck are you? What are you doing here?' the man who had hit him shouted in English.

'I recognise him,' said a second man. 'I saw him in the camp.'

'Let's take him inside,' the first one said.

One of the men picked up his phone and he was marched at gunpoint by the three men to the house and into a room where the bald man he guessed was Valmir sat on a sofa clutching a large glass of brandy. The one who had told the others to bring him to the house spoke to him in Albanian.

Valmir said something back in Albanian and Ibrahim felt a sudden push and staggered towards the sofa.

'Now, you have a choice,' said Valmir. 'We do this the easy way or the hard way. Understand?'

Ibrahim nodded.

'Good. Either way, you will tell us what we want to know. So, first of all, who are you?'

'My name is Farrokh Bahrami. I am refugee. From Iran.'

'What were you doing spying on us?'

'I... I wanted to know what happened when they took people to the boats. I wanted to know if it was safe.'

'And why did you follow them here?'

'I...I thought they were going back to the camp. I got lost.'

'Lost, eh? Hmm. And where did you get the moped?'

'I stole it. From a house in the city. A few days ago.'

Valmir got up off the sofa and came towards him until he was inches from his face. He could smell the man's breath. There was a strong stench of garlic and meat. He said something in Albanian and one of the men searched him. They found his bum-bag containing his passport and cash. The man handed the passport to Valmir.

'British!' he said, looking at the passport. 'Ibrahim Mahmoudi? You are a fucking liar!' Suddenly he grabbed him round the throat. Ibrahim could hardly breathe. He was choking and struggled but the man's grip grew tighter. 'Lies. Fucking lies. I told you we can do this the easy way or the hard way. You have chosen the hard way.'

'OK, OK, I'll tell you,' said Ibrahim, struggling to speak. 'I am a journalist. I am working on a piece about refugees. It's the truth.'

Valmir shook his head looked at the men who had brought him in. 'I don't believe this shit. Take him away and persuade him to tell the real truth.' Then he let go of Ibrahim's throat and pushed him away.

It was a relief to be able to breathe normally again but Ibrahim knew it was only temporary. He was seized by the two men and taken out of the room and along a corridor. Then he was pushed down a flight of steps until he found himself face down in a cellar. The men followed. He felt a kick to the ribs. Then another.

He was picked up and placed on a chair which was bolted to the concrete floor. He was tied tightly to the chair with cable ties. They dug deeply into his wrists and ankles. In one corner was a sink with a long hose attached to the tap.

One of the men turned on the tap and water started gushing out over the floor. He picked up the hose and brought it to Ibrahim's face. His mouth was forced open by one while another pushed the hose into his mouth and down his throat. Again, he felt himself choking, but this time the sensation was of drowning as well. He was sure he was going to die.

After about thirty seconds or so, the hose was pulled out.

'Ready to talk?' said the man with the hose.

'Ibrahim spluttered and coughed. He tried to get his breath back. The hose was spraying water over him and it was raised to his mouth.

'Yes. Yes,' he said.

The water was turned off.

'The truth this time. Who are you? What do you want?'

Ibrahim told them. 'I'm a private detective from London. Someone hired me to find out who the people smugglers here were, and where they are based. I had to send him their location. His number is on my phone. That's all I know.'

'Who hired you?'

'Moore. His name is Stephen Moore. From Cambridge. But he told me his name was Michael Brown. I don't know any more. That's the truth.

Please don't kill me.'

'Why does he want to know who we are?'

'I don't know. Honestly,' said Ibrahim, though he had his own ideas. Moore must have been hired by someone. Was it a rival gang wanting to move in on this gang's operations? Perhaps.

As soon as Ibrahim had given up his purpose and means of communication, he was dragged back up to the room to see Valmir again. The Albanian gang leader came up with a plan. The snag might be that as soon as they had sent the message, the recipient could call back to confirm it was really Ibrahim who had sent it, or ask some questions. Ibrahim was instructed as to what to say if the call came.

They chose an isolated farmhouse twenty kilometres away which was approached by a track with tree cover on both sides. Perfect. Four of the gang drove over there and disposed of the elderly couple living there, then called the base to confirm it was secured. Now they used Ibrahim's phone to send the location of the farmhouse.

They waited a few moments, then the call they were expecting came through. They had instructed him in exactly what to say. 'Tell him everything is fine. You better sound convincing. Or else.' One of the men told him, holding a gun to his head. 'Understand?'

Ibrahim nodded. A gun was held to his head. 'Now answer it.' The phone was put on speakerphone.

'Hello,' Ibrahim said.

Stephen said, 'Ibrahim, is everything OK?'

'Yes. Did you get my message with the location? That's their HQ.'

'What's the place like?'

'Just an old farmhouse. I didn't see any guards or anything there.'

'How many smugglers did you see?'

'There's only six of them.'

'Is the leader there?'

'Yes.'

'Did you get his name?'

'No. But he looked like he was in charge.'

'Are you still there?'

'No, I'm back at the camp now.'

'OK. Stay there. I'll phone you tomorrow. You should be able to go home then.'

'Thanks. I'll be glad of that.'

Two men were left behind to look after Ibrahim. The rest of the gang, ten of them including Valmir, all heavily armed, drove off in several vehicles to join their colleagues at the farmhouse.

After Stephen spoke to Ibrahim, he forwarded the GPS coordinates to the team leader, Wayne Morgan. It was what they both had been waiting for. They swung into action. The team quickly assembled and packed their weaponry into two vehicles, a Toyota Land Cruiser and a Land Rover Discovery. Morgan had checked out the destination on Google Maps: an isolated farmhouse east of Calais. The nearest other inhabited buildings were at least three kilometres away.

The drivers keyed the location into the satnavs and they set off.

When they saw vehicles approaching, the Albanian gang let rip with everything they had. Machine-gun fire and hand grenades obliterated the convoy and its passengers. Then the gang looted their vehicles for weaponry they could make use of and disappeared as quickly as they had appeared.

Back at their base, Ibrahim had already been dealt with.

THIRTY-FIVE

It was a fucking disaster, in fact, that's what it was, Stephen thought, looking at the breaking news report on his phone. Operation Seagull had gone tits-up! The French authorities were saying that eight bodies had been found in two vehicles, a Land Cruiser and a Land Rover Discovery near Calais, including one Briton. They had all died in an apparent hail of gunfire and explosions. Plus a dead elderly French couple.

He knew immediately what would have happened. The smugglers must have caught Ibrahim and tortured him, and used his phone to send him the location of the "target". He'd wanted to make double sure it was accurate. That's why he had called him. Mahmoudi may have sounded slightly nervous but he'd just been tailing a gang of people smugglers, for God's sake. That would unnerve anyone. Wouldn't it? he thought. His gut instinct told him everything was OK, so he had forwarded the GPS coordinates to Morgan. But it had resulted in a clusterfuck of the highest order.

He had tried to phone Mahmoudi again but the line was dead. As, presumably, he now realised he had been by that point. Had he divulged who he was working for to the smugglers before being killed? Did he know Stephen's real name? Probably. He was a detective, after all. Fuck. They could be coming after him. Even if they didn't, the French authorities might be able to trace the operation to his door. He opened the safe and took out the file he kept there with current Cerberus paperwork, and the burner phone and SIM cards he used. He put the documents through a shredder, smashed the burner phone with a hammer, then cut up the SIM cards and dumped the lot in the bin. What now? He needed to phone Simon and get protection, that's what.

Fucking Simon! he thought. It was all his idea. He recalled the last time he'd met him. The previous month, he had walked across Westminster Bridge, casting a glance towards the City with the dome of St Paul's visible in the distance and, as he always did when crossing the Thames this way, recalled the poem he had to learn by heart at school. The church domes were no longer quite the prominent objects that they had been two hundred or so years ago when Wordsworth had composed his famous sonnet: the skyline had altered dramatically in the past few decades with several "monstrous carbuncles", as someone had once described them, rising into the sky nearby.

Still, that was progress, wasn't it? The onward march of capitalism and all that. The many odd-shaped towers were statements of fiscal muscle and corporate power. He recognised that and respected it. It was what made London the great economic powerhouse that it was, despite some of the financial companies having relocated to mainland Europe post-Brexit.

He had arrived on the south bank of the river and approached the bench where Simon, his old school friend, had said they could meet. It was a cold, crisp day with a clear blue sky. He was slightly early. No matter, it was a lovely day and he could just sit and enjoy the view. A young female jogger ran past. He enjoyed that view as well, unable to keep his eyes off her exquisite rear until she disappeared down the footpath.

Simon arrived and Stephen was summoned back to reality from his erotic fantasy. 'Sorry, the fucking Cobra meeting ran late and Jayne was in a foul mood,' Simon said, when he sat down on the bench beside Stephen. 'It's these bloody small boats. Still, as far as our little scheme goes, she's given it the green light. It's all agreed. So, you can have the five hundred grand for Operation Seagull.'

'That's great. I've started making the arrangements already, just need to firm them up now I know the money is safe. I've got a PI who's going to pose as a refugee. Then there's the rest of the team. I'll have to pay my team half up front.'

'That will be OK. We can advance you half now, the rest on a successful outcome. You'll have to provide an invoice, of course. Something suitably vague like "Asylum Seeker Security Arrangements" should cover it.'

'No problem. I'm looking at the mission happening sometime next month. There's a bit of organising to do beforehand but we should be ready to go in about three or four weeks or so. '

'Perfect,' said Simon.

THIRTY-SIX

Jayne Steele got the phone call from Simon as she was being driven to the office in her ministerial car from her flat in Chelsea. She'd already heard on the radio that there had been an incident near Calais in the early hours of the morning. Clearly the plan to eliminate the smugglers had backfired and the team who had attempted to eliminate them had been wiped out. French police were on the scene and initially were treating it as a fight between rival smuggling gangs.

'It's a total fuck-up, Simon,' she said.

Simon said, 'Stephen has been on the phone to me. He's panicking. He's worried that the French police will be able to trace him. Or the smuggling gang.'

'Shit!' she said.

'He's worried. He wants protection. From us.'

'What kind of protection?'

'He wants us to keep him out of it, to tell the French government he was working for us and that it's top secret. In other words, he wants a cover-up. He says if he doesn't get that and he goes down for this, then he will take us down with him.'

'Does he?'

'Yes. He's blaming me, saying it was all my idea. What do you think we should do?'

'Leave it with me. I'll arrange protection for him. Does anyone else know about your friendship with Moore?'

'Just his wife, Olivia Andrews. They're separated. She lives somewhere in Cambridge, I believe. I met her a few times when I came to visit Stephen. And when I worked at the Foreign Office, I used Stephen's men to eliminate a Real IRA cell based in Dublin. Stephen may have told her about it.'

'Jesus. Olivia Andrews. OK, I'll need to go now. I think I need to stop off somewhere on the way to the office. I'll see you later.' She made a call and re-directed her driver where to go.

In the back seat of the chauffeur-driven Jaguar, Jayne put her hands to her head and sighed deeply. She was only in her late forties but suddenly felt much older. How had it come to this? She was the fucking Home Secretary, for fuck's sake. Get a grip!

When the current PM was forced to finally go, she was confident of replacing him. She would offer tax cuts and a promise to halve the immigration numbers. The only likely serious challenger would be the Chancellor of the Exchequer. But he was seen as too cautious for the rank-and-file Tory members who were overwhelmingly elderly and white. He was also too brown for them.

She had so wanted to be the next PM, the current one's future looking decidedly bleak, enmeshed in his latest scandal about who paid for his Caribbean holiday. The party was surely going to get rid of him soon, then she could step up. But not unless she proved herself capable in this post.

But, at the back of her mind now, she was worried. This Calais shitshow could blow all her hopes out of the water. She kept going over the past and wishing she'd rejected the plan. Her mind went back to the day in her office when all of this had started.

That day's headline in the *Daily Mail* had stared at her from her desk. One single word: "Invasion". A word she had used herself in speeches. The previous day, five small boats had been intercepted in the English Channel carrying over three hundred asylum seekers. The Tory-supporting papers were apoplectic with rage. What *was* the Home Secretary doing about it? they demanded to know. And the problem was that the numbers would only increase as the weather improved, although the issue was now a year-long problem. Yesterday had been a calm sea so the boats had been launched by the people smugglers based in France.

Something had to be done. But what?

She ran her hands through her dyed-blonde bob and then massaged her scalp. This sometimes helped stimulate ideas, she found. She'd come up with some good ones in the past. She was sure of it, though, for the moment, she was struggling to think of one that had worked. 'There must be something else we can come up with,' she said. 'I can't just sit here and accept that these illegal immigration numbers are going to keep going up. The press is having a field day! The Norwegian barge we hired to put them on had an outbreak of Legionnaires' disease and got shut down. Then the old military camp we put them in was closed after the press went to town. They said it was overcrowded. That was the bloody point. It was meant to be a deterrent. I didn't want to spend good money putting those scum up in luxury hotels. And so what if there were a few cases of Monkey Pox? It's not like we were exterminating them. Though, maybe that's an idea.'

Across the table, her companion simply stared at her through his round spectacles. Her special advisor, Simon Parkinson, didn't want to say anything too risky in case he became the object of her wrath. His boss had a reputation for completely losing it when she was angry and just now seemed to be one of those occasions.

She looked at him in disbelief. 'So? What have you got to say? Don't you understand? As Home Secretary I'm the one who carries the can for this. I'm the one the papers are blaming. "Why hasn't she done what she said she would?" they are saying. We said we'd stop the boats, didn't we? Stop the Boats was meant to be a three-word winning slogan like Get Brexit Done. Well, we could conjure a trick about Brexit, it was always open to interpretation, but it's a bit more difficult to lie about the boats. There's something to be seen. Well, I'm not going to fucking take it, I tell you!'

She thumped the table with her clenched fist. 'I promised I would bring those numbers down. I might even have said I'd stop it happening altogether. But what's happened? Instead, the numbers have gone through the fucking roof. Asylum seekers my arse! Terrorists and criminals more like. But that doesn't stop the fucking lefty lawyers persuading the courts that these people deserve to stay here. Look at your idea of deporting them to Rwanda. What's happened? Those lefty lawyers took the cases to the European Court of Human Rights and stopped it in its tracks. Bloody ECHR!'

'What about doing a deal with the French, seeing if we can process them over there, hold them in camps on the other side of the Channel?' said Parkinson.

'That would never work!' she snapped. 'The French hate us! No, I need a proper solution. Something that will stop those boats crossing from France in the first place. God, my head hurts,' she said rubbing at her temples. 'Brexit was all about controlling our borders. Instead, look what's happened. Immigration numbers have increased, not helped by these bloody people-smuggling gangs.' She closed her eyes and sank into a reverie of the halcyon days of a few years ago when she and her colleagues in the Leave campaign had toured the country and TV studios proclaiming that Brexit would be the panacea to all the nation's ills. A sunny upland future was promised, free of nasty EU laws which hindered enterprise and business. And control of our borders was at the heart of it. Because, when it really came down to it, all that mattered to the public was stopping migrants from coming here.

That's what mattered to the ordinary voters, she thought. That and promising millions more for the NHS. Neither had happened, of course. The drop in EU migrant workers that did happen had only led to a shortfall in workers in the care sector, hospitality and agriculture with cafes and restaurants closing because of staff shortages and food being left unpicked in the fields and going to waste. And the economy had taken a hit now that we couldn't just trade freely with our European neighbours. It had all just been a dream, an illusion, an absolute failure.

And with its failure she now saw her own future career prospects tanking, flushed away by the tide of small inflatables crossing the Channel. It didn't matter if she'd manipulated the police figures to show there were more bobbies on the beat. No, the headlines focused on these bloody boats.

'We've tried Royal Navy patrols, turning back the boats. What happened? Either they avoided them or we got even worse headlines when the boats sank and they all drowned. Then there was the stupid wave-machine idea. To send them back to France. That proved to be a complete non-starter. So, what now? Give me something. And fast. That's what I pay you for.'

'We could change the law. Put forward a bill to remove all illegal immigrants, even asylum seekers, even if it clashes with the ECHR.'

'Too slow. It would get stuck in the Lords. I need something that produces a quick result!'

Parkinson paused, mulling something else over in his mind. 'There is something else that we haven't tried,' he said, finally.

'Yes, I'm listening. What is it?'

'Well, as long as there are people willing to pay money to cross and people smugglers in France offering to provide boats to take them, the problem won't go away. The French police don't have the resources to stop them, even if they wanted to, which they don't. They can't possibly police the whole stretch of coast.'

'So, what are you proposing, Simon?'

'We eliminate the smugglers.'

'Eliminate them? How? What are you getting at? If it's paying the French to employ more guards on the beaches, I can tell you the Treasury won't stand for it.'

'No. I don't mean arrest them. I mean *eliminate* them.'

'You mean kill them?'

'Well, yes, but I wouldn't use that word, Jayne.'

'So how would we do that?'

'Special operations. Like we did in Iraq and Afghanistan.'

'You mean use the military? The SAS? I'm not involving the MOD on this. I know exactly what the Defence Secretary would say. And MI5 wouldn't get involved in an overseas mission. MI6 wouldn't want any part in this, either. And the last thing I would want is for the Foreign Secretary to have a whiff of such an operation.'

'I know someone who runs a service for this kind of thing. It would be a private arrangement, outwith the security service. Totally discreet and confidential.'

'OK. I'm listening. Tell me about it.'

'Well, erm, it's a private military outfit. It's run by an old friend of mine from school days, Stephen Moore. You will know of him. He has a political consultancy, SM Political Intelligence. But on the side, very discreetly, he is a director of a company providing security services, bodyguards and the like. It's called Cerberus. The company also offers an additional service which has been used by private contractors and even some governments: eliminating troublesome elements or individuals, when they don't want their own fingerprints over it, if you catch my drift.

'Assassins, you mean? Mercenaries?'

'Yes, I suppose so. They're all ex-Special

Forces. He recruits them very carefully.'

'Hmm. Interesting. Flesh this out, Simon. I need to know that it would work. And ensure absolute confidentiality. The last thing I want is for this to blow up in our faces. And by our faces I mean my face, am I clear?'

'Of course.'

''I mean it, Simon! Be discreet. And keep my name out of it, no matter what you do. Let me know the costs of the operation. Get an invoice. Something vague. I'll put it down as security expenses. No one will bat an eyelid.'

'Terrific!'

'This better work, Simon. Taking out some of these smuggler gangs. This could be the answer I'm looking for. Even if it's just a temporary fix. Those numbers could plummet. I'm tingling just thinking about it. I'm almost as excited as thinking about a planeload of illegal migrants getting shipped off to Rwanda.'

But now, after this complete fuck-up, her career was finished, unless she got this sorted pronto.

THIRTY-SEVEN

Jayne met Charles Willoughby at his office in Thames House on Millbank. Willoughby was head of MI5, a tall, patrician figure in his early sixties, with grey hair and glasses. Jayne thought he always looked world-weary, as if he had seen and heard it all, and she had never seen him at all worried about anything. She was rather in awe of him.

'What was it you wanted to talk to me about, Jayne? It sounded urgent. I always think of you as having a very cool head but you sounded pretty worked up on the phone. It must be something serious.'

'It is! There's been a bit of a balls-up, Charles and I need your help.'

'Oh, really, Jayne?'

'Yes.'

'OK. Tell me.'

'You'll have heard on the news this

morning about a shooting incident overnight near Calais,' she said. She told him about the plan to eliminate gangs of people smugglers and how it had failed at the first attempt. 'I should never have listened to Simon. He has a friend he was at school with. Stephen Moore. Runs a security company. He's being troublesome now that it's all gone tits up! There's also his estranged wife, Olivia Andrews. She knows too much.'

'I see. And you'd like them taken care of?'

'National security is at stake, Charles. I'm sure you understand.'

'I completely understand, Jayne.'

'I wouldn't want anything to come out about the operation that links Moore's outfit to the government.'

'Hmm. OK. Leave it all with me. We'll need to cover our arses in the aftermath. I'll pull in a favour from SO15. Their boss owes me big time for some help I've given him. I'll get them to take over the police investigation. Not too soon, mind, I'll tell him to leave it a couple of days. Don't want anyone nosy to get a sniff of a cover-up. If there's anyone else we think might cause problems we'll put surveillance on them as well and deal with them if necessary. Don't worry, Jayne. It'll all be kept under wraps.'

'Thank, Charles. I knew I could rely on you.

You've never let me down.'

'Of course. But you'll owe me for this one, Jayne. I'll have to pull a few strings. Quid pro quo and all that. How about something in the New Year Honours list when you get to be PM?'

'How about a knighthood?'

'I'd rather a peerage.'

'Consider it done, Charles.'

*

The MI5 special ops team arrived in Houghton just after 2 a.m. the following morning, parking their van near the house. The van carried the logo of the UK Power Network. The house was detached and sat in its own sizable grounds so there wasn't any immediate worry about neighbours, the nearest other house some distance away. One man stayed in the van as a lookout. The two others approached the front door. The alarm system operated on a wi-fi connection so they were able to hack into it and immobilise it from outside. They had done this sort of thing many times before and one of them was an IT expert, specially chosen for this task.

Once inside the house, two of them crept upstairs to nullify the householder, having studied the floorplan of the building in studious detail. They were clad entirely in black and wore earpieces, headtorches, gloves and balaclavas and moved in virtual silence, communicating with hand signals. As they entered the bedroom, Moore suddenly sat up in alarm.

'Who the fuck are you?' Moore said.

'Shut the fuck up!' said one of the men holding a Glock pistol fitted with a silencer to Moore's head. Then there was the muffled sound of a gunshot.

The whole operation hadn't taken long and, once the CCTV was disabled, and the memory wiped, they made their getaway.

On Sunday evening, just before 9 p.m., two people paid a call on Olivia Andrews. They gained entry by buzzing her at the entrance with a gloved hand and claiming to be police detectives who wanted to speak to her about her husband. To avoid identification from the camera positioned above the doorway, they wore FFP2 masks. The agents, a man and a woman, the woman carrying a large handbag, showed Olivia their warrant cards when they got to her door saying they were from Special Branch, who were taking over the case.

She let them in. Once the door was shut, the man suddenly grabbed her from behind with an armlock and twisted her neck until there was sickening crack. He hung onto her and gently eased her body to the floor.

Having checked that the coast was clear, the pair carried her out to the stairwell, slid a noose around her neck and tied the other end of the rope they'd brought with them in the handbag to the banister. Then they bundled her over the side and let her drop. The pair stood there looking over the banister for a moment. Then they left.

TUESDAY

THIRTY-EIGHT

BBC News

There were reports of a shooting at an address in Finsbury Park last night. No one was injured in the attack which occurred around 7 p.m. A Metropolitan police spokesperson said enquiries into the shooting are continuing and appealed for any witnesses to come forward.

*H*elen had taken a few days' leave now that the Moore case had been handed over to SOI5 and was out of her hands and she set off for the station. At the end of the road where she lived, smoke started pouring out from under the bonnet. She stopped the car instantly and turned the engine off, then phoned her breakdown company and waited for them to come. The mechanic who arrived said, 'There's an odd electrical fault. You're lucky it didn't burst into flames.' Her car was towed to a garage for repair, and she phoned a taxi to take her to the station.

She'd missed the train she had intended to catch and the next one had been cancelled, so the one she got on was rammed; she couldn't get a seat and had to stand the whole way. She sent Finn a text to say she was running late.

She tried to relax and not panic. What had happened to the car was probably just an accident but she was suspicious. She'd been in good spirits before it happened. She'd had a nice evening the night before, sharing a take-away Chinese meal as a family. Then the children, Alice, fifteen, and Andrew, fourteen, went off to their rooms to do what teenagers these days did: occupying themselves on their phone (Alice) or playing internet games (Andrew). She and Robert had sat up late drinking wine. When they had gone to bed, they had made love. Had they been too noisy? she worried. Would the kids have heard them? Probably not Andrew, forever with headphones on. Alice, though, had given her some sly looks this morning, as if to say, *I know what you were two were up to last night!*

At King's Cross she walked to the Tube station and was standing in the crowd on the platform as the train came rushing into the station, when she suddenly felt a shove from behind. She felt herself falling helplessly towards the track and saw the approaching train only seconds away. There was nothing she could do.

She would be crushed beneath its wheels. Just then, a hand seized her by the collar, pulling her back to safety.

She clung to the arm of the man who had caught her, a tall young black man wearing an enormous set of headphones. Helen was struggling to get her breath back. 'Thanks. Someone pushed me...,' she said, looking round. But the crowd was too thick for her to know who it could have been and now the carriage doors were opening. The crush of bodies around her moved like a tide as people clambered off the train and those on the platform surged forward. She remained stationary, like a rock on the seashore as the tide ebbed and flowed around her until she was left alone on the platform. She looked for the man who had saved her to thank him but he was gone, like everyone else.

She wondered about CCTV. There were cameras overlooking the platform. Maybe they would have captured what happened. But the chances were that it was impossible to see what really happened. There had been a crowd of people squeezed close together. All it would take was a hand somewhere behind her. Of course, it might just have been an accident, someone, impatient, trying to make sure they got through the crowd and onto the carriage, but after what had happened to the car she felt certain that she was in danger. Had she been followed all the way from home? she wondered.

Still, she should report it and see what they came up with, she thought to herself, even if whoever was responsible would surely have made sure the CCTV didn't reveal their identity. Hooded. Probably masked too, as still some passengers were. It would likely be a futile search, but she went back up the escalator and found the Transport Police office and reported it nevertheless. When she told the officers she was a police officer herself, showing them her ID, they seemed to take it more seriously. They took her contact details and said someone would be in touch with her later.

She boarded another train and stayed on past her stop, changing lines and carriages, hopping on and off to evade any possible pursuer. She got off at Leicester Square station and made her way to Trafalgar Square, constantly looking behind to see if she had a tail. There didn't seem to be any one obviously following her, but then again, they wouldn't make it obvious, would they?

Finn's journey across London by train and Tube was equally tense. The shooting the previous night had unnerved him and he constantly surveyed the other passengers for any sign that he was being observed or in danger. He also deliberately changed lines several times, jumping in and out of carriages on the Tube at the last minute until he was sure that no one had followed him.

When Helen arrived, he was already there, tucking into a large slice of cake. He hadn't seen her and was absorbed in his phone screen.

'You look like you're enjoying that,' she said, sitting down opposite him.

'Oh, hi. ... Sorry... shouldn't speak with my mouth full,' he said.

'That's OK. Take your time. I'll grab a coffee then we can talk. Do you want anything?'

'No thanks.'

She went to the counter and ordered a flat white then returned to the table.

'I'm sorry I'm late. My car broke down on the way to the train station.'

'I got your text. What happened?'

She described how smoke had suddenly poured out from under the bonnet. 'The mechanic said I was lucky it didn't burst into flames.'

'How old is your car?'

'It's only a year old.'

'Sounds suspicious to me. Like someone is out to get both of us.'

'Why? What's happened to you?'

'Last night all shit broke loose in my apartment. Someone was shooting at me.'

'I read about a shooting online on the way here. Tell me more.'

He described the previous night's events to her.

Helen said, 'First you get shot at. Then my car is sabotaged. Then someone tries to push me in front of a train on the Tube platform.'

'What? You're joking.'

'Do I look like I'm joking? I felt a hand at my back just as the train was coming into the station. Fortunately, a young man who was standing beside me grabbed me by the collar. Otherwise, I wouldn't be here.'

'Jesus! Are you OK?'

'Yes. Just a bit shaken up.'

'That must have been terrifying.'

'It was. But, well, I'm here, in one piece, that's the main thing, so we better get on with it. Before I share some things with you, tell me what you know. Or what you think you know.'

Finn felt he could trust her, unlike the

detectives who'd come to his flat. There was just something trustworthy about her and she had seemed interested in what he'd told her in Cambridge. So, he told her what he thought he'd figured out. 'I've found out that there's a company, Cerberus Security Services, that Stephen Moore owned. But there's nothing online that I can find about what they do. Security could mean anything, I suppose. But I reckon Moore hired someone to kill Clark and Powell when they were about to expose his links to it, though I'm not sure why he wanted to keep it so secret. Powell must have found out about it from Olivia. Then he's told Clark. I was going to file my story about it but then you phoned and I decided to hold off until I'd spoken to you. I'm hoping you might be able to fill me in on more details about what's going on.'

Helen looked around the room, seemingly checking that nobody was trying to eavesdrop on their conversation. 'You're right. I think Moore believed that Powell had put Clark onto him and had information about Cerberus. Both men died within days of each other. It was you who first mentioned Cerberus to me. I then learned more about it from Olivia.' She told him about the apparent suicide of Olivia Andrews. 'It certainly appeared to be a suicide, but I'm suspicious. Unfortunately, there's nothing else to go on and my boss isn't interested in an investigation.'

'It does sound suspicious, especially coming after her husband's murder.'

'Totally. Obviously, you are in danger, too, Finn. And I really shouldn't be doing this as it will cost me my job if it gets out, but I can't ignore what I think is going on. I've struggled with this, and have never done anything like this before, but I really believe it has to be exposed. But you must treat what I tell you as coming from an anonymous source. I need you to guarantee that.'

'Of course.'

She took a memory stick from her bag and passed it across the table to him.

'What's on that?' he said.

'Information about Cerberus Security Services and Stephen Moore. Contracts, bank statements and phone records. Moore apparently started this business, Cerberus Security Services, a few years ago. The company's registered offshore in Jersey, and Moore kept it pretty secret. There's nothing about it online, as you said, not even a company website. But from what I've been able to find out from the contracts, they did a lot of private security work, mainly in Africa and the Middle East, employing security guards, that sort of thing. But I suspect that they did a lot more than that.'

What kind of thing?'

'Employing mercenaries. Undertaking private black ops work, like that operation in France. The French police have traced those men killed near Calais to Cerberus. Obviously, the operation there went badly wrong. The French police suspect it was an operation against people smugglers.'

'People smugglers? You think Moore organised an operation against people smugglers. Why?'

'Good question. I know you will be working on a story and I hope this will help you get to the truth of what is happening. You're lucky to be alive after what happened last night. I don't know how they found out that you were working on a story about all this but I now suspect there's a tap on my phone.'

'You think this goes where? Organised crime?'

'I'll explain all that in a moment. The investigation into Stephen Moore's death has been taken over by SOI5, the Met's Special Branch in other words. My super is happy with that and doesn't want me to continue with the investigation, which is why I contacted you. We've had to hand everything over.'

'The reason being?'

'I've been told that they've taken it over

as it's too sensitive for us to handle. National security.'

'And you don't believe that?'

'No. I don't trust the truth to come out now that Special Branch are involved. Which is where you come in. To expose it. On the stick, you'll find details of the Cerberus bank account in Jersey. I've discovered that the dead men were all paid from the Cerberus bank account, as was the rental for the house they used as a base. There's also a payment to a man called Ibrahim Mahmoudi. There was another body found in the same area in France, who was killed around the same time as the others. That man was Ibrahim Mahmoudi.'

'The private investigator who was found dead in France? I've been reading about that murder online.'

'Yes. He was identified when his description appeared in the media, and his wife contacted the French police. I think that Mahmoudi must have been hired by Moore to help the mission in some way. His body was found in an old quarry. He'd been shot in the head. According to the French police, he'd clearly also been tortured beforehand.

'Moore's phone records, which are also on the stick, show that he contacted Mahmoudi's office last month. He may have hired him to obtain information about the smugglers. Moore and Mahmoudi must have been operating on separate phones from then on, though, as nothing else shows up in the phone records. But here's the really interesting thing. The bank statements show a payment of two hundred and fifty thousand pounds received from the Home Office.'

Finn shook his head in disbelief. 'What the fuck!' he said.

'Interestingly, Simon Parkinson, the Home Secretary's special adviser, was also one of the people Moore spoke to, according to the call records. Parkinson phoned him at the start of last month. He attended the same public school as Moore, Winchester College. And he worked for a Home Secretary obsessed with stopping the boats controlled by people smugglers, at any cost.'

'Wow! So, what you are saying, if I'm following you correctly, is that it's the Home Office who was behind the France operation and you think the operation in France was initiated by the Home Secretary, Jayne Steele, and her spad?'

'It's difficult to prove, but the call from Parkinson and the payment to Cerberus from the Home Office would suggest so, I'd say. It's certainly suspicious. Who else would hire men employed by Cerberus to try to take out a smuggling gang? You'll see now why I don't swallow the national security explanation.' She took out a piece of paper from her bag and passed it to Finn. 'These are Parkinson's and Mahmoudi's numbers so you can identify them on the call list.'

'Thanks. This is incredible. Mind you, I wouldn't put something like this past Steele. She's truly off the wall and fixated on immigration. It's well-known that she's ambitious too and fancies the top job. The right-wing papers have been giving her a hard-time on the number of refugees arriving on our shores, so in some ways, I'm not surprised of she was taken in by such a plan. Highly risky, though, as it's turned out. This will do for her, she'll now be toast.'

'I'm sure she and her spad will deny everything.'

'Doesn't matter. The perception will be that she had something to do with it.'

'OK. So, who do you think killed Moore then? Steele and Parkinson?'

Helen nodded. 'Yes. With help from the security services. It all stinks of a cover-up. I think that's why the Moore case has been taken off my hands.'

'Blood hell! And they were also trying to kill me last night, then?'

Helen nodded. 'I'd say so. From their point of view, anyone who is a threat to the state is a legitimate target. SO15 has close links to the security service. They obviously think that you are investigating Moore and want to take you out before you expose anything. They will have seen the statement you gave me when I handed the case over yesterday and noted your interest in Moore and Cerberus. But you were hugely lucky. They weren't as efficient as those who killed Moore. So, be very careful, Finn. This whole thing is extremely dangerous. But I think that getting the story into the light as soon as possible is the only way to keep yourself safe.'

'And you, too,' said Finn. 'You're clearly a target as well.'

Helen nodded. 'Yes. Me too. Incidentally, you might be interested to know that Brian Clark phoned Moore's office the day before he was killed. When I asked Moore about it, in the course of the investigation, he said the reporter was asking him how he thought the Conservatives would do at the next election. But now I'm not so sure that was the reason.'

'Hmm. Yes. I agree. It probably was about Cerberus, after he'd been told about Moore's connection to it by Powell. Would Moore really have had Clark and Powell killed to prevent that being revealed? He could have, I suppose. He wouldn't want any publicity on a company that was linked to mercenaries. But what I don't get is why did Powell want to expose Moore's link to Cerberus in the first place?'

'I don't know, either. He must have really hated him for some reason, I guess.'

THIRTY-NINE

*F*inn and Helen caught a taxi outside the National Gallery in Trafalgar Square. In the taxi, Helen phoned her husband, asking him to meet her at the station in Cambridge, explaining her car had broken down earlier. The taxi dropped Helen off at King's Cross, then took Finn to the Chronicle's offices. At his desk, Finn plugged the memory stick Helen had given him into a computer and studied the files inside. It all became clearer. He tried to piece together the timeline of events. The payments. Exactly as Helen had said. He started to scribble it all down on a sheet of paper. So many deaths! Clark, Powell, Moore, Olivia and so on. He felt particularly sorry for the elderly French couple and the private detective, Ibrahim Mahmoudi, and wondered what had led to his death. He felt no sympathy for the mercenaries who were killed; they knew what they were getting into.*

He went to tell his editor, Iain, what he had, and that he was going to write up the story and file it. Iain couldn't believe it at first but then said he would try to contact Steele and Parkinson for comment before Finn's copy went into the next day's edition. Finn would submit a freedom of information request to the Home Office regarding any payments to Cerberus Security Services and what they were for. However, he fully expected to be told this information could not be made public or disclosed for reasons of "national security". It didn't matter. They had enough proof. The Cerberus operation in France was clearly about trying to take out people smugglers. That was obvious. What was now also apparent was who was behind it. In addition, it looked like Moore's murder was part of a cover-up by the person who had wanted the French mission: the Home Secretary, Jayne Steele.

He then got a WhatsApp text from Amy with an attached link to a story breaking on the BBC website:

ORKNEY BUILDER HID
COCAINE IN BAGS OF CEMENT

The boss of a building company in Orkney has been arrested and charged with the supply of Class A drugs after police swooped on his Kirkwall home and warehouse and discovered £500,000 worth of cocaine hidden in bags of cement which he had imported from Europe.

David Laing, 44, appeared in court today and made no plea. The police operation was led by a specialist team from Glasgow after they received an anonymous tip-off that the builder was importing cocaine into Orkney from Rotterdam amongst his building materials and then distributing it around the Northern Isles and the mainland of Scotland.

Finn replied in a text: *'I wonder where the anonymous tip-off came from?'*

He then phoned Grace.

'I just heard about Laing being arrested for drug-smuggling. I think we've got Amy to thank for that.'

'Yes. I'm writing up a piece on it right now. Peter is incandescent about it all.'

'Do you think he knew what Laing was up to?'

'I don't know. He's saying nothing, just growling about the place. I'm keeping out of his way. But that's not the only thing that's going on up here. The police have arrested a man called Jamie McLeish and charged him with Callum's murder.'

'What? Who's McLeish?'

'He works for Laing as an electrician. He's a thirty-five-year-old from Stromness. I told you

Laing wanted Callum to sell him his land so he could build luxury homes. Looks like Laing obviously thought if he could do away with Callum, he could get his hands on the land and build his housing development, and so got McLeish to do his dirty work for him. No doubt he offered him a tidy sum.'

'What's the evidence?'

'I've heard they found Callum's wallet in a bin and it had McLeish's DNA on it. Apparently he had a previous conviction so his DNA was on the police database. A knife has also been recovered by divers from the harbour and the police are saying they think it's the murder weapon.'

'Sounds pretty conclusive. Yes, Laing will have paid him handsomely to kill Callum. Bastards. Let's hope both Laing and McLeish go down for a very long time.'

'Could Laing have got this man McLeish to kill Powell as well, do you think?'

'I don't know. I was working on the assumption that Powell's murder was linked to Clark and Moore. But it's a possibility, I guess.'

'Are you any closer to finding out who killed Powell, then, if it wasn't MacLeish?'

He then told her how Moore's secret company, Cerberus Security Services, apparently used mercenaries, and was involved in the massacre in France. 'It's a big story. You'll read all about in the *Chronicle* tomorrow. But I think Powell found out about Cerberus and put Clark onto Moore, who may have had them both killed. It's all a bit circumstantial, though, and I could do with some more evidence, so I'll keep that theory under my hat for the time being. Watch this space!'

FORTY

When Finn's article was published, he knew he would find himself at the centre of a media storm. Every news and broadcasting outlet would want a piece of the action and he'd be bombarded with demands to share his source for the story. Which, of course, he would refuse to do. He'd keep his own counsel, not even disclosing the identity of his informer with Iain, his editor. He knew that within the police force in Cambridge, suspicion would automatically fall on Helen, which he was sure she would deny, and there would probably be an internal investigation into the leak, but would they be able to prove that she had provided Finn with the documents showing a link from Moore's disastrous mission to the Home Secretary? He hoped not.

In any case, the story would be out, which was the main thing. Once it was in the public domain, they surely would also both be safe? Helen had also known she was taking a great professional risk in leaking the story, believing that it was for the greater good. Would the police service really wish to punish her for helping to expose malfeasance in government? For complying with a cover-up? He thought the Chief Constable would probably want to try to draw a veil over the matter. There were other ways in which newspapers might have come across the material, they might conclude: through private investigators, hacking or whistleblowers in government departments.

But as he worked on the article, he began to suspect that something was wrong. Helen had agreed to text him to let him know she had arrived back in Cambridge safely. But no message had come. He had tried calling her several times but her number went straight to voicemail. Perhaps she had simply forgotten, he thought, just been relieved to have got home. Switched it off. Or it was out of battery. She'd probably call later. He got on with writing the article and tried not to worry about it.

At quarter to four he received a call on his mobile. It was Helen's husband, Robert, in Cambridge. 'Is Helen with you?' he asked, sounding panicked.

Finn immediately realized something must have happened. 'No. I met her earlier and she went to catch the train. I was beginning to worry, though. She said she would text me when she got home. But I haven't heard anything.'

'It's strange. I was supposed to meet her at the station. She had told me she was catching the 14.12 train from King's Cross. The train arrived on time but she wasn't on it. I thought maybe she had missed it and would catch a later one. I tried calling her but she didn't answer. I figured the battery on her phone had run out, that's why I hadn't heard from her, so I waited for the next train, but she wasn't on it either. And I still can't get hold of her on the phone.'

'Well, I dropped her at King's Cross in time to catch that train,' said Finn.

'I'm worried. It's a direct train. There are no stops between London and here, so she can't have got off somewhere.'

'She can't have got on it then. By the way, how did you get my number?'

Robert said, 'Helen told me last night about the case she had been working on, the Stephen Moore murder. And about the case being taken off her hands and that she was meeting a reporter today in London. She left me a note of your name and number.'

'She was very brave,' said Finn. 'Not many police officers would do what she's done.' Finn wondered if he should tell Robert about the two incidents that had happened to Helen earlier in the day: the car almost bursting into flames and the push at the Tube station? But he decided not to, no sense in making him even more worried than he already was. But what on earth could have happened to her? Abducted? Killed? Fuck, he shouldn't have let her go into the station.

'Have you phoned the police?' Finn asked.

'No. Not yet. I was just about to.'

'Well don't.'

Helen was aware that she was being paranoid, but who wouldn't be? After all, already that day, she was sure someone had tampered with her car, then she'd almost been shoved under the wheels of a passing Tube train. So, she was convinced that someone must be following her as she walked through the station and onto the platform to board the Cambridge-bound train waiting there. As she boarded the carriage, she surreptitiously glanced down the platform at the other approaching passengers, trying to determine whether any of them were potential assassins. Of course, there wasn't anyone that obviously stood out as fitting that category. Why would they? They'd be a bloody useless assassin if they were.

She boarded the train and found a seat. The carriage was quiet at this time in the afternoon. Later it would be rammed again with commuters returning from work to Cambridge. But now, there were only a handful of others seated further up in the carriage, all engrossed in their own activities: a woman in her mid-thirties reading a picture book to a pre-school child; an elderly couple sharing a crossword; and a young couple in their late teenage years or early twenties, students Helen concluded, very much in love, laughing, kissing, their eyes fixed on each other and their arms entwined. Those were the days. Helen thought, with a smile. Carefree and careless, with the whole world and your life ahead of you.

Helen began to relax. It had been a relief to hand over the material to Finn. Now, it was literally out of her hands. He would be back in his office, speaking to his editor, reading through it and shaping it into an article which would splash across the newspaper and into the world.

She took her phone out of her pocket to text Robert, telling him she had caught the train. Just then someone sat down beside her to her left and she felt something hard press against her groin.

'I wouldn't do that if I were you,' a voice said.

She turned to look at the person. He was

dressed in a dark blue suit and raincoat. He had fair hair, swept back, with a pale complexion and pale blue eyes. Eyes which seemed to freeze her with their stare. He had a long thin face and it looked like he had cut himself on his Adam's apple while shaving. Panic seized her. She felt like screaming. But instead, she tried humour. She wouldn't show this bastard that she was scared.

'Is that a gun in your pocket or are you just pleased to see me?' she said, grinning and nodding at the bulge in his jacket pocket where his right hand was clearly holding something.

Nothing so much as a smile, though, crossed his face. 'I *am* pleased to see you. And you're right. It *is* a gun. I wouldn't do anything stupid, if I were you. I'm quite prepared to use it.'

'Your people have already tried to kill me twice today. But I don't have a clue why.'

'Don't you? Perhaps you could start by telling me what you told that journalist you met earlier, and what you've given him?'

'Journalist? What journalist? Can I remind you that I am a senior police officer.'

'A police officer who has been leaking classified information to the press.'

Helen said nothing. She simply stared at him.

'So, this is what we're going to do,' he said. 'First, hand me your phone.' He prodded her with the gun. Helen reluctantly fished her phone out of her pocket and passed it to him. He took it in his left hand and held the power button down to switch it off and put it in his pocket.

Just then an announcement came from the PA system in the carriage: *This service is the 14.12 for Cambridge ...*

The man said, 'OK. Now, we're getting off.' She felt the barrel of the gun pushing hard into her side as he pulled her up to her feet with his other hand. She grabbed her shoulder bag, and stood up.

'Now let's go. And don't try anything stupid, remember.' He took his hand out of his pocket and gripped her wrist tightly.

At the ticket barrier, he flashed an ID card and the station staff opened the gate to let them through. Outside the station, he led her towards a black SUV with tinted rear windows. A BMW. A man in the driver's seat glanced at them as they approached the vehicle and nodded. Using his left hand, the man with the gun opened the rear passenger-side door. 'Get in,' he said.

'Where are you taking me?'

'Somewhere we can talk. Get in.'

She felt sick and afraid. Very afraid.

'Why don't you want me to call the police?' asked Robert.

'Helen doesn't trust them. Neither do I. A unit in the Met have taken over the investigation and they have close links to the security services, so if we let them know she's missing and we're worried they'll likely come after us.' He didn't say that he had also been a target.

'So, what do we do? I can't just hang about this station forever?'

'Sit tight for now. I'll head over to King's Cross and ask around if anyone has seen her and I'll let you know if I find out anything.'

Robert sighed.

'Look, I know it's hard but Helen is tough. Whatever situation she's in, I trust her to get out of it.'

'I hope you're right.'

The man released her wrist and pushed Helen towards the open door. If she got in there, that would be it. She'd knew she'd never be seen again. They'd take her somewhere, interrogate her, then, no doubt, kill her and dump her body somewhere it would never be found.

She quickly turned round and elbowed him in the throat, then kicked him as hard as she could in the knee. He collapsed to the ground and she sprinted out into Euston Road. Cars swerved, a bus slammed on its brakes, taxi horns blasted but she made it across to the other side and kept on running without looking back.

She ran along Birkenhead Street then turned right into St Chad's Street, all the time thinking how glad she was she'd adopted wearing trainers and jeans today. If she'd opted for a skirt and heels, she'd already be caught, fallen over or been mown down by the traffic. At the end of the street, she came into a square. What now? She spotted a hotel, The Argyll Hotel. It would have to do. She stopped, had a look around. No pursuers in sight. She walked up to the door and pressed a buzzer on the intercom. Just then the black BMW drove into the other side of the square. She snuck into the outer porch and pressed the buzzer again, holding onto the handle. There was no answer. She heard a car behind her and looked round. There it was. The black BMW.

Finn caught a black cab outside the office and asked the driver to take him to King's Cross by the quickest possible route. 'There'll be a large tip if you can get me there in five minutes.'

'You must be joking mate. At this time of day?'

'OK, but see what you can do, will you?'

There was a sudden click. Helen felt the lock of the door release and almost fell into the hallway. The young woman, immaculately made up and wearing a smart pin-stripe suit standing behind the reception desk stared at her in amazement. She must have looked a sight: panting, bedraggled, sweaty.

'Can I help you?' the young woman said in an east European accent.

'Yes, please help me. There are these men. They're after me. Is there somewhere I can hide?'

'Through there,' said the receptionist, pointing along a corridor. 'Toilet.'

Helen found the toilet and locked herself in. She could hear buzzing from the front door. The men who were after her clearly weren't going to give up. Hopefully the receptionist wouldn't let them in.

Then she heard a crash which sounded like the door had been kicked in.

Helen opened the window in the toilet and squeezed herself out and found herself in a mews lane which led to a street. She dashed along it until she found herself back where she'd started, on Euston Road. She felt she was in a maze. She looked round and spotted the black BMW coming back along the street towards her. I've got to get out of here, she thought, seeing a taxi rank and Tube station opposite, and dashed across the busy road. This time, she wasn't so lucky. A taxi, which had just turned the corner from Pancras Road, tried to stop but it was too late.

Finn leapt out of the taxi and dashed for the station entrance. He sped around the large hall, his eyes searching everywhere for a sight of Helen in vain. Then he tried asking the station staff. He didn't have a photo of her but could describe her: in her forties, dark hair in a ponytail, dressed in skinny jeans, Adidas trainers and a cream jacket. They all shook their heads until he reached the barrier at platform six. The two of them, a man and a woman, looked at each other, then the woman said,' Why do you want to know?'

Finn hesitated then said, 'It's my wife. I was meant to catch the train with her back to Cambridge but I got held up and now she's not answering her phone.'

The man said, 'She was taken off the train by a detective. He showed us his ID.'

'When?'

He looked at his watch. 'Oh, must be two hours ago now.'

Finn dashed off to the exit but felt it was hopeless. She must have been apprehended as she got on the train or on it before it departed. In two hours, she could be anywhere. Still, someone might have seen something.

There was a taxi rank outside, with several taxis queued in a line. He went along the line, asking them if any of them had seen her being taken out. He was in luck. The second one he asked nodded but it wasn't good news. He said a woman who sounded like her had been run down by one of his colleagues as she ran across the road in front of him. She'd been taken to hospital in an ambulance with blue flashing lights.

'Which hospital would that be?' asked Finn.

'Probably the Royal London,' he said.

Finn thanked the driver and immediately jumped into the cab at the front of the line, directing him to the Accident and Emergency department of the Royal London Hospital.

Once there, he went to reception and asked if Helen Richardson had been admitted?

'Are you a relative?' he was asked by the

receptionist, a middle-aged woman in glasses with a kindly expression.

'No,' he said. 'I'm a friend. I heard she was knocked down at King's Cross. I wanted to know if she was OK.'

The woman tapped at her keyboard and stared at the screen in front of her. 'She was taken straight into surgery. I'm afraid you will just have to wait. Do you know her next of kin?'

Finn gave her Robert's phone number then took a seat and phoned Robert to tell him. Finn watched the flotsam and jetsam of the walking wounded stream through the doors of A&E: builders who'd driven a nail through their hands, cyclists who'd fallen off their bikes, five-a-side footballers injured in a rash tackle and so on.

Sometime later Robert phoned back. 'Apparently, she suffered a serious head injury from the accident and they had to remove a blood clot. It's fucking awful. I don't know if she'll pull through. I'm in the car now on my way to London. I can't believe it.'

'I'm sorry,' said Finn. There wasn't much more he could say. The best thing he could do for both of them, he thought, was to head back to the office and finish his article and file it as quickly as possible.

WEDNESDAY

FORTY-ONE

STEELE AND PARKINSON LINKED TO FRANCE SHOOTINGS

Exclusive by Finn Morrison

Questions are being asked of Home Secretary Jayne Steele, and her special adviser, Simon Parkinson, about their role in a botched raid on a farmhouse in France in the early hours of Friday morning which left eleven people dead. Two of the dead were an elderly French couple, eight are believed to be members of a team of mercenaries who, French police believe, were planning an attack on a people-smuggling gang, and the other is a private investigator from London. There are close connections between Steele's special adviser, Simon Parkinson, and the believed organiser of the raid, the late Stephen Moore.

Stephen Moore, the owner of SM Political Intelligence, was found dead on Saturday morning at his home in Houghton, just outside Cambridge. He had been shot in the head. His wife, Olivia Andrews, an academic and historical novelist who wrote under the pseudonym Rebecca Rossetti, was also found dead on Sunday morning, having apparently taken her own life.

It has since been revealed that Moore operated a covert business called Cerberus Security Services, a private military contractor registered in Jersey, which offered a service for individuals, businesses and governments. The range of services provided is not known but there are suspicions that it involved armed intervention using mercenaries in overseas countries against those identified as a terrorist threat. The Chronicle has seen contracts that the company agreed with several governments in Africa. Moore was the sole company director of Cerberus Security Services.

The Chronicle has received details of the company's bank statements, which show payments from prominent politicians and top businessmen in Central America, Asia and Africa. The sums paid into Cerberus's bank account in Jersey are substantial, amounting to over £5 million in the last three years alone. During that time, several opposition figures or rebels in these countries have mysteriously disappeared. The account's statements show that a payment of £250,000 was received from the Home Office two weeks ago. Payments of

£20,000 were made to each of the men who died in the shooting in France on Friday. Cerberus Security Services also rented the property which the team used as a base. There is also a payment of £10,000 to Ibrahim Mahmoudi, the private detective whose body was found in the same area.

Being based in Jersey, Cerberus Security Services also managed to avoid paying UK tax. When asked what the payment to the company was for, a Home Office spokesperson said that this could not be disclosed for reasons of national security.

Ibrahim Mahmoudi, was found dead in a disused quarry east of Calais. Moore's phone records show that he made contact with Mahmoudi's office on 7 March. It's not known exactly what the private investigator was doing in France, but the suspicion is that he was hired by Moore to assist the mission but this somehow backfired and he was killed.

Cambridgeshire police initially investigated the killing of Stephen Moore but this paper has since been told that the investigation into his death has now been taken over by SO15, the counter-terrorism branch of the Metropolitan Police. The Home Office and the Met refused to confirm this.

Questions are being asked whether Moore's killing was actually part of a cover-up. Likewise, his wife's apparent suicide has caused speculation as to, in the circumstances, whether or not she really did take her own life.

Steele is well known for her anti-immigration rhetoric, describing the increase in small boats carrying illegal migrants as an "invasion" and the country being overrun with "hordes of so-called asylum seekers." She has frequently spoken of her determination to stop the boats by whatever means necessary.

Steele's special adviser, Simon Parkinson, had a close personal friendship with Stephen Moore that went back to their days at their exclusive top public school. Moore's phone records reveal that Moore was phoned by Parkinson on 3 March.

Steele's role in the events is unclear, as is that of Parkinson. But it seems more than a coincidence that Moore's company, Cerberus, was paid the sum of £250,000 by the Home Office after a phone call from the special adviser and shortly before a supposed raid on people smugglers was to take place.

Jayne Steel and Simon Parkinson were approached for comment.

FORTY-TWO

Finn had moved back into his flat and, although he didn't feel entirely safe, now that the story was out in the public domain, he felt a lot safer than he had previously. He had gone out for a run in the park, then showered and tried phoning Robert to get an update on Helen's condition but there was no answer, so he sat down with a coffee and his laptop and started to work on the first-hand piece about Powell, finding Moore's body and everything that had happened over the past nine days, when Grace phoned.

'Great article. Just read your piece about the Home Secretary online,' she said.

'Thanks.'

'You really nailed it. Where in the name of fuck did you get all that information?'

He laughed. 'It's confidential. You don't really expect me to tell you, do you?'

'Hah! No! Anyway, what a piece!'

'Thanks. So, what's new with you?'

'Well, I have found out something too, something very interesting! Something you will want to know,' she said.

'OK. Yes? Go on. You're keeping me in suspense.'

She told him what her friend Kirsty had just told her. 'You know those mercenaries killed in France that you wrote about? The eight men found dead in their vehicles. The Cerberus team.'

'Yes. What about them?'

'Well, one of them happened to be in Orkney around the time Powell disappeared.'

'What the fuck! You're joking!

'No, I'm not.' She went on to explain what Kirsty's mother had told Kirsty. 'The man is being named as Wayne Morgan, but Kirsty says he booked into her mum's B&B under a different name,' said Grace. 'David Fletcher. Said he was there to do some birdwatching. Paid cash. Stayed one night. Sunday the twelfth of March. Kirsty's mum saw his mugshot in the newspaper and says it's definitely him. What do you think of that? Powell disappeared the next day. A mercenary. The contract killer. Could he be the man who killed Powell?'

'I think we're onto something, that's what I

think.'

Finn reckoned that whatever business had led Morgan to Orkney was extremely shadowy to say the least. It had to be more than a coincidence. And he didn't believe in coincidence in investigations. Had Morgan been hired to assassinate Powell? he wondered. It appeared likely. Why else would he be in Orkney? Birdwatching? Under a false name? Not likely. He was a mercenary. One of Moore's team. Morgan would most likely have been hired by Moore as a hit man for the killings in both Cambridge and Orkney, to keep his offshore business secret.

'But what I don't get is why do you think Powell wanted to expose Moore's secret?' said Grace.

'I can't help thinking it's got something to do with what Callum told me about when I met him. Callum told me that Powell had never gotten over the death of a young woman who he was in love with in Beirut and probably used it as the basis for his first novel. Powell and Moore were both in Beirut together, so I'm thinking Powell could have had a reason to blame him for her death.'

After he spoke to Grace, he looked at the Cerberus bank account details again. Eventually, he spotted something.

He phoned Powell's widow, Laura, and told her what Grace had told him about Wayne Morgan being in Orkney at the time of Jeremy's death and what he had uncovered in the bank records. 'This man Morgan was a mercenary. He was one of those killed in the shooting near Calais. You'll have heard about that.'

Laura said, 'So, it wasn't an accident. Just as I suspected. I was right. There really was a hit-man, Jeremy was murdered. But why would anyone want Jeremy killed? I don't understand.'

'I think he knew too much. Jeremy found out something when he was in Cambridge last month, about Stephen Moore's Cerberus business which he wanted to keep secret, and I reckon he told Brian Clark about it.'

'But why would he do that?'

'That's a very good question.'

WERE POWELL AND CLARK KILLED TO PROTECT A DEADLY SECRET?

Exclusive by Finn Morrison

Last Saturday morning, I walked into a room and found Stephen Moore lying dead in his bed. The Cambridge businessman had been shot in the head, in cold blood.

I had gone to Moore's house just outside Cambridge to question him about what he knew about Jeremy Powell. I had been asked to investigate Powell's death, which Police Scotland had dismissed as an accident, the famous author assumed to have simply stumbled off a cliff in bad weather.

But there was something that wasn't right about that theory from the start. What had happened to his dog? The writer had gone for a walk with his labradoodle one afternoon and not returned. A few days later his body had been washed up on a beach with head injuries but there was no sign of his dog.

Powell and Moore had been friends a long time ago, when they were students together and also when they worked in Beirut. After he left the Middle East, Moore returned to Cambridge and set up a company, SM Political Intelligence, a political consultancy specialising in using data to target election campaigns. They have been involved in elections in several African states. As revealed in this newspaper yesterday, Moore also operated another company, Cerberus Security Services, registered in Jersey. This company appears to have provided security guards, bodyguards and other personnel to overseas clients, but is believed to have also organised groups of military mercenaries for specific missions, including the one in France last week which backfired catastrophically. Moore also had a close connection to Simon Parkinson, a special adviser to the Home Secretary, Jayne Steele, who has made it her priority to "Stop the Boats".

Moore was murdered shortly after the debacle in France in which eight mercenaries employed by him were massacred in what is believed to have been an ambush by a people-smuggling gang. Was Moore assassinated as part of a cover-up? If so, who was responsible?

Questions are now also being asked about one of the mercenaries killed in the Cerberus operation in France, Wayne Morgan, in connection with the deaths of Jeremy Powell and Brian Clark. A witness has now identified Morgan as being in Orkney around the time of Powell's death. Was he responsible for Powell's death? The circumstances certainly seem suspicious. Could Morgan have been also responsible for the killing of the Cambridge journalist, Brian Clark, who was gunned down and killed in his flat on 11 March this year, two days before the disappearance of Powell on 13 March?

It is now known that Clark had met with Powell a few days before his death and that he had a phone call with Moore the day before he was shot. Cambridgeshire Police believed that the killing was a case of mistaken identity as part of a gangland dispute involving drugs but his links to Moore and Powell now suggest a possible contract killing.

Morgan, a former British soldier, was a known associate of Moore and, according to the Cerberus company's bank statements, like the seven other members of the team who were killed, received regular payments from Moore's Cerberus account. The Cerberus bank account shows that Morgan was paid two amounts of £25,000, one on 12 March, the day after Clark's killing, and the other on 14 March, the day after Powell disappeared. Powell's body was found a few days later. Did Morgan kill both men? If so, why?

It is thought that Moore may have hired Morgan to target and assassinate Powell and Clark believing that they had incriminating knowledge of Cerberus Security Services, which Moore wished to keep secret because of its role in using mercenaries abroad. It is believed that Clark was planning to expose Moore's directorship of the company after receiving information from Powell about it. It is, however, not known exactly why Powell wanted to expose the clandestine business interests of his former friend, though what happened between them in the past may lie behind it.

In this investigation, I have been greatly assisted by Grace Campbell of the Orkney Times. It all began when I returned to Orkney to attend my grandmother's funeral ...

ONE MONTH EARLIER

FORTY-THREE

Monday 13th March

*I*t was windy and wet and the sky was darkening, so Jeremy didn't intend to go too far. As he walked along the coastal path, his thoughts went back over the previous week. That night in Cambridge, as he had lain in bed, he had tried to remember how the events eighteen years ago in Beirut had unfolded.

Beirut was just about the noisiest place Jeremy had ever been in. And the hottest. The streets were choked with people and vehicles, everyone constantly on the move, or at least the traffic would have been if not for the traffic jams. Horns beeped and people shouted. Market traders called out from their stalls to passers-by. Outdoor café tables were packed with men playing chess, backgammon or having heated discussions about life, the universe and everything. Diesel fumes choked the air and the heat was oppressive. But he loved it. Despite the car bombs, the power cuts and the scorching heat. The country was in a constant state of upheaval with protests against the Syrian occupation and assassinations of political figures a regular event.

He rented an apartment in the Badaro district, a quiet area of the city, which he thought would be a good base to work from. He had been in the city for a couple of months when he ran into Stephen Moore at an event hosted by the British Council, a talk by an expert on antiquities. They hadn't seen each other since university, when they had been friends.

One Saturday afternoon he had arranged to meet Stephen to go for lunch and, as they were approaching a café, Stephen said, 'Look, see those two girls sitting over there. Students of mine. Let's go over and say hello. Isn't the black-haired one a stunner?'

Jeremy turned to discreetly look to where Stephen pointed. Two young women, who looked to be about twenty years of age, were seated at an outdoor table, smiling and laughing and talking animatedly together. One was a brunette, the other had jet-black shoulder-length hair.

Stephen was right. Both girls were pretty but the black-haired one looked particularly beautiful, he thought.

'Oh, hello, girls,' said Stephen. 'Having time out from your studies today? I hope you're enjoying yourselves.'

Both young women smiled shyly.

'This is Nasreen,' said Stephen, indicating the brunette. 'And this is Laila. Girls, this is my friend, Jeremy.'

'Pleased to meet you,' said Jeremy. So, Laila was the name of the more attractive one, thought Jeremy.

'Jeremy is a journalist,' said Stephen. 'I'm sure he'd be interested in talking to you two girls about life in Beirut for young people, that sort of thing, wouldn't you Jeremy?'

Jeremy hesitated. This had taken him completely by surprise. 'Well ... I suppose so. That's if it's alright with both of you. I wouldn't want to put you to any trouble.'

'Why don't we have some coffee and cake, eh?' said Stephen, pulling up a chair and sitting down. 'You girls don't mind if we join you, do you?'

'No. Of course not,' said Laila. Nasreen didn't look too sure. She smiled at Stephen. He smiled back. And sat down.

Jeremy went home that evening with his

mind in a swirl. All he could think about was Laila's smile. Her face. Her shape. And her voice. In fact, everything about her.

Over the next few days, he became obsessed with thinking about her. He thought of phoning Stephen and asking him how he could get in touch with her and picked up the phone but then put it down again. He would feel foolish. He found himself often hanging around the Hamra neighbourhood where the American University was located, as classes were finishing for the day, hoping he might bump into her. Finally, one day, he spotted her, walking with Nasreen, both of them carrying backpacks. He followed them, feeling like some kind of stalker or pervert. But he couldn't stop himself.

Eventually, at a street corner, the two women separated and Jeremy saw his chance. He raced around the block thinking that if he came down the street in the opposite direction from the way she was now heading he could make it look like a coincidence that he ran into her.

When he got round the block, completely out of breath, he couldn't see her. Maybe she had gone a different way. He stood frozen to the spot. This was idiotic, he told himself. He should really just forget her. He started to walk along the street. He should just go home and do some work.

Then suddenly there she was in front of him. She had stepped out of a baker's shop, carrying a loaf of bread, straight into his path. In fact, it was her who spoke first as they faced each other.

'Hello,' she said. 'It's Jeremy, isn't it?'

'Eh...yes...yes. Laila, isn't it?' he stumbled.

'Yes,' she laughed.

'I didn't expect to see you here. Do you live near here?'

'No, I'm just heading home from university. I live with my family in Achrafiyeh.'

'That's a nice area.' There was an awkward pause. 'Well, it's nice to see you again,' said Jeremy. 'I very much enjoyed our chat the other day. It was enlightening finding out so much about young people's lives in Beirut. I had no idea there was such a vibrant music scene.'

'Maybe you would like to experience it for yourself,' she said.

'I definitely would,' said Jeremy.

'There's actually a very good concert in a couple of days' time. On Friday evening. Would you like to go? I can get tickets.'

Jeremy couldn't believe it. 'Of course. That would be great, thanks. I'll give you the money for the ticket, naturally.'

She shook her head. 'You don't need to do that. Anyway, it's a Lebanese singer called Asha. She's terrific. You'll love her.'

She told him the details of the venue and the time and arranged to meet beforehand in a nearby café.

Jeremy went home that night to his apartment feeling like he was walking on a cloud. He couldn't wait for Friday night.

The gig led to a meet-up for coffee in a café. Then to a quiet restaurant by the sea for lunch. Gradually they progressed to the point where Jeremy invited her to his apartment one Saturday afternoon. They ended up in bed, of course. After sex, they talked and talked. About his family, her family; his brother, her sisters. His parents. Her parents. He found out that her father was a businessman and her mother a housewife. They would strongly disapprove of her seeing a man, she told him. They had to keep it secret.

They began to meet regularly at his apartment. They talked about books, films, music. Politics. And, of course, they had sex. Then she would go home to tell her parents that she had been at the library studying. Or at the cinema with a friend.

They talked about the political situation

in Lebanon and the Middle East. About Israel. The Palestinians. The intifada. Jeremy had felt unsure about the state of Israel before he arrived in Beirut. On the one hand, as a European, he felt some weird residual sense of guilt about what had happened to the Jews in Germany during the Second World War. The Holocaust. Something was owed to them, surely, he had thought. But, on the other hand, the Palestinians had been displaced. Millions became refugees after 1948. Those that remained were treated as second-class citizens by the Israelis. It was basically an apartheid regime. The Six Day War had occupied more territory, stealing it from its rightful owners. There had even been massacres of Palestinians by the Israeli Defense Forces, the IDF, at refugee camps. Some even in Lebanon. As a Middle East correspondent, he was expected to travel around the region and so he had travelled to the West Bank and into Gaza. He had witnessed the terrible conditions that Palestinians were living in and having their homes demolished to make way for Israeli settlers. It was an illegal occupation and the world needed to know about it, he soon had realised.

He saw the dire conditions of the Palestinian refugee camps in southern Lebanon. His reports became more polemical. At the same time, the political situation in Beirut was sectarian and incendiary. Rival political factions clashed in the streets. There were daily protests and demonstrations. Battles with the authorities. Bomb blasts. A leading politician was killed when a car bomb exploded as his vehicle passed it. It looked like the civil war, recently ended, was about to resume.

Against this backdrop, they made passionate love to the sounds of Coltrane and Parker on his stereo, at weekends, or when she skipped her lectures for the afternoon during the week. The windows of his apartment open to allow some air into the hot, stuffy bedroom as their hot and sweaty bodies writhed on the bed.

One such afternoon, Jeremy told her that he was going to Gaza in a couple of days.

'Could you do something for me?' Laila asked.

'Of course. What is it?' said Jeremy.

'I'll tell you tomorrow. It will be helping the people there.'

'You're involved in the struggle then?'

'Of course. Either you act or you do nothing and let the suffering continue.'

The next day, she arrived at his apartment with directions for him.

It took him five and a half hours to drive

from Beirut to Tel Aviv. There, he met the men, whose names he never learned, in greasy overalls in a backstreet car workshop, which Laila had directed him to. His Skoda was fitted up for him to drive through to Gaza, its panels removed and secreted with piles of cash. US dollars. Jeremy watched as they finished fitting the panels and hid the cash, wrapped in plastic, inside. Then he was off, driving to the Erez crossing to take him into Gaza.

He felt like a carrier pigeon. In the First World War, that's how they relayed messages from headquarters to the front, wasn't it, he thought. How many of those carrier pigeons got shot? he wondered. The thought unnerved him. When he arrived at the crossing from Israel into Gaza, he felt sure his vehicle was going to be taken apart and searched. He handed his passport, travel permit and press credentials to the heavily-armed Israeli soldiers and felt the sweat trickling down his back. It wasn't the heat, either, though it was unbelievably hot that day.

It seemed to take ages for them to process his papers. Then he was asked to go over to an office. Inside, it was cool, the air conditioning hitting him with an icy blast the moment he walked in the door. A man in military uniform sat behind a desk. He stared at him for a second then looked at his passport and Press Association documentation. Then looked back at him again.

'Sit down,' the man barked.

Jeremy sat on the chair in front of the desk.

'Why do you want to visit Gaza?'

'I'm a journalist. It's my job. There have been recent rocket attacks from there, as you know. And your forces have mounted air raids in response. I've been asked to go and see what the situation is.'

The man, who Jeremy thought was probably in his forties, stroked his chin. And nodded. 'These Hamas terrorists always start it, you know that, don't you? We defend ourselves, that's our right, isn't it?'

Finn said nothing in reply. He wanted to tell the man, who hadn't introduced himself but looked like a senior military officer, that Israel occupied land that was previously Palestinian territory which they had been evicted from. That they felt that they were defending land that had been stolen from them. That the Israelis treated Palestinians as second-class citizens, or barely citizens at all. He wanted to say a whole lot about the matter, but what was the point? The guy had an entrenched view.

Eventually, the officer sighed and stamped his passport and gave it back to him with his press papers and permit and he was allowed to leave. He got back into his vehicle and drove into Gaza.

Whole sections of Gaza City were literally bombsites. For the past week there had been aerial bombings by Israeli jets in retaliation for rocket attacks fired from within Gaza City. The streets were heavily potholed and the traffic was often at a standstill, one time as a funeral procession passed by, the crowds of wailing mourners carrying a coffin draped in a Hamas flag and with a large framed photograph of the dead man being carried by a mourner at the head of the procession. The coffin jostled and bounced on the arms of the crowd as it passed amid shouts and chants, then the procession was gone and Jeremy carried on into the heart of the city.

He found the address that Laila had told him to go to, a house in an alleyway off a main street. He'd had to remember it as she didn't want to write it down for him to carry or to draw a map in case it got found at the crossing. What if they had found a map? They'd have torn his car to bits.

In the alleyway, he eventually found the house, which had been difficult as there didn't appear to be any signage, the only identification being the green-painted door he had been told to look for. He knocked and waited.

The door was opened by an elderly woman

who peered at him through her spectacles and asked him, in Arabic, who he was.

He replied in the way he had been instructed, with the phrase, 'I've come to repair the TV.' The woman eyed him suspiciously then shouted something over her shoulder and disappeared.

A moment later, two men in their early twenties appeared in the hallway and told him to come in. As soon as he came in, one of them slammed the door shut and the other turned him round forcibly and pushed him against the wall. His messenger bag was taken off him, as well as his mobile phone and car keys. A hood was thrown over his head and he was plunged into darkness. He was aware of hands frisking him from head to foot, then something hard being poked into his back. It felt like a gun. His hands were handcuffed behind his back then he was turned around and pushed down the hall, the gun prodding him in the back all the way.

He was aware of a door opening and being led outside, so he surmised that he was now at the rear of the house. A push sent him into what felt like the back of a van. He fell face first to the floor and lay there, with a boot on his back. A voice told him to stay where he was. The van's doors closed.

Then the noise of the engine started and

they were off. The vehicle shook and jumped violently as it made its way, Jeremy rolling from side to side, the boot pressing into his spine.

After about fifteen minutes the van stopped and the engine was switched off. He heard voices outside and then the van's doors were opened and he was hauled to his feet and led outside. Hands at his back steered him forwards. He stumbled and fell, hitting his chin off the ground. Someone grabbed his arm, pulled him back up to his feet and pushed him forwards again. He was led into another building and marched along a what he thought must be a corridor and through a door then down several flights of steps. He realised that he must be down in an underground tunnel. From there he went through another door which slammed shut behind him. He heard the sound of it being locked and bolted.

Time passed. He heard the occasional voice in the corridor outside but mostly it was silent. He had no idea how long he was there in this room, presumably a cell, though as he was still hooded, he had no idea what it was like. It smelled fetid, though. He was thirsty but also needed the toilet and tried desperately not to piss himself. He sat down on the hard, concrete floor and tried not to be scared but it was pointless. He was petrified. Would he ever see the outside world again? Would he ever see Laila again?

But had Laila, in fact, sold him out? Deceived him. Was this whole thing a trap, designed to make use of him to transport the money then hold him as a hostage to free a prisoner in Israel or elsewhere? He had been so sure that what he and Laila had was a genuine loving relationship but maybe he had just been naïve. She had been very eager to start seeing him, hadn't she? Too eager?

No, he told himself, he couldn't believe that. If it was true, then he was in real danger. He tried to convince himself that it wasn't the case but doubts kept surfacing in his mind.

Eventually he heard the sound of the door opening. The handcuffs around his wrists were unlocked and the hood removed. He could now see that it was indeed a cell, with a bucket in a corner but nothing else. A single strip of light on the ceiling illuminated the room. There was also no furniture: no bed or a table, not even a chair. Two men in military fatigues stood there, both carrying weapons, AK-47s, by the looks of them, Jeremy thought. One of them asked him if he needed anything. He indicated that he needed to use the bucket and the man nodded. After he'd used it, he asked for water. The man handed him a bottle which he hung from his belt. Jeremy took a long drink of the water and wiped his mouth with the back of his hand.

'Thank you,' he said.

They then interrogated him, asking him for details of his occupation, where he lived in Beirut, who he knew there, the reason for his journey and so on. He told them about Laila. They asked how he knew her. He told them how they met and how she'd asked him to carry something through to Gaza and where he had been told to go to in Tel Aviv to fit up the vehicle.

They seemed satisfied with his answers but said nothing and left, bolting the door again. At least now he could see, and his bladder had been emptied. But he wasn't sure what was going to happen next. He looked at his watch. It was only two hours since he had arrived at the house in Gaza but it felt much longer.

A while later the same two men appeared again. 'Come with us,' one of them said.

Jeremy followed them out of the cell and along the corridor into another room. A middle-aged man was seated at a desk. He had a thick bushy beard and was wearing army fatigues and glasses. On the desk in front of him lay Jeremy's mobile and messenger bag, its contents spilled out over the desk.

'You can have your belongings back, Mr Powell. I'm sorry for any discomfort we have caused you,' said the man in English. 'You'll understand that we have to be careful and take precautions. We had to check that you really were the journalist we were expecting and not an Israeli spy.'

Jeremy nodded. 'Yes. Of course. I understand.'

'Please have a seat,' said the man.

Jeremy sat down on a chair.

'I would introduce myself but that might be taking our trust in you a little too far, eh?' He laughed and picked up a cigar box and opened it. 'Care for a cigar, Mr Powell?'

'No thanks, I don't smoke.'

'Shame,' said the man. 'These are the finest Havana cigars, sent to us from our comrades in Cuba. Always makes me feel like Fidel Castro every time I light one up.' He laughed and picked a cigar from the box and lit it. Thick pungent smoke filled the room and Jeremy began to cough.

'Thank you for coming here today. What you have brought us is most welcome. The US dollars you had in that car will help us to buy urgent medical supplies for our hospitals. We have to have everything shipped in to escape the Israeli blockade; you understand? You will have saved lives.'

'And it will no doubt also help you to buy ammunition, weapons and chemicals to build rockets and bombs.'

'You have a problem with that?'

Jeremy shook his head. 'No, though doesn't firing rockets into Israel just inflame the situation, if you pardon the pun? It provokes the Israelis into responding, sending over their planes to bomb here, turning parts of your city into a wasteland. Where does it get you?'

'If we do nothing, the Israelis will just ignore the issue. We will gain nothing.'

'But look at Northern Ireland. The IRA gave up the armed struggle and their weapons. There's peace now. Isn't that better?'

'But the IRA lost. Where is the united Ireland they wanted?' He shook his head. 'No. We won't give up until we have got rid of Israel and have a free Palestinian state. Mr Powell, I hope that we can continue with our friendship and meet again, but I would warn you to wait a while before venturing here again. We do not want to draw the Israelis' suspicions about your motives.'

'I understand,' said Jeremy.

'You are a journalist and have no doubt told the Israelis why you came here was to report on conditions in our city. So, you will have to do that. We can help you. You will want to see how the Israelis have deliberately targeted our schools, our hospitals, claiming that they are military targets. This is lies. We can show you the pain and misery that they cause. What we can also show you is how we are defending ourselves. How we look after our people. They will not break us, no matter how hard they try. And one day we will win.'

'I appreciate your help.'

'I hope that you find our hospitality to your approval. And please, when you return to Beirut, give my thanks to Laila.'

One day, Stephen phoned him and they arranged to meet for a drink. Jeremy hadn't seen much of Stephen since that day when they had met Laila and Nasreen.

'Remember those two students of yours we met one day?' said Jeremy.

'Yes,' said Stephen.

'Well ... I've sort of been seeing one of them.'

'Do you mean *"seeing"* as I think you mean?'

Jeremy laughed and shook his head. 'It's amazing. I think I'm in love with her.'

'Who? I mean, which one?'

'Laila. She's so beautiful. And intelligent. And funny.'

'You really are smitten, aren't you? How long has this been going on?'

'A couple of months.'

'So that's the reason why I could never get to see you, you lucky bastard.'

'It's a secret, though. Stephen, I mean it. You can't tell anyone. Her parents would go mental if they found out. They're very strict with her.'

'Don't worry. Your secret's safe with me. You could do something for me in return.'

'Of course, what is it?'

'I know you and Olivia used to see each other. You wouldn't happen to have her phone number, would you? I'd like to get in touch with her.'

'Why do you want to contact her?'

'I'm planning on having a trip back to England in the next few months sometime and I thought I might look her up. See what's she's up to. You don't mind, do you?'

'No. Of course not. Water under the bridge and all that.'

'Thanks. That's awfully decent of you. How come the pair of you split up anyway. You always struck me as a perfect couple.'

'I think that was the problem. We were too alike. We just got bored with each other. Differences attract, eh?'

'Like you and Laila, eh? Here's to the two of you.' Stephen raised his glass of wine in a toast.

'And here's to you and …Olivia!' said Jeremy. 'You always did have a fancy for her, didn't you?'

'She is bloody good looking.'

'Good luck with her, mate. Hope it works out for you.'

'Cheers, Jeremy!'

One day, a few weeks later, Laila appeared at his apartment in a distressed state. She was in tears.

'I received this text last night,' she said. She held out her phone.

He read it. Clearly it was blackmail.

"We know you are a militant supporting the work of Palestinian terrorists. If you don't want photographs of your affair with an English journalist to be shown to your father you will

cooperate. We need to have copies of everything you send in future and a list of all your associates and contacts. You have twenty-four hours to reply or else the photos go to your father."

'What will you do?'

'I won't do anything. I am not going to work for the enemy.'

'Who do you think is behind this?'

'The Americans? The Israelis? I don't know.'

'But what if they do what they say? Give the material to your father.'

'This is a bluff. There's no way they will give my father anything. If they do, I will explain to him that we are in love.'

'But what if he won't accept us?'

She shrugged. 'I will leave home and come to live with you.' She stared at him 'You want me to, don't you?'

'Yes, of course. But you would be giving up your family.'

'I know. But I love you,' Laila said and embraced him.

'I love you too,' said Jeremy. 'But we have to be careful.'

'You are right. You cannot risk taking

anything else to Gaza.'

Jeremy offered to come and talk to her father but Laila thought she should speak to him herself first.

'I'll see you tomorrow afternoon', she said. 'Three o' clock.'

But the following day, Laila did not show up at his apartment at three o' clock as planned. Jeremy could not get hold of her. Something was definitely wrong, he thought. Later, he heard on the news that a young woman had fallen to her death from a tower block. Something instinctively told him that it was Laila. He tried ringing her mobile again and again but still got no answer.

When the body was identified later as her, it was reported on the news as a suicide. But Jeremy knew the truth. Her father must have been told about their relationship. Laila had dismissed the threat as a bluff, but whoever it was who had been behind it, they had done what they had threatened to do and her father had punished her in the most extreme way.

He'd been drinking heavily all day since hearing about her death when Stephen called round to see him that evening.

'Laila is dead,' said Jeremy. 'She fell from a tower block.'

'Yes. I heard that at the university today. Tragic. It's awful when a young person takes their own life.'

'They're reporting it as suicide but I think there's more to it. I think her father found out about the two of us and had her killed. She told me he wouldn't approve of her seeing me.'

'You think so? Maybe he put a tail on her and found out where she went when she was seeing you.'

'No. That's not what happened. She was being blackmailed.'

'What? You're kidding.'

'No. She was an activist and she told me she'd received a text telling her that unless she cooperated with the sender, then photographs of her seeing me would be sent to her father.'

'Shit! That's unbelievable. What did she do?'

'She called their bluff, whoever, *they* are. She decided to ignore it. That was brave but reckless and ultimately the wrong decision.'

'What did these people want?'

'Laila was active in a group supporting the Palestinians. She knew people in Hamas. According to this message, they wanted to know her contacts and information.'

'Bastards. And you think that they then passed material about the two of you onto her father?'

'They must have.'

Stephen nodded. 'It was probably Mossad who was behind it. They have spies everywhere. Even, it's rumoured, within the university. They'll have known she was active in radical circles and had her followed and then seen the two of you together. Listen, Jeremy, the best thing you can do is forget her.'

'Fuck off, Jeremy, how can you say that? I loved her.'

'I'm sorry about what's happened to her but the rumour at the university is she's slept with half the boys in her year.'

'That's a lie.'

'Anyway, you'd never have married her, would you? There's plenty more like her. Beautiful young Lebanese women. You'll find someone else. I can even help you find one. I'm with a really hot one just now. I'll get her to introduce you to one of her friends. How about that?'

'You are unbelievable! How can you say that? Just fuck off, Stephen, for God's sake, will you! Get the fuck out!'

Jeremy had checked that Olivia was sound asleep. He got out of bed, picked up his phone, switched on the torch app and went into the living room. He had a look around. There was a desk with a laptop. He searched through the drawers until he found what he was looking for, a folder containing papers related to the secret company Stephen ran, that Olivia told him about. He photographed the contents with his phone then slipped it back in the drawer and crept back to bed. Thankfully, she was still asleep.

What Olivia had told him the night before made perfect sense. Stephen had worked for the intelligence service, MI6, while he was in Beirut, spying on students. The revelation brought back the memory of how he had grieved for Laila. He couldn't believe that he hadn't twigged it at the time. Stephen was the only one who knew that he and Laila were going out. He'd told him about her. Then a few weeks later, Laila had received the blackmail threat. Stephen had planted the idea in his head that it had been Mossad who had been behind it all. But if it had really been the Israelis, why had they allowed him to pass through security checks into Gaza without intercepting what he was carrying for Laila?

No. It had been Stephen all along who was responsible for her death, he decided. The duplicitous bastard! He'd deceived him. Betrayed him. Had the bastard even set him and her up from the very start when he introduced him to her? That supposedly accidental encounter at the café might not have been so accidental after all, he thought. Now eighteen years later he knew how to make him pay.

The next day, he met Brian Clark in his hotel bar, as arranged. The journalist had approached him when he had arrived to give his talk the night before and handed him his business card, asking if he could have an interview. At the end of the interview, Jeremy said, 'You also might be interested to knows that one of your city's businessmen is operating a private security company involved in some shady business. Stephen Moore. Of SM Political Intelligence.' He told Brian what he knew about Cerberus Security Services. 'You won't find anything about them online. They must operate mainly by word of mouth or via the dark web. They do so-called security work overseas. Sounds dodgy to me. Anyway, this will definitely be something he doesn't want to be made public. I'll WhatsApp you the proof. Use it as you like. But make sure you keep my name out of it, OK?'

'Of course. Thanks.' Said Brian. 'Sounds intriguing.'

Jeremy WhatsApped him the photos of the

Cerberus documents then left to catch the train to London, visited his parents and met up with a friend. He didn't mention Cerberus to anyone. On Saturday, he read that a man had been shot dead in his home in Cambridge. He had a strange feeling. He tried ringing Brian without success.

By the following morning, as Jeremy boarded his plane to Edinburgh to connect with an onward flight to Kirkwall, the dead journalist had indeed been confirmed as Brian Clark. The press reports said the police thought it could be case of mistaken identity related to drug gangs operating in the area, but they were keeping an open mind and the investigation was at an early stage. But Jeremy had a good idea why he'd been killed.

Jeremy wondered if Stephen had guessed that he had supplied Brian with the information. If so, his life was in danger. On the other hand, Stephen may have concluded that Brian uncovered what he knew about Cerberus himself, in some other way through hacking the dark web, for example. So, he thought he'd just be vigilant and hope that Stephen would be satisfied with having got Brian out of the way.

*

Stephen was waiting impatiently for the phone call that would tell him the mission was complete. One half of it had been successful, getting rid of that that fucking reporter, Clark, who had called him up to ask him why his company, Cerberus Security Services, was so secret? Was his company involved in anything illegal? What exactly did they do in Africa?

How the hell had he found out about Cerberus? Stephen refused to comment but managed to delay things by offering a meeting with him on the following Monday. That would give him time to put a plan in place.

'Come to my office at nine o' clock on Monday morning and we'll talk then and I can tell you all about what Cerberus is about. I can assure there's nothing illegal. I assume you won't be publishing anything in the meantime until we meet.'

'OK,' said Clark. 'See you on Monday.'

The call unsettled him. It was important to stop this in its tracks, to literally snuff it out. With this vital government contract to wipe out a people-smuggling gang underway, the last thing Stephen needed was publicity about what Cerberus was up to. Business had been declining, especially in Africa, where a Russian mercenary group was extending its reach, and his political consultancy wasn't doing so well either. There was caution from clients about where the data they were using to target ads on social media was obtained, and politicians were nervous about being accused of using personal data that users hadn't consented to be shared. He badly needed the government income.

How the hell had this journalist found out about Cerberus? He then did a bit of investigating himself, and found out that Clark had just had a piece published on the Cambridge Mercury website, an interview with the writer Jeremy Powell. Apparently Powell had delivered a talk at St George's College earlier in the week. Fucking Jeremy Powell! Of all people.

Then, a friend of his had said he'd seen Powell with Olivia in a restaurant in Cambridge the evening of the talk. He quickly realised that Olivia must have been the source for the leak about Cerberus. She must have let something slip about it to Powell, who then passed it on to Clark. The bitch, he thought. But, fortunately, she didn't know all the details of Cerberus, though, thank God, and what it really was. And the reporter hadn't indicated exactly what he knew. Olivia had seen some documents once and asked about them. Signed contracts, suitably vague about what the work entailed but still, something he wouldn't want in the public eye. He knew exactly why Powell wanted to disgrace him, though. It all went back to, Beirut, naturally.

Stephen had gone to the safe and checked. Yes, as he suspected, there were several contracts missing. He'd put them in the safe after she had noticed them, but she must have gone in there one day and taken them. Fuck! She must have stolen them and shown them to Jeremy. At the time, he'd given her only a vague description of what they were for and what Cerberus was all about, making it sound almost beneficial to society.

In fact, it had started out a bit like that, offering personal protection to dignitaries – politicians and top businessmen – who often didn't trust locals or some of the people close to them to provide security. It wouldn't be the first time that a head of state had been assassinated by one of his own bodyguards, secretly in the employ of a rival or actually a member of a terror group. Cerberus provided personal security which was completely confidential and safe. It was expensive but these people could afford it. They valued their lives more than anything else of course.

It had initially been a step from providing data on electorates gleaned from social media for political parties in Africa to help influence elections in their favour to providing security guards for the politicians. It was only a small further step to go from providing security and protecting potential targets to eliminating the source of the threat altogether. Wayne Morgan, whom Stephen had met in East Africa, provided the contacts with other mercenaries and often personally led a mission; Stephen was the brains, providing the strategy. It was a great combination and they worked around the world. The rewards were lucrative.

So, what to do? he had thought. One, he had to get rid of Clark. And Powell, too. So, he got in touch with Morgan. He wasn't cheap but he always did an efficient job. Which he did. Then he paid a hacker to wipe Clark's cloud account clean. Which he would also arrange for Powell's account, once he heard he was dead.

But, thinking about Charlotte, for whom he had a soft spot, he couldn't force himself to eliminate Olivia. He balked at having her killed. He could undoubtedly ensure her silence in the matter of Cerberus with a good pay off in the divorce settlement. She was always keen on money more than anything else. He was sure she would keep her mouth shut if he paid her enough. Besides, how would she connect Clark and Powell's deaths with Cerberus? No, he was sure he could relax with regard to her.

He went round to see her in her new apartment by the river and demanded she hand back the contracts. He couldn't ask her anything about Jeremy, ask if she'd seen him, told him anything. That would throw suspicion if the plan didn't go as expected. Things could always go wrong, though. If things went awry, he didn't want her to think it had anything to do with him. There was no knowing what she might do. He knew she was fond of Jeremy. They had once been lovers. They had probably shagged only a few days ago.

She was surprised to see him but invited him in and they sat down. 'I've gone through the safe and there's some Cerberus contracts missing. I know you took them, Olivia,' he said. 'Just hand them back. I'll make sure you get enough in the divorce settlement, if that's what you're worried about. I've also transferred you a significant advance this morning, you'll see it on your bank account if you go online.'

Reluctantly, Olivia went to her desk and retrieved the folder containing the documents. She handed it over to Stephen. 'I only took them because I was angry with you, Stephen. I don't care now. You mean nothing to me anymore.'

'Look, I'm sorry about the way things worked out between us, Olivia. I really am.'

'I don't want to discuss it. Now, if you don't mind, I have things I'd like to be getting on with.'

He made his way to the door and turned

to face her in the doorway. 'Olivia, I need to trust you,' he said.

'Oh, fuck off, Stephen,' she said, slamming the door in his face.

Now, as he waited for the call from Morgan to tell him that he had accomplished the mission in Orkney, Stephen's mind switched to Naomi. She was an employee of his from Egypt, half his age, gorgeous and seemingly in love with him. She was also terrific in bed. He couldn't believe his luck. Even if it had ended his marriage when Olivia found out about her. He still hadn't worked out how she knew. Some jealous bastard must have blown the whistle on him.

Naomi reminded him of Laila. Beirut. Stephen had already been there a year, lecturing at the university but also secretly spying on the students for MI6, relaying information on them and their political connections to his bosses. He had been tapped up by the security service at Cambridge while still an undergraduate. He'd passed the series of selection tests with flying colours and, after graduating, been trained in surveillance and how to operate undercover. His was instructed to continue with his academic career as a cover and then posted to Beirut, lecturing at the American University, but also keeping an eye out for militants. He met Jeremy by chance at some reception or other event, he couldn't quite recall what. Stephen hadn't known until then that he had been posted to Beirut as a foreign correspondent. Jeremy told him that he'd been there for a month already. They started hanging out together, then one day he introduced her to Laila, who was with her friend, Nasreen.

A while later, he and Jeremy were out drinking when Jeremy told him his news. 'Remember those two students of yours …I've been seeing one of them.… Laila.' Stephen already suspected Laila was an activist with links to Palestinian militants and Jeremy's relationship presented him with an opportunity. He had a word with Richard Spencer, head of the MI6 station in Beirut about it. Stephen had a good idea of the surveillance they would then have carried out. The surveillance team would occupy a place across the road, positioning their tripod and camera so there would be a good view of their comings and goings, maybe even some intimate interior shots if Jeremy kept the shutters open.

They would then have sent Laila a text telling her what information they possessed on her and that she needed to supply information on her contacts within the activist network she was involved in, or her father would know all about her relationship with Powell. They would give her a limited period to reply. But she didn't. Jeremy had told him so afterwards.

She was found dead at the foot of a ten-storey building, apparently having "fallen". Her father claimed that he had found a suicide note written by his daughter left in her bedroom, which he had destroyed in his grief. The father, of course, had an alibi as to where he was at the time. Not that the police would likely have bothered with investigating him. He was a wealthy businessman with plenty of connections amongst the authorities. And money to bribe them with. Stephen had a good idea what had really happened. He had no doubt paid some henchmen to abduct and kill his daughter.

But that was all in the past. For now, all he could do was wait for that call from Morgan.

*

Morgan parked just down the road from Powell's house, where he was able to spy on it from. Just after three o' clock he saw Powell leave his house to take his dog for a walk. He was in luck. Powell was on his own No one else was about. He got out and followed.

He felt the weight of the gun in his jacket pocket with his right hand. He could see Powell and his dog about a hundred yards ahead of him and increased his pace. Rain lashed his face and the wind threatened to lift him off his feet but he maintained his focus on the figure ahead.

As he got within a few yards of him, Powell must have heard something, and turned round and stared at him.

'Hello,' said Powell.

Morgan pulled the gun out of his pocket. The look on Powell's face told him that he knew who he was and why he was there. Powell made a move, dropping the phone he had in his hand and grabbed Morgan's arm holding the gun and shook it. The gun went off and an animal yelped. The pair of them tussled, Powell trying to get hold of the gun, but Morgan smacked him on the head with it and Powell staggered backwards towards the cliff's edge and seemed to lose his balance. One second, he was there, the next he was gone.

Morgan inched over to the edge. Powell had disappeared into the sea. He looked around. No one was there to see what had just happened, except for a dead dog lying at his feet, a crimson patch spreading out over its white fur. He picked up Powell's phone from where he had dropped it in the struggle, switched it off, and removed the SIM card which he would destroy later along with the handset as instructed. He then rolled the dog over to the edge and dropped it into the sea. Hopefully it would never be seen again. There was some blood on the ground from where the dog had been shot but, as it was raining, it would soon be washed into the ground. Satisfied with the job, he made his way back along the cliff path to the village.

No one was about when he returned to his car. There was a darkening sky by the time he drove off. He put his foot down on the accelerator and sped off. On the edge of the village, a woman almost stepped off the pavement in front of him but stepped back at the last moment. He breathed a sigh of relief. It would have been unfortunate, to say the least, if he'd been involved in a hit-and-run after completing the assignment so successfully which he'd come to the isles to carry out. Even if the stupid woman reported it, he'd be long gone before they could trace the stolen car. He would go straight to the ferry now. He'd stolen the car in Inverness, after driving north in his own car overnight from Cambridge straight after killing Clark. He'd changed the number plates and driven to catch the Scrabster ferry in the morning. He'd dump the car back in Inverness, after changing the plates back, and then drive his own car back to London.

No, it had all worked out perfectly, he thought to himself. This one would even look like an accident. So, there was nothing to worry about. If Powell's body was ever found, he wouldn't even have any bullet holes in him. And he'd read that the police thought his shooting of that Cambridge journalist might be related to gangs. What idiots the cops were. Jumping to the obvious conclusion on a crime-raddled estate. But the result was a good one for him, nevertheless.

The only worry was the dog. If it was ever found, they'd find a bullet in it. But he'd been careful. He'd used a different gun from the one he'd used in Cambridge, so there was no possibility of the police establishing a connection.

Stephen had been worried that the shit was going to hit the fan. He had been in a panic but Morgan had assured him he could deal with it. And he had. He would call him with the good news. Now that the two potential threats he'd spoken about had been eliminated, the journalist and the author, he and Stephen could relax again and look forward to a bright future for Cerberus. There was talk of an assignment in France, to take out some people smugglers. That sounded like it would be a blast!

EPILOGUE

Finn walked out of the back door and into the bright sunshine of the garden. There was a touch of warmth in the air. Flowers were in bloom. He gazed out across the sea to the smaller islands in the distance. He felt glad to be alive. And glad to be back on the isles. It felt like home.

After the events surrounding Cerberus, six weeks ago, including being shot at in his London apartment that night, he'd realised he needed to get away more from London. The investigation into who had shot at him had, predictably, got nowhere. Thankfully, Helen survived. Her operation was a success; the surgeons had saved her life. She had been lucky. As had he. The security services had obviously wanted to kill them both to prevent the story leaking, to protect themselves, and the Home Secretary. But once his article was published, he felt that both he and Helen were a lot safer. The story was out.

He'd decided not to put his gran's place on the market after all; he'd keep it as a bolt-hole, somewhere to escape to every now and again. A weekend and holiday home. He could even work from there some of the time, remotely, as so many people now did since the pandemic. Interviews could more easily be conducted by Zoom than taking expensive and time-consuming journeys around the globe in any case. And Amy had adopted his gran's dog, Kiki. The attempted assassination he'd experienced in London had also made him feel less safe there, but it was really the beauty of the isles that called him back. It was almost as if his gran's final gift to him was to bring him back to the place he belonged.

He filled the cafetiere with coffee, sat down at the kitchen table and took out his mobile. His jaw fell open as he read the breaking news on the *Chronicle's* website:

STEELE AND PARKINSON FOUND DEAD IN NORFOLK

The former home secretary, Jayne Steele, and her special adviser, Simon Parkinson, have both been found dead in Steele's home on the outskirts of Burnham Market in her North Norfolk constituency.

Steele, 48, was sacked from her post after revelations were published in the Chronicle revealing close links between Parkinson and Stephen Moore, whose personal security business, Cerberus Security Services, is thought to have been responsible for, what French police believe, was an attempted attack on a gang of people smugglers in France. Eight members of the raiding party, a private investigator and two elderly French pensioners were killed. Moore, himself, was found shot dead in his home the following day.

A Norfolk Constabulary spokesperson said that Steele and Parkinson had both died from gunshot wounds. According to the spokesperson, it appeared that Steele may have used a pistol to kill Parkinson then turned the gun on herself. The spokesperson added that they are not looking for anyone else in connection with the deaths.

Steele was divorced and had two daughters, both in their twenties. She was previously married to Conservative MP, Sir Trevor Whitelaw. Parkinson, 45, was married to the journalist Liz Perkins.

Steele initially refused to leave her post, saying that the claims that she had anything to do with the Calais operation were completely false, but then she was sacked by the prime minister in a Cabinet reshuffle.

Because of Steele's well-known views on countering the people smugglers, there had been speculation that she had hired Moore's company, Cerberus Security Services, to carry out a mission to eliminate the gang in France. A payment of £250,000 was made to the Cambridge businessman's company by the Home Office. Her special adviser, Parkinson, was a close friend of Stephen Moore's and they had been at a top public school together.

A Downing Street spokesperson said that the prime minister was very sad to hear the news and that his thoughts were with the families of Steele and Parkinson.

The spokesperson said that the PM knew nothing about any vigilante missions against people smugglers in France, but reiterated that the government was intent on halting the flow of illegal immigrants and that stopping the boats remained a top priority.

Finn thought that some on the internet would already be speculating that the Prime Minister had had a hand in their deaths. It was usually the case that conspiracy theories weren't based on any kind of fact, but in this case, Finn thought, in this case, there might be some truth in such a theory. The Prime Minister wouldn't want anything to come out that would embarrass the Tory party, and perhaps he didn't feel assured that the pair would keep their mouths shut if prosecutions followed. The French authorities had reportedly been seeking to interview the pair in connection with the Calais operation.

Therefore it was best to avoid any whiff of scandal associated with the government, even if it was a former minister who was involved.

Whatever had really happened, Finn was sure that Steele and Parkinson's deaths hadn't happened as described. As Helen had said, as well as the operation in France against the smugglers, they would have been ultimately responsible for Moore's death, with assistance from the security services, who had no doubt decided to tidy things up by disposing of the pair once they were seen as becoming a liability.

He put his phone down and focused on the day ahead. Amy was coming round to dinner later, with Kiki, along with Grace and her new partner, Kirsty. He would cook langoustines, fresh from the sea.

Author's Note

The shooting of Brian Clark in the story is based on the real-life murder of a relative of mine, Dr Michael Meenaghan, a forensic scientist at Oxford University, who was tragically shot dead through his kitchen window on 10th December 1994. There was no known motive for the shooting and police speculated it could have been a case of mistaken identity or a hired hitman. His killer has never been identified.

The right-wing anti-immigration rhetoric of the Conservative government escalated in 2022 and 2023 while I was writing this novel. On 31st October 2022, in the House of Commons, the Home Secretary, Suella Braverman, described asylum seekers arriving in small boats as an "invasion" a day after a firebomb attack on an immigration processing centre in Dover.

Acknowledgements

Thanks to Maureen for all her support and taking the time to read through the drafts, spotting the many mistakes and suggesting many improvements. I wouldn't have been able to write this book without her. Thanks also to Mathew for so assiduously reading a draft and giving me really useful feedback one night in a Glasgow pub over a few beers.

All characters are fictitious. Any resemblance to real people, events or places is entirely coincidental.

Printed in Great Britain
by Amazon